Against the Boards

CANADIAN PLAYED
BOOK ONE

CYNTHIA GUNDERSON

BUTTON PRESS

Copyright © 2023 by Button Press

All rights reserved.

No part of this book may be reproduced in any form or by any electronic or mechanical means, including information storage and retrieval systems, without written permission from the author, except for the use of brief quotations in a book review.

With Gratitude

Editing and Critique
Scott Gunderson, Stacie Mason, Jordan Truex

Cover Design
Mitxeren

Author Note

A huge thank you to readers on Booktok for jumping in with my storytelling and giving me the push to write this series!

While I use real NHL teams and places in this story, all characters are fictional. The Calgary Flames have been changed to the Calgary Blizzard in this series because the team becomes central to one of my future plot lines. You'll know what I'm talking about when you get to the end of book#3, Stickhandle With Care.

I hope you have as much fun reading these as I had writing them! Welcome to Cow Town.

xo Cindy

Find extended author notes in special edition copies at www.CindyGunderson.com

A love letter to home.

CHAPTER
One

EMMA STARED at the wall of kale. Red, curly, *lacinato*. This was why she didn't buy vegetables. Too many choices and not enough...instruction. She closed her eyes and pointed, then plucked a bundle of verdant leaves from the display. *Greens are cheaper than skincare.* That's what Vaughn was always telling her. He'd be thrilled to hear she'd listened for once and would hopefully tell her how to consume this.

The strawberries looked scrumptious, and *those* she knew what to do with. Dip them in melted chocolate chips, obviously. That, or give them an oil sheen along with a spritz of water and glycerin to make their colour pop on camera.

Emma sighed. She'd accepted years ago that she couldn't force her brain out of work mode purely because she was grocery shopping for sustenance instead of props. *That one berry in the corner could use a swipe of lipstick to cover up the bleached spot at its tip.*

"Excuse me." A woman reached past Emma to grab a bunch of grapes.

"Sorry." Emma scooted over and flashed a smile, then moved on to the avocados. She'd filled each of her mesh produce bags, which meant it was time to check out. Limiting herself to seven bags was how she reminded herself that she was cooking for one and didn't need to bring home enough fruit for an entire hockey team.

Growing up, she'd shopped with her mother, who was always cooking for a small army, and that training was still her default. Her brothers ate like junkyard dogs, especially during hockey season. *Two bunches of bananas? No, we need four at least. Now, help me load eight gallons of milk into the cart!*

Her oldest brother Sean took full advantage of the fact that their mother had never adjusted. Sharla Thompson still made pots of spaghetti that could feed half of downtown Calgary. Or Sean's Elite League hockey team every Sunday night. Same difference, really.

Her phone buzzed in the pocket on her left thigh. She switched her shopping basket to her right arm and slipped it out. *Speak of the devil.*

"Hey, Mom."

"Emma! What are you up to this fine March morning?"

"Trying not to wish I was in Cancun instead?"

Her mother laughed. "Well, I'm glad you're not in Mexico. I heard there were a couple of carjackings the other day, and not near the border either. In a touristy town—Rob, what was the place called?" Emma stifled a grin as her dad yelled from the other room. "Well, he doesn't remember, but the point is, I'm glad you're here this weekend so we can see you Sunday night."

Emma stepped into line behind a man holding three cases of mineral water. *Thirsty.* And mineral deficient, apparently. She didn't know that was possible living in Alberta. "Mom, I haven't come to a Sunday Supper in ages—"

"No, the Snowballs have a tournament in Saskatoon this weekend. The team won't be back until well after supper. We wanted to spend some time with just you. You're welcome to bring Lindsey and Vaughn if you like."

Just her? When had that ever happened? She was the third of six children, and while she wasn't going to pretend her life had been anything but charmed, her parents had only forgotten *one* of their children in the Claresholm Seven-Eleven. At least the guy behind the counter then hadn't been a serial killer, or she wouldn't have the current privilege of watching Mineral Man pay for his future kidney stones in loonies.

"Sure, I can reach out to them." Emma pinned her phone between her cheek and shoulder as she emptied her basket onto the counter.

Her mother's refrigerator door slammed. "Now, I know Vaughn is going to ask what we're having, and it's not all gluten-free, but I was planning to make Jell-O salad and green beans."

Emma sighed. "Mom, gluten-free doesn't mean he can't eat regular food—"

"I know, I know. I just want to make him feel comfortable."

The idea of watching Vaughn pretend to enjoy Jell-O salad was almost worth lying to him about the menu. "Sounds great. Can I text you later? Just checking out at the grocery store."

"Oh, sorry, I won't keep you. Love you, Ems."

"Love you too. Give Dad a hug for me."

Emma paid for her groceries and strode out the front sliding doors, her runners crunching over the re-frozen slush still shaded by the brick building. *Two more months until summer.* She could hold out till then, couldn't she?

Every year she had this conversation with herself. It was only a matter of time before she gave in, sold her apartment, and high-tailed it to Vancouver like both of her younger sisters. If Vaughn and Lindsey would go with her, she'd leave tomorrow. Except she'd need her parents to come, too, and then Sean would be annoyed, but when wasn't he annoyed with her life choices?

Something skittered across the ground, and Emma stuttered a step. *A credit card?* She opened the back hatch of her CRV and dropped in her groceries, then picked it up.

A driver's licence. Emma flipped it over and blinked at the gorgeous face staring back at her. Umm . . . that was not a driver's licence photo. Even in black and white, this was a straight-up headshot for GQ. *Maybe it was because of the black and white?*

First of all, this guy was definitely smiling, and *was he even looking at the camera?* Had the employee at the Registry found this man to be so beautiful that he'd snapped a candid? Emma wouldn't have blamed him.

She wiped the muddy water from the plastic and read the name. Tyler Bowen. *Yes, please.* Born in 1991. March. *Tyler just had a birthday.*

Emma dropped her hand and pursed her lips. Was she really reading someone's personal information in the middle of a Co-op parking lot? She was a bonafide voyeur. It's pathetic that this was the most exciting thing that had happened in her love life for weeks.

She closed the back, locked the car doors, and retraced her steps into the store. As she searched for the service desk, a thought sent heat flashing through her. *Was this man still here?* In the store? If he'd dropped it on the way in, he could still be browsing the aisles.

She stood on her tiptoes and did a quick sweep. He was probably short. *Ugh, why did all the hot guys have to be short?* Emma glanced down at the card in her hand. One hundred and ninety centimetres. What was that, six-foot-three? Her stomach swooped. *Never mind.*

She turned back to the guest services line and wove through the tape. A girl who couldn't have been older than sixteen with bubble gum pink hair stood behind the counter, scrolling on her phone.

Emma cleared her throat, but the employee didn't look up. After a few more seconds of *Baby Got Back* bumping from the girl's phone speaker, Emma spoke up. "Excuse me?" The employee finally looked up. "I found this driver's licence in the parking lot."

The girl shrugged. Maybe if Emma choreographed a quick

dance and made a few attention-grabbing transitions, she'd find her more interesting.

Emma tapped the licence on the counter. "I was hoping to turn it in?"

"Oh, okay. I'll take it." The girl reached out to take the licence from Emma, her fingers adorned with an array of colourful plastic rings that must hinder her typing significantly.

Emma pulled back. "Is there any way you can locate the owner? Maybe he's still in the store?"

"Uh, I don't know. I guess I can call the manager." The girl shrugged and picked up the store's intercom phone, mumbling something indistinct into the receiver. A moment later, a stout middle-aged man approached them, his nametag askew. *Merl.* Of course, he was.

"Hi there!" He greeted Emma with a friendly smile. "What seems to be the problem?"

"Oh, no problem. I found this driver's licence in the parking lot, and I wondered if the person who lost it might still be in the store." Emma's cheeks flushed, judging herself on Merl's behalf. *She was being kind.* If she lost her driver's licence, she'd hope someone would do the same thing, wouldn't she? "His name's Tyler Bowen."

"Righty-o, let me call that over the speaker here." Merl picked up the phone and pressed a button. "Howdy-do Friday afternoon shoppers, it seems one of you may have dropped a very important piece of personal property in our parking lot. If Mr. Tyler Bowen could make his way to the guest services desk, we'd be happy to get your driver's licence back to you. Again, a driver's licence for Mr. Tyler Bowen. Thank you, and please note the sale on Doritos in aisle eleven."

Emma stared at Merl as he dropped the handheld back on its perch and slapped his hands on the counter. *Had he been a popcorn salesman at carnivals in the fifties?*

Merl grinned. "Awful neighbourly of you to bring that back

into the store. We can put it here in our lost and found. I'm sure you're ready to move on with your day."

"You have a lost and found?"

Merl pulled open a drawer behind him, and the girl with pink hair shifted out of the way without looking up from her phone. "It'll be locked up tight."

Emma frowned. "So you'll keep this here until someone comes and gets it?"

"That's correct."

She glanced down at Tyler's picture. "What if he doesn't come?"

Merl put a hand on his hip. "We hold on to things for thirty days, then we have to dump the junk and skedaddle. There's not enough storage back here for all the lost toys to have a permanent home." He chuckled.

"No, of course not." Would Tyler know this was where he'd lost it? Or would he give up and make an appointment at the Registry? Emma shuddered. "I think I'll wait a moment and see if he shows up."

"You could take it to the police station," an old woman called out from behind them. Emma turned to see her gnarled hands wrapped around a plastic container of donut holes. *Blasphemy.* The only donuts worth eating were Tim's. Emma's stomach grumbled.

"You know, that's a great idea." Emma flicked the plastic card against her fingers. "I'll take this down to the station. Thanks so much for your help."

Merl saluted her as she exited the store and crunched back to her car. Once in the driver's seat, she looked up the closest RCMP. *Seriously?* All the way east to Country Hills Village?

Emma glanced back at Tyler's licence. Sage Valley. That was just north of her neighbourhood. Was she really going to drive clear to the highway to go to a police station when she could just drop it off at his doorstep?

Her heart picked up speed. That was a *neighbourly* thing to do, wasn't it? Emma started the car. Merl would definitely approve.

Emma parked on the street. The townhome was cute and well-kept, with shovelled walkways and steps. She blew out a breath, then pulled on her toque, picked up the licence from the passenger seat, and strode up to the door. Her knees felt weak as she knocked, hoping the lip gloss she'd applied in the car wasn't too obvious.

Footsteps sounded inside. A moment later, the door swung open to reveal a woman in her late forties, her hair pulled back into a messy bun. *Married.*

Emma gave an awkward wave. "Hi, I'm sorry to bother you, but I found this driver's licence in the Co-op parking lot and thought I'd drop it off. Does a Tyler Bowen live here?"

The woman reached out and lifted the licence to peer at the address. She raised an eyebrow. "I wish he did, but no. We just moved in a few weeks ago. Maybe he didn't get his address changed?"

Emma should've been disappointed, but her heart flipped hopefully in her chest. *Not married?* "No worries, thanks so much."

"Good luck." The woman smiled and pushed the door closed.

Emma groaned and stalked back to her car. This was stupid. She should've left the licence at the grocery store and been done with it or taken it to the police station like Betty White had suggested in the bakery.

This wasn't a cheesy rom-com, and she most definitely wasn't a Kate Hudson look-alike or whoever was acting in those movies these days. *When had she last sat down and watched a rom-com?* Maybe she was overdue.

No, the reason she'd *stopped* watching them was because of

moments like this—unrealistic expectations born of addictive plotlines and excellent editing. This was Calgary. In the middle of March.

While it had lifted her spirits to know that men with faces like Tyler Bowen, who was only three years older than she was and apparently shopped at the same grocery store, could exist in this world, it was time to pop the bubble. She'd go home, unload her groceries, eat a protein bar, and drive to the RCMP at Country Hills. Because what else did she have to do on a Friday night besides avoid rom-coms and learn how to chop kale?

Ten minutes later, she pulled into her parking garage and rode the elevator up to her apartment with groceries in hand and Tyler's licence slipped into her leggings pocket next to her phone. She was following her plan to a T until she made the mistake of sitting down on her new loveseat. It was too comfortable with its high-performing fabric and fuzzy throw blanket, and her legs were dead from shooting all week at the studio.

She needed to get up. Return the licence, then she could shower and pull on pajamas and watch non-romantic movies as long as she wanted. She checked one last notification on her phone. Lindsey had sent her a reel, which meant she'd be watching either a cute animal video or a clip of Ryan Reynolds. In her current deprived state, she hoped for the former.

Emma clicked and wasn't disappointed. A seal slapping its belly with the caption, "Me every night after dinner." She sent three cry-laugh emojis, then lifted her finger to swipe out of the app. Her finger hovered as that feeling of *I'm about to steal a cookie from the cookie jar* washed over her.

Instead of leaving her social media feed, she navigated to the home screen and clicked on the magnifying glass. She glanced around her living room, suddenly positive that there was a hidden camera somewhere. Could she ever admit to *anyone* that she was doing this?

Emma's heart raced as she typed "Tyler Bowen" before she could talk herself out of it, then pressed the search button. *It was only his name.* Public record. She wasn't going to send him a friend request or—

Her breath caught in her throat. There he was. Six-foot-three Tyler. His dark hair mussed, that same chiselled jawline from his photo. Hazel eyes. *Whaaaaat?* She probably could have read that on his licence, but since she was a *good person*, she hadn't looked. She exhaled in a rush and clicked on his photo.

There weren't any pictures or updates besides his profile picture and a few articles someone had tagged him in. All hockey-related. *Did he play?* He looked to have all his teeth, but her brother Carter had fooled plenty of girls with his tooth attached to a retainer, so she couldn't know for sure if they were real of not.

Her thumb hovered over the message button. He didn't seem to be posting regularly on social media, but he had commented on the articles. Maybe he got notifications? If she sent him a quick note letting him know she'd found his licence, there was at least a chance he'd see it. And if he didn't write back by the time she folded the load of laundry in the dryer, she'd hop in the car and drop it off at the police station.

Decision made. Emma tapped the button and began typing.

> Hi Tyler, you don't know me, but I know a lot about you!

She snorted and deleted that last part.

> Hi Tyler, you don't know me, but I found your driver's licence in the parking lot of the Co-op off Country Hills Blvd. today. The store was planning to hold on to it, but I thought you were adorable and wanted to see you in person

Delete.

> Hi Tyler, you don't know me, but I wanted to save you a trip to the Registry if possible. If I don't hear back, I'll drop it at the police station in the Village. The grandma picking out donuts in the bakery told me that was the place to drop it, and I decided to trust her

> However, her decision to purchase grocery store donuts is suspect and, frankly, un-Canadian

> Emma

She did a quick scan for typos, then pressed send and set her phone on the side table. Her heart raced as she walked into the hall and opened the door to pull her clothes from the dryer. *Why were her hands shaking?* That message would probably end up in the voids of the internet, and in a half hour, she'd be driving to drop his licence to an officer.

Emma had folded exactly two towels and one long-sleeved shirt when her phone dinged. Probably Lindsey again, and while the seal had been adorable, she wasn't especially in the mood.

Another ding.

She looped her black jeans over her arm and marched back to the end table for her phone. Emma read the banner on the screen, and her jeans hit the floor.

A message.

From Tyler Bowen.

CHAPTER Two

SHE MISTYPED her PIN twice after her Face ID failed, probably because her smartphone had never seen this particular expression on her face before. When her screen finally unlocked, she devoured his message faster than her chocolate peanut butter protein bar.

> Emma, while trusting Grandma is always the right call, I'm glad you reached out. I'm leaving town for the weekend, and my ID would come in handy
>
> Only for driving, of course, no extracurriculars. Not sure how quick officers are at returning those, especially by Mountie and horse in this kind of weather

Emma laughed out loud and had to steady the phone to read the rest of his message.

> I can meet you to pick it up if that works. Sounds like you might be partial to Tim's, plus then we'd be in a public place so you wouldn't have to worry about being murdered (I'm not a murderer, but I don't expect you to trust me on that)
>
> Shaganappi and Symons Valley? If that's not convenient, let me know what is
>
> Thanks, T

Emma dissected every sentence of his message. *He was funny.* Hot and witty? She didn't think that was allowed by the personality gods. And where was he going for the weekend? Had to be something fun if he was alluding to needing his ID for more than driving.

She checked the time and started typing.

> T, I appreciate the anti-murder sentiments immensely, though if you told me you were bringing honey crullers, I'd probably ignore a number of felonies. Does five o'clock work?

Over the top? She didn't care. This was too much fun. Messaging a hot guy about when she was going to meet said hot guy and eat donuts? It was already past four-thirty, but if he was leaving town, she didn't want to hold his licence hostage. Plus, she was still starving, and that trumped taking a shower.

As much as she was tempted, she would *not* get dolled up for this. For years she'd wasted time trying to look perfect for social outings, and the only thing *that* had gotten her was a guy who was embarrassed to have her on his arm when she didn't wear mascara.

No. Even tall, hot Tyler with hazel eyes would have to see her post-workout if he was interested in anything more than a hookup. This was the easiest way to weed men out in her experience. Which she had very little of since Alex, but it seemed like a good strategy on paper.

Her phone lit up.

> See you in fifteen

She swiped over to his relationship status. *Single.* Though, who knew when that had last been updated? Emma put her phone in her pocket. A girl could dream a little longer.

This was happening.

She was meeting Tyler.

He was *grateful* she'd tried to return his licence. Her mind raced with a hundred different thoughts as she stood staring at her screen. Should she be early? A few minutes late? Could she time it to arrive perfectly on time? Doubtful, and *what kind of psychopath arrived perfectly on time?*

She stuffed the licence back into her pocket, grabbed her phone and her keys, and left her black jeans lying in a heap on the living room floor.

———

Tyler planted himself in front of the counter at Tim Hortons. He was the only person under sixty in the establishment, which wasn't surprising for a Friday at five o'clock. He was guessing none of these white-haired women were Emma unless she hadn't changed her profile picture in approximately forty years.

What was it she said she liked? Honey crullers? He stepped up to the glass and scanned the display until he found the placard. A definite old-person donut. Maybe she *was* sitting here having her bedtime snack after all.

The door opened behind him, sending a blast of cold air against his back. He wanted to turn around and check who had entered but also didn't want to seem desperate. He was aloof. Just going with the flow. Emma knew what he looked like, at least from the neck up, and could approach him first if she wanted.

"Are you ready to order?" the pimpled employee asked.

Tyler straightened. "Yes, I'll take two honey crullers and..." he stalled, not sure what she'd want to drink. Coffee this late in the day? Since he wasn't a coffee guy, he didn't know what the best drinks were here anyway. The teen behind the register set two plates on a tray with the crullers he'd ordered. If she got to choose the donuts...

"Two London Fogs, please."

"That all?"

Tyler nodded and tapped his card to pay, then picked up the tray and stepped back to let the next person in line order.

"London Fog? I didn't peg you as a tea guy."

Tyler turned, and his pulse jumped. Emma, looking very much like her age in her most recent profile picture, stood behind him in grey leggings and a black puffy coat. Her hair was darker now, but it looked natural. He liked it better this way.

"I'm a tea guy." Was that really the first thing out of his mouth? He put out his hand, and she shook it. "I'm Tyler."

"I know." Her eyes widened, and her cheeks flushed. "I mean, I knew what you looked like because—" She pulled her hand back. "I'm sorry, that sounded creepy."

Tyler laughed. "Not creepy. I knew what you looked like too. From your profile picture."

She nodded and glanced down at the tray in his hand. Her eyes lit up. *Holy hell, she was cute in person, with her workout clothes and hair pulled up.* Emma grinned. "You ordered me a cruller?"

"Honey cruller, and only so you'd forgive the felonies I plan to commit later."

"Impressive. You upped the creepiness of this in one sentence." She laughed and played with the zipper of her coat. Like she didn't know what to do with her fingers.

"London Fogs." The employee behind the counter called out.

Tyler turned and was about to set down the tray when Emma

leaned in and took the drinks from the employee's outstretched hands.

She grinned. "Keep buying me supper, and I'll start stealing driver's licences left and right."

"This is supper?"

Emma shrugged as she walked to the corner table furthest from the door—a perfect choice. "I think I earned it. Went to the gym and bought kale after work."

Tyler chuckled and sat down across from her. "Where's work?"

"A photography studio on ninth."

"Down by the Saddledome?"

Emma nodded and removed the lid from her tea, then leaned over and blew on the creamy liquid. "What do you do?"

That was a complicated question, but he'd gotten better at sticking to the basics over the past year. "Internet securities."

Emma's brow furrowed. "That means nothing to me."

He grinned and picked up the cruller. "Are these any good?"

"Do I look like someone who would fall in love with a crappy donut?"

Tyler gave her a skeptical look and took a bite. The cruller was crispy on the outside but buttery soft inside. The layers melted on his tongue. "Holy shit."

Emma beamed at him. "Exactly. Now explain internet securities."

He swallowed, wishing he didn't have to talk so he could take another bite. He might have to get one of these to go. "Companies hire me to test their infrastructure. I try to break into their secure assets and information, and when I get in, give them a report on how they could protect them better."

Emma raised an eyebrow and pulled a piece off her donut. "When?" She popped it in her mouth. "You said 'when,' not 'if.'"

"Freudian slip." Tyler winked, and a blush rose to her cheeks.

Her lips curled as she tested the temperature of the tea with a small sip. "Mmm, what's in this?"

"You've never had one?" he asked. She shook her head, and warmth spread across his chest. He liked being the one to introduce this girl to something new. "It's Earl Grey, vanilla, and steamed milk. What did you peg me as, by the way?"

"Hmm?" Emma took another sip.

"You said you didn't peg me as a tea guy."

She grinned. "Ah. Right. No, I definitely had you slotted as a Bieber Brew type of guy."

Tyler laughed out loud, barely swallowing his tea in time to avoid a spit-take. "A cold brew? Have you looked outside?"

"The fact that you knew what it was tells me all I need to know." She shot him a look through her lashes, and suddenly his hands were tingling. Something in his expression made her laugh out loud before she took another sip. He wondered what she'd found so hilarious.

"What do you do at the photography studio? You're the photographer?"

She shook her head and leaned back in her chair, tearing off another piece of her cruller. "No, I'm a food stylist."

"That means nothing to me."

Emma barked a laugh. *Three.* He'd counted three different laughs since they'd met. "You know when you see commercials of burgers or ice cream sundaes? All slow motion and perfect?"

"You do that?"

She held out her hands and tipped her head as if waiting for a round of applause. *Adorable.* "I've shot for Timmies before."

Tyler pointed at the picture of steaming coffee above the menu lines. "Did you style that picture?"

"No, they contracted me years ago. I doubt my work is still in the rotation."

He took another bite of his donut, purposefully trying to eat it slower than usual. "So you're like me."

Emma's eyes dropped to his chest and lingered before she looked back at her tea. *Was she checking him out?* "How so?"

"You're a contractor. Moving from job to job."

She nodded. "I used to bounce around a lot, but now I'm only contracted through that studio. They have enough clients that I haven't had to find my own gigs for a couple of years now."

"You work with the same photographers there?"

Emma nodded. "Two of my best friends."

He grinned. "Not the worst."

"Do you enjoy that luxury?" She held her cup with both hands and folded her leg under her before taking a longer drink.

"I have the luxury of working alone at home with my computer."

She pursed her lips. "Seems . . . healthy."

He laughed, watching the way her fingers moved over the insulated cup. "That's why I have hockey."

Her eyes narrowed as she leaned in. "You play?"

"Are you trying to figure out if my teeth are real?"

Emma's mouth dropped, and her skin flushed pink. He liked that too. "No. *Maybe.*" Her face split into a wide smile. "Not that I'd judge you for it. All my brothers play, and Carter, my oldest brother, is missing at least one of his incisors."

"*All* your brothers?"

"I have three and two sisters."

"Big family." He took another drink.

"Do you have siblings?" she asked.

Tyler exhaled. "Nope. Only child."

"Wow. I have no idea what that must've been like."

"Less stolen clothing items and more rides in shotgun."

She chuckled, but then her face sobered. He wondered if he'd said something wrong. Emma sighed and flicked her hand in the air. "Sorry, I was just lost in the fantasy of having a private bathroom as a teen."

Tyler took the last bite of his infused-with-the-nectar-of-the-gods donut and wiped his hands on the napkin. He glanced at his watch.

Emma noticed. "I'm sorry. You said you were going away for

the weekend, and here I am going on about my siblings." She brushed her hands on her napkin and reached into the pocket of her leggings. She pulled out his licence and slid it across the table. He couldn't help but think about how it'd been pressed against her thigh the whole time they'd been talking.

Tyler picked it up. "I appreciate you getting this back to me."

She motioned at the table. "I feel more than appropriately thanked. You really didn't need to do this."

"But I found a new favourite donut."

She replaced the lid on her cup and tipped it. "And I found a new favourite drink."

He smiled and watched her until she blushed under his gaze. Emma looked away and reached for her coat. "Where are you going this weekend anyway?"

"Saskatoon. Hockey tournament."

Emma froze. She dropped her coat back onto the chair and whirled to face him. "Which league?"

"Elite."

She blinked. "Which team?"

Tyler grinned. She might be even cuter when she was serious. "Snowballs. I joined when I moved to Calgary at the beginning of last summer. Why?"

Emma slumped onto the table and dropped her head in her hands. She muttered something unintelligible under her breath, then sat back up and forced a smile. "Your captain is Sean Thompson, right?"

Tyler's brow furrowed. "Yeah, how did you—"

"Sean's my older brother."

CHAPTER *Three*

THE SHRILL SOUND of Tyler's alarm pierced the silence, jarring him awake at five o'clock the next morning. He rubbed his eyes, swung his legs over the edge of the bed, and planted his feet on the chilled floorboards. He really needed to buy a rug.

"You up?" Knuckles rapped on the door. Brett had probably been up for an hour and had already finished a workout. Since Tyler moved in a few weeks ago, he hadn't witnessed Brett miss a day of lifting, even when they had doubleheaders. The dude was a machine.

"Yep. Thanks, man." Tyler stretched his arms over his head and popped his back. He was still a little achy from Thursday's game.

He lifted his phone off its charger on his nightstand. Fifteen new text messages, but not one he wanted to answer. Kelli asking if he wanted to go on a pub crawl this weekend. Tamar wishing him a late happy birthday. Misty asking when he'd be playing the next home game.

After this tournament, they'd be at home or in South Calgary for the next three weeks, but he wasn't going to tell any of them that. He blew out a breath and dropped his phone on the bed, then searched for his pants.

They had just over a six-hour drive today, one game at four-thirty tonight, and potentially two on Sunday if they won. Which they should. Their first match-up was with some team from Regina, and they didn't have a great record.

The game he cared about was Sunday afternoon for the championship, most likely against Pucks Deep. They'd traded W's in their first two match-ups of the season, and it was time for the Snowballs to get one up. But he couldn't get ahead of himself. They had two games to win before they'd get a shot at them.

He pulled on a waffle-knit shirt, a puffy vest, and his navy toque. The vest made him think of Emma, which sent a shot of adrenaline through his sluggish veins. Last night felt like a fever dream. *Sean had a hot younger sister?* How had *that* never come up in dressing room conversation? Either the other guys didn't know, or Sean had already threatened to castrate them if they made a bid. He was guessing the latter.

He stalked into the kitchen and was about to grab a bowl and spoon when Brett called his name.

"Made you this." He handed him a tall cup with a straw. "Forty grams of protein right there."

Tyler took a drink. It was good. Chocolate with only a slight green aftertaste. *I went to the gym and bought kale after work.* Tyler cleared his throat. "Thanks, man. You lift already this morning?"

Brett nodded and dropped into one of the four chairs around the kitchen table. Nothing in this townhouse belonged to Tyler besides the furniture in the bedroom. Brett had the place outfitted well before he'd moved in, and that suited him perfectly. He didn't plan to stay in Calgary long and would probably sell his bed and shelves before moving back to Toronto.

Brett kicked his feet up on the table. "Where were you last night? I was going to see if you wanted to hit the bar, but you weren't here when I stopped home."

"You went to the bar at five?" Tyler took a drink.

"No, we went to Moxies, then Dusty Rose. Ginger was playing." He waggled an eyebrow. Tyler shook his head. "Dude, you know she wants to hit that." Brett ran his hands through his hair. "It's silly, bud. You know that, right? How you can walk through any door and have every woman salivating over—"

"Yeah, I get it. Thank you." He grinned and drank the last of his shake.

"Foul." Brett laughed, clapping him on the shoulder as he rinsed out his cup and placed it in the sink. He leaned in. "Do you want to tell whoever you left in the sheets that she's not allowed to eat my leftovers?"

Tyler shoved him, and Brett laughed, pushing on his shoes and grabbing his duffel. Their hockey bags, sticks, and skates were still in the truck. One less thing to carry down the steps. He stalked back to his room and grabbed his overnight bag.

He hadn't brought someone home in . . . well, a week, and Brett was still giving him crap. *Why hadn't he brought someone home in a week?* He'd had plenty of opportunities. Ginger wasn't the only one making a play, his unanswered text messages were proof of that. Work had been busy, but that excuse felt hollow even as he thought it.

He slung his bag over his shoulder and followed Brett down the stairs and out the door. *He didn't want to bring someone home.* That was the honest, pathetic truth.

It was being around Troy again. Seeing his father flirting with the real estate agent at one of his properties when Tyler knew he had a girlfriend back at his apartment made Tyler's own flirtations sparkle less. He hated what Troy had done to his mom before they split, and seeing the man in action felt like a cheap shot against the boards.

He might not be boyfriend material, but at least he wasn't that guy. He never cheated on women because he never got serious with them. He couldn't hurt them if they never had expectations in the first place.

"Bud, unlock my door. It's cold as balls." Brett blew into his hands.

Tyler opened the door to his truck and hit the button. They threw their bags in the backseat on top of their frozen equipment and got in, then started south toward Sean's.

The image of Emma's eyes peeking out at him from under her lashes flashed in his head as they passed the Tim Hortons on Shaganappi. He'd thought about sending her a message last night after he got home but hadn't known what to say. Would that be weird? It seemed like she'd enjoyed herself as much as he had.

Tyler rechecked his notifications at the next light. Emma hadn't sent anything last night, and there wasn't a message yet this morning. *Why would she be up this early on a Saturday?* She was probably still dead asleep. In her bed. Wearing—

"It's green, bud."

Tyler hit the gas.

The passenger van was packed. Tyler somehow scored shotgun after they filled up with gas in Kindersley, and he nearly sighed as he stretched out his legs.

"I'm surprised André didn't fight you for that seat." Sean grinned and called over the seat. "Probably because he knows who won the war the first time."

André balled up a napkin from breakfast and threw it at the back of Sean's head, and laughed. "Faire le boss de bécosses!"

Sean ducked. "What the hell does that mean?"

"Your country is bilingual—you should know!" André pulled a cigarette from his pocket, but Country swiped it.

"Not in the van, *Francois*."

André threw up his hands. "I can't live under these conditions."

Tyler laughed. André joined the team last year but was still one of the new guys, like him. How he could smoke a pack a day and still beat most players on the ice to the puck was beyond him. Probably because he was still technically in his twenties.

Then there was Country. He'd never played pro, but his stick-handling was better than half the guys Tyler skated with in Toronto. Country attributed it to years of roping on the ranch but had never explained how those two things could possibly be related.

"Guys, we should play that licence plate game. I do it with my kids all the—" Curtis stopped talking when groans erupted around him. He reached for Darcy's earbud, but before he could rip it from his ear, Darcy grabbed his wrist.

"You want to keep this hand, eh?"

Curtis grinned and mouthed, *'Do you want to play a game?'*

Darcy dropped his arm and rolled his eyes, then returned to staring at his phone. Darcy was a dick, but Tyler understood why Sean kept him around. He mostly kept to himself as long as people didn't piss him off, and he was a killer defenseman.

Brett reached between the seats for the cord plugged into the stereo. "Time for some pump-up music."

Tyler yawned and looked over his shoulder. Fly, Steve, and Suraj were all dead asleep in the backseat. They were going to appreciate this turn of events. "We still have three hours to drive."

"Never too early to get amped."

Sean flicked open a text message on his phone and glanced at it just as a heavy beat punched through the speakers. He looked back at the road, then over at Tyler. With his knees steadying the wheel, he typed a quick response and set his phone back in the console.

He turned to Tyler and said something but the music swallowed his words.

Tyler reached out and twisted the volume dial to the left. "What?"

"When were you going to mention you met my sister?" he repeated. His eyes were hard, and Tyler's throat went dry.

"Wait, you met Emma?" Brett's head was suddenly back between the seats. "Is that where you were last night?"

Darcy pulled out his earbud.

Tyler shrugged. "I didn't know she was your sister." *How did Sean find out he met Emma?* Tyler glanced at Sean's phone sitting in his lap. "Did she tell you what happened?"

"Something *happened?*" Mike piped up from the middle row. Why did he feel like he was suddenly on trial?

Sean's jaw tensed. "It doesn't matter what Emma told me. Why didn't you say something?"

Tyler bristled. "Probably because I was half asleep when I crawled into this van."

"Were you half asleep for the past three hours?"

Tyler scoffed. "Am I supposed to disclose information on every person I meet? Did I miss that on the team paperwork?"

Brett snorted. "Ask Suraj how asking for Emma's number went for him."

"What the hell, Brett!" Suraj threw his hands up in the backseat before adjusting his pillow. *Not as asleep as he'd looked.*

Tyler drew a deep breath and exhaled. "Listen, I get it, but it wasn't like that. She found my driver's licence in a parking lot and messaged me. We met up at Tim Horton's so I could grab it before we left."

They had to show ID at check-in for the tournament, and while he didn't think they'd kick him off the ice, he was grateful he wouldn't have to jump through hoops to play.

"That was it?" Sean scratched the scruff on his chin.

"Did you get her number? Suraj wants to know," Country drawled.

Sean shook his head and glowered at them in the rearview mirror.

Tyler turned in his seat. "Wait, if you all know her, why have I never seen or heard of her before?"

Brett sat back and skipped past the next song on his playlist.

"She used to come to plenty of games, but we haven't seen her much this season. You probably crossed paths in exhibition."

Tyler shook his head. He'd only joined the team in October. "Anyone else have a sister I should stay away from?"

Fly piped up. "My sister's forty-two and just got divorced. She'd probably send me a gift card if I gave you her number."

Tyler laughed and shook his head. "Sean, I'm sorry, man. I wasn't trying to hide it. I only met her last night."

Sean nodded. "She's been through some stuff. Dated a hockey player. Total D-bag. She doesn't need that in her life."

Tyler turned back to the front and nodded once. Point taken. Sean thought he was a D-bag. First, he hadn't heard that term since the nineties. Second, *why did Sean think he was a D-bag?*

He thought back to Brett's comments that morning. Sure, he didn't get serious with women, but that didn't mean he treated them poorly.

Tyler pulled out his phone, opened his messaging app, then clicked on Emma's picture. His thumb hesitated momentarily, but then he started to type.

CHAPTER Four

> Don't get involved with Tyler

EMMA STARED at the text message from Sean and rolled over onto her back. She wasn't looking to get *involved* with him. She was only curious. She typed out, *Fine, but is he single?* then deleted it. She hadn't asked too many questions already, had she?

Emma scrolled back through the last few messages. No, she'd only asked whether he was new on the team and about his situation. Totally normal, non-invasive questions after meeting someone you had a mutual connection with.

A notification popped up on her phone. Emma's heart felt like it was connected to an air pump and someone had just slammed down the handle. *A message from Tyler.* She swiped up.

> Seems it's a well-known fact on the Snowballs that nobody on the team is supposed to share honey crullers with you

> Please don't mention how far we went. If Sean knew about the London Fogs...

Emma clapped a hand over her mouth. *Sean told him she'd texted?* What. The. Hell?! She was going to murder her brother. Didn't he understand discretion when it came to private messaging?

Now Tyler was sitting in that van filled with *the entire team,* and they all knew she'd texted Sean asking about him. She dropped her phone on the bed next to her and draped an arm over her eyes. Such an idiot.

No. She wasn't the idiot. Sean had made a big deal out of nothing, and she wouldn't be rude just because he was. She picked up her phone and let her thumbs go to work.

> Oh, he'd be intimidated. I don't think he and Kelty have even made it past Timbits
>
> Seriously, though, I'm so sorry. I texted to ask when you joined the team since I didn't recognize you
>
> Didn't mean to put you on his naughty list

Her heart flapped against her ribs as she stared at the screen. The chat jumped as the words *typing* appeared under her message. She turned onto her side and folded her pillow to prop up her head. She held her breath as Tyler's message appeared.

> I've been on plenty of naughty lists, but never my captain's
>
> That's a first.
>
> Two firsts in less than twenty-four hours. I think you're a bad influence on me

She giggled—*giggled*—and pulled the phone closer so she could type.

> I don't think I've ever been told I'm a bad influence, so I think we're even with firsts

> You guys in Sask yet?

Tyler responded immediately.

> Still two and a half hours out

> Good luck tonight. I haven't been to a game in forever, but a little birdie told me you're gunning for the finals this season

> Was it Suraj? He's not supposed to have your number. I'm telling Sean

Emma snorted, then coughed and nearly dropped her phone off the bed.

> Shhh. Put that tasty morsel in the lockbox with the Fogs

It took Tyler a minute to respond. When he finally did, it was only one sentence.

> Maybe you should change that, by the way

Emma frowned.

> Change what?

> How long it's been since you saw a game

Emma didn't realize she was holding her breath until her lungs began to burn. She exhaled and waited for her vision to clear.

> I'll think about it

After a few minutes with no response from Tyler, Emma returned her phone to the nightstand and rolled over onto her pillow. Today was wide open, which suddenly seemed like a special brand of torture.

She threw off her sheets and scampered into her closet. This called for her yoga mat and spandex. Stat.

On Sunday in the late afternoon, Emma stood on the step sandwiched between Lindsey and Vaughn, their breath misting in the chilly air. Calgary's winter sun was a beautiful but disappointing illusion. Unless a Chinook was blowing, its warm glow gave no respite from the cold.

"Emma! Lindsey and Vaughn, I'm so glad you could make it! Come on in." Emma's mom, Sharla, shuffled to the side to let them in. Rob, her dad, sat in his favourite recliner with his reading glasses on. He kicked down the footrest and set his paper on the coffee table.

"Smells delicious." Lindsey sighed as they hugged all around. They unbundled themselves and hung their coats on the hooks by the door.

Sharla beamed at them and clasped her hands in front of her. "I hope you like it. I made shepherd's pie, Jell-O salad, rolls, and Nanaimo bars."

Emma nudged Vaughn on their way into the kitchen. "I'm going to watch you eat the Jell-O You know that right? No dropping it into your napkin."

"It's made with *horse hooves*," Vaughn hissed.

"Mmm." Emma stifled a laugh at Vaughn's horrified expression. His eyes darted around the table, looking like a cat who just found himself on an ice rink.

Lindsey playfully elbowed him. "Did your mother never cook for you?"

"I'm from California. We ate out of Trader Joe's freezer."

"You knew a trader with a freezer?" Sharla asked.

Vaughn pursed his lips. "It's a grocery store," he answered, then muttered under his breath, "but so much more than that."

They sat down around the table, which Sharla had decorated for spring. With long, harsh winters, Albertans were forced to be a perpetually hopeful people—which was a nicer way of saying irrationally optimistic.

Emma's phone buzzed in her back pocket as she sat down. Out of habit, she pulled it out and checked the screen, then nearly swallowed her own tongue.

"Emma, is everything okay? We're about to say grace."

Emma blinked and looked up. "Mmhmm." She slid the phone under her thigh and clasped her hands on the table. Rob recited a short prayer, then Sharla invited them to dig in. Emma's heart pounded as she passed her plate for her dad to load up a serving of shepherd's pie.

"Since Lindsey and I are both here, I'm dying to know who that message was from," Vaughn murmured as he took a pathetically small portion of the green Jell-O with little pieces of pineapple floating in it.

"What, you don't think I have other friends?"

Lindsey snorted. "Not who would text you on a Sunday afternoon."

Emma scoffed. "I will have you know that I spotted a guy at the gym the other day and he said we should do it again sometime."

Vaughn nodded seriously. "That's basically second base for you."

"I know, right?"

Sharla looked up. "Emma, you're dating someone?"

"No. I'm very much not dating someone." Emma took a large portion of Jell-O salad and grinned at Vaughn before setting her plate down on the table. She took a deep breath. She should tell them, shouldn't she? About Tyler and the licence? It wasn't like it was anything to be embarrassed about since it ended well.

"That message was actually from a guy on Sean's hockey team," she stated with as much nonchalance as she could muster. Rob's eyes widened, and Emma held up a hand. "I found his driver's licence in a parking lot—I had no idea he was on the Snowballs."

"Well who is it? We know all those boys." Sharla watched her eagerly.

Emma swallowed hard. "Tyler Bowen. We met up at a Tim Hortons so I could give it back—"

"You met up with a stranger to give back a driver's licence?" Lindsey looked horrified. "Emma, do we need to review those commercials from the Concerned Children's Advertisers?"

Vaughn's hand flew to his chest. "Umm, no. I kid you not, since you showed me those, those puppets have shown up in my dreams more than once."

Sharla laughed. "I used to love those songs!"

"Focus!" Lindsey snapped her fingers. "Emma, you could've been murdered!"

Emma laughed. "No, that's why we met at a Tim Hortons. He even brought that up."

"He brought up the possibility of murder?" Vaughn gaped at her while holding a forkful of mashed potatoes.

Emma held up her hands. "I think we're forgetting the point. I'm a hero. I returned this poor man's licence and then found out he was on Sean's team, so . . .not a murderer."

Rob grunted. "Isn't Tyler the pretty one?"

Emma pursed her lips to keep from laughing. *Her dad thought Tyler was pretty?* Well, he wasn't wrong.

"Oh, those boys are all handsome, Rob."

Not as handsome as Tyler.

"Aren't you going to answer it?" Lindsey asked.

Emma pretended her phone wasn't burning a hole into the bottom of her thigh. "I didn't want to be rude."

Rob pulled out his phone. "I haven't heard anything about the tournament from Sean. Their game should be over."

"Fine, if you insist." Emma tried to avoid looking eager as she pulled her phone out and swiped up.

> Game ended on a power play. We lost by one. Second place

Emma groaned. "They lost in the finals." Sharla sighed, and Rob's face dropped. Emma pretended to be disappointed, but that was the opposite of what was blooming in her midsection. *Tyler had messaged her to tell her about the game.*

> I should've told you at Tim's, I'm notorious for having bad luck. I probably passed it on when I handed you the licence. Please apologize to the team for me

She didn't know Tyler well enough to gauge whether he'd be devastated by this loss or if he'd take it in stride. Sean had always been the former. They knew to stay out of his way for at least six hours after a hard loss, though his being with Kelty had shortened the time span significantly.

"At least they get to play them again Tuesday," Rob muttered.

"Who?" Lindsey asked.

"Pucks Deep. The rival team in town."

Emma put a hand on Lindsey's arm. "There are three teams in Calgary, but C-Biscuit hasn't been as competitive the past few years." Though they'd been friends for years now, Lindsey and Vaughn still had very little interest in the hockey part of Emma's life. They'd come to a few games here and there but would rather be at a theatre production or art show.

It was kind of a miracle they'd become friends in the first place, considering how different their post-work interests were. Emma loved creating beautiful and compelling photos, but for her it was mathematical. Scientific. She didn't feel the composition of it in her gut like they did.

Her phone buzzed.

> Does that mean we need to hold some kind of seance?

> Tyler, I know you're from out of town, but people here don't typically meet with mediums until at least the third date

"You're grinning." Lindsey took a bite of her roll.

Emma looked up and put her phone back on the chair under her leg. "Sorry, I saw a funny meme."

Lindsey raised an eyebrow, and Emma pretended to be deeply involved with her ground beef and green beans. Lindsey was the only one that scrolled social media feeds in their relationship, and they both knew it.

CHAPTER *Five*

EMMA STOOD SHIVERING outside the ice arena, her breath pluming above her in the air. It was Tuesday night. As her dad noted on Sunday, the Snowballs were set to play Pucks Deep for the second time in a week, and this was the game that counted. Losing to them in the tournament didn't affect their provincial standings, but it did mean that Sean would be out for blood tonight. Those were always the best games to watch.

She wrapped her scarf tighter around her neck and stared at the entrance. Once she walked through that door and sat behind the boards, Tyler would know he'd had something to do with her showing up. *Was she okay with that?*

Though, after the tournament, this game would be packed for the rematch. It wouldn't be difficult to play it off as a game she'd already planned to attend if she needed to. The Elite League had plenty of fans, especially since there were three teams here in Calgary. They were also hosting the playoffs this year, which meant everyone was even more invested than usual.

Emma strode toward the doors, avoiding a frozen puddle beside the curb. The warmth of the arena enveloped her instantly as she pushed into the airlock, as did the familiar sounds and smells of the place. Echoing voices layered over each other. The thump of bodies against the boards. Smells of buttered popcorn and funnel cakes that caused cavities simply through inhalation.

Taking a calming breath, Emma descended the stairs and pushed through the doors leading to the stands. As she scanned the rows of seats, her eyes landed on a petite woman with striking features, her dark hair pulled back into a ponytail. Kelty, Sean's girlfriend, waved when she saw Emma approaching.

Kelty's face split into a wide smile as she stood and pulled her into a hug. She pulled back, and her dark eyes sparkled in the overhead lights. "Emma! I can't believe you made it! It's been way too long."

"I know! Couldn't miss this one." Emma sat down on the bench next to her.

"Tell me about it. Sean was pissed when they lost in the finals Sunday."

Emma groaned. "What time did they get home?"

"Late. I was already asleep, so I'm not sure of the exact time." She picked up a thermos of hot cocoa and took a drink. "If they don't win tonight, I'm sleeping at your place."

"Done."

Kelty passed her the thermos, and Emma took a drink. The cold metal bleachers bit into her skin through her jeans. She was out of practice. She owned a foldable seat pad, but it was sitting at home, forlorn in the front closet.

"Did you have supper with your parents Sunday since the team was out of town?" Kelty asked.

"I did! Lindsey and Vaughn came with me."

"Friends from work, right?"

Emma nodded. "I think you may have met Lindsey at my birthday in the fall."

"Red hair. Loves to wear green. I remember."

A voice crackled to life over the PA system announcing the

national anthem. The bench shifted as people rose to face the red and white flag hanging from the rafters. A little girl walked out onto the ice holding the hand of one of our players.

"Wait, is that Ryan's daughter? Is she singing?" Ryan had been on the team almost as long as Sean, and the last time she'd seen Amaya, she'd been barely out of diapers.

Kelty grinned. "Yep! She's six now. Isn't that wild?"

Emma watched as Ryan skated over to get the mic from behind the penalty box, then took it out to his daughter and stood next to her while she sang.

Six. How long had it been since he'd gotten divorced? Amaya's little voice soared through the arena, and she only mispronounced 'patriot' and 'glorious,' which was understandable since she probably hadn't graduated Kindergarten.

Minutes later, the game began with a face-off at centre ice. Sean squared off against the Pucks Deep centreman. The referee dropped the puck, and after a scuffle of sticks, Sean tapped it back to Ryan. His hair hung out the bottom of his helmet, so even though they didn't have names on the backs of their jerseys, Emma could always spot him.

She recognized Tyler immediately. His height set him apart, but the way he held his body cinched it. His easy, relaxed manner at Tim's the other night seemed to grow exponentially on the ice. He leaned and glided—none of the harsh, jerky movements she saw from other players. He wore a number four on his jersey, and Emma wondered if it had any significance.

Country sprayed ice as he stopped beside the boards and received a crisp pass from Ryan near the blue line. He danced around two Pucks Deep players with a series of dekes, and the crowd erupted as he shot past centre ice.

His stick slapped the ice sending the puck in an arc around the edge of the boards where André was ready to receive it. He took a shot, deflected by a Pucks Deep defenseman. The fans groaned with disappointment, then cheered as Curtis knocked a player into the boards and stole the puck.

Emma's heart raced. *She'd missed this.* With three brothers playing competitive hockey, she'd seen more games than she could count, which was why it'd been easy to convince herself that she didn't need to make an effort to see more. But being in this chilled arena, feeling the heaters radiating overhead, hearing the sounds of blades against smooth ice and the puck knocking against the boards. It felt like coming home.

The crowd continued to grow through the first period, and after watching the Snowballs play a man down for a minute or two, those in blue roared while those in gold booed as André exploded back onto the ice. The score was still at zeroes, and Emma knew Sean had to be getting antsy.

Pucks Deep had the puck, and their forwards flew into formation. They wove and passed between themselves, keeping the puck wide of the defence, then took a shot from the far side. Boyd, the Snowballs' goalie, split his legs and blocked it with his left pad. Half the crowd screamed their approval.

Ryan took the puck behind the net, then back again. He found Curtis who then spotted Tyler cutting the neutral zone and sent a tape-to-tape pass. Tyler split the defence and beelined to the goal in two hard pushes.

Emma rose from the bench, watching each graceful pump of his legs. With a quick move to his backhand followed by a swift return to his forehand, Tyler faked a shot through the five-hole, then flicked it over the now sprawling Pucks Deep goalie.

A horn blasted through the arena, and Emma couldn't help but scream right along with it. Kelty bounced up and down, clapping her hands as the Snowballs on the ice swarmed Tyler, then moved as a puppy pile back into their own territory.

A group of women screamed and trilled on Emma's right, and she leaned forward to see the sign one of them was holding. *#4, Drop mitts with me!*

Emma gagged. Puck bunnies. Of course they were cheering for Tyler.

"How long has this been happening?" Emma murmured to Kelty as they sat down.

Kelty rolled her eyes. "André still has his regulars, but it's worsened since Tyler joined."

"How do they even know? Is there an underground group sharing new recruits I don't know about?" If there was, then why wasn't she on it?

Kelty laughed and picked up her hot chocolate. "Oh, word gets out quick in this town, you know that. And most of it *is* Tyler's fault. He's the life of the party when they go out on the weekends."

Emma's ribs closed a little tighter over her lungs. Was that what Sean's text message was about? *Don't get involved with Tyler.*

He hadn't seemed like one of *those* guys at Tim's the other night, but usually, that *was* the red flag. Players always seemed like they weren't playing you until you spent the night, and then they suddenly stopped returning your messages.

The Snowballs continued their aggressive play, with Ryan making key defensive stops and Boyd coming up with a couple of highlight-reel saves. Pucks Deep didn't make it easy, though. They continued pressing, looking for opportunities to level the score.

They'd always been the team to worry about, and since Jordan Wheatfill became their captain, Sean was even more dead-set on beating them. He and Jordan had played against each other in high school. Jordan's team won Provincials Sean's senior year, but that wasn't why Sean hated him. That came two years later when Jordan slept with his girlfriend.

Every close call, every shot, every save evoked a collective gasp, a shout, a cheer. Pucks Deep scored late in the second, but Tyler sent a laser between their goalie's legs at the beginning of the third, taking advantage of the knowledge he gained off of the fake he made earlier. *That sneaky bugger.* Somehow the Snowballs staved them off, and fans erupted in a wave of baby blue when the final buzzer sounded. The team swarmed the ice, hugging each other and raising their sticks.

"Glad you came?" Kelty grinned at her.

"Hell, yes." Emma threw an arm around her shoulders and added her voice to the cheers.

It didn't take long for the crowd to filter out of the arena. Emma and Kelty moved in the sea of blue and gold across the street to One Place after the game. The whole team would be there. They always were. Even if players couldn't stay for long, they made an appearance and greeted Pat behind the bar before heading home. Tonight, she doubted any of them would leave early.

The pub was bustling with activity, its dim lighting casting a warm glow on the exposed brick walls adorned with vintage hockey memorabilia. Laughter filled the air as patrons clinked glasses while classic rock drifted in the background.

They moved past the booths and, with a wave to Pat, made quick work of moving the tables in the back. Once they were pulled together to form two long tables, they set up the chairs and dropped into two seats at the end.

Emma ordered six plates of loaded nachos to start while Kelty stood at the bar to transport pitchers of beer as Pat filled them behind the bar. "Sean's going to be over the moon tonight."

Kelty nodded to the door where the players began to trickle in, still riding high on adrenaline from their win. They greeted friends and fans with hugs and hearty pats on the back, their smiles contagious. Emma scanned each face, not realizing until she didn't find one in particular that she'd been hoping to see it.

Emma and Kelty took two of the nachos, cups, and pitchers back to the table. Sean grinned from ear to ear, and Emma made a point to compliment him. She loved seeing him like this. His life hadn't gone as planned over the last decade.

Sean knew he'd never be able to go pro with hockey after getting in a motorcycle crash his senior year and never quite regaining his speed. He went to Mount Royal and graduated with a business degree, then worked with a friend at a tech startup company. They paid him well, especially in stock options, but when the company went belly up a couple of years later, that didn't help much.

For all their faults, none of her brothers were prideful. They were simple. Kind under their burly exteriors, and Sean the most tender-hearted of the three. Nobody would know it by looking at him. He didn't say much, and when he did open his mouth, it was usually to make a joke. But when Emma found out Alex had been cheating on her, Sean had been the first one on her doorstep. Not Lindsey. Not Vaughn. He'd even brought her a bag of dark chocolate—all the wrong brands because he never ate it himself—but it was the thought that counted.

"Emma, you're eating cheese now?" Sean put a hand on his chest in mock horror as she lifted a chip coated in queso from the plate. "I thought you were counting macros."

Emma flipped her middle finger at him and shoved the chip in her mouth. It was the memory of that bag of dark chocolate that kept her from throat-punching him in moments like these.

Cheers lifted at the front of the bar, and Emma's heart stuttered. *She knew.* Before he even walked through the door— freshly showered, his dark hair still damp and curling over his ears— she knew that Tyler had walked in.

One hand was shoved in the pocket of his coat as he strode toward the back tables. The lights glinted off a few lingering water droplets on his neck, and heat flashed through Emma's middle. This was not good. She hadn't had a physical reaction like this to anyone in . . . probably ever.

She cleared her throat and looked down at the chips, hoping the flush in her cheeks wasn't as noticeable as it felt.

Compliments, hand slaps, hugs, and fist bumps sounded around her as she feigned interest in a pile of jalapeños. A chair scooted across the floor next to her, and then out of nowhere, a solid, warm arm landed on her shoulders.

"You know it was Emma that saved my ass this weekend, right?"

Emma's head shot up, her eyes wide. Tyler was there next to her, so close she could smell his soap and could've licked the water from his neck. She snapped her head forward, her mouth suddenly feeling like it had been swabbed out with a handful of cotton balls.

"I dropped my licence in a parking lot, and she gave it back to me before we left."

The whole team hooted and hollered. Sean cleared his throat, and Tyler's grin faded a bit. He pulled his arm back and slid his chair a few inches to the side.

Kelty looked between Emma and Sean. "Did you know this?" She punched Sean's shoulder, and he grunted. She looked back at Emma. "You didn't feel like telling *this* story while we were sitting together for three periods?"

Emma swallowed. "I didn't think it was that big of a deal."

Kelty ignored her. "How did you track him down? Did you know he played on the team? I want to hear all the details!"

Tyler reached for a glass and stood, walking toward the water cooler next to the bar. Emma glanced up at Sean. He stared daggers at Tyler's retreating back, then looked back at her. Before she turned her attention back to Kelty, he mouthed, *Keep it in your pants*, then reached for a pitcher of beer.

Emma's eyes widened, and the chip she held between her thumb and forefinger crumbled, dropping black beans and a sliced olive onto the table. *Keep it in her pants?* Was he serious?

She drew a deep breath, her nostrils flaring. "You know, I think Sean wants to tell you his side of the story." Emma stood and snatched one more chip layered with queso, leaned over the table, and shoved it in her mouth right in front of him. She yanked her coat and purse off the back of her chair and marched toward the door.

She was still seething when she got home, replaying Sean's comment in her head. Was that seriously what he thought of her? That she was one of those girls with the signs saying *I'll drop my panties for #4!*

Ugh. Yes, Tyler was hot. Yes, over the past few days, she'd thought way more than she should have about his hands on his Tim Hortons cup, but that didn't give Sean the right to tell her where to *keep her things*.

This was why she'd stopped coming to the games in the first place. Ever since she broke things off with Alex, Sean was like a helicopter parent anytime he saw her out with any male with a pulse. Especially a guy with a pulse who also happened to play hockey.

Emma took the elevator up to her apartment, unlocked the door, and slipped inside, looping her purse over the hooks. She took off her coat and boots, then stomped into the kitchen and grabbed the washcloth next to the sink. A little rage cleaning always helped in situations like this.

She wiped down the cabinet doors, then moved on to the appliances, following up with a microfiber cloth to prevent streaks. Her arms started to complain just as she finished. She dropped the rags on the counter and filled up a glass of water, then leaned up against the counter and gulped it down.

Her phone dinged in her purse. She set the glass down and walked over to grab it. Tyler Bowen's name showed on the message banner. The hair on the back of her neck prickled. She swiped up and read the message.

> Hey. Just wanted to apologize. I saw you leave and realized I probably made you uncomfortable. I wasn't thinking, I'm sorry
>
> Hope you enjoyed the game -T

Emma pursed her lips and started typing.

> You didn't make me uncomfortable. Sean was being Sean, and I have an early shoot tomorrow.
>
> The game was a blast! I think you forgot to mention at Tim's that you're one of THE players on the team.
>
> Next time, lead with that.

She pressed send and flicked off the lights in the kitchen, then walked down the hall to the bathroom. Her phone dinged again as she slipped a headband over her hair to keep it back while she washed her face.

> Excellent advice. It would seem your marketing acumen isn't limited to burgers and ice cream

Emma laughed and turned on the water. When it was warm, she splashed it over her face and scrubbed with a squirt of face wash. She reached for her towel and dried her skin, then picked up her phone from the counter. There was a second message below Tyler's last one.

> What do you mean Sean was being Sean?

She sighed. How to explain that in a few sentences? *Sean is my only brother that lives close and he saw me devastated after my last relationship. He doesn't trust me to make good decisions when it comes to men since that wasn't my only relationship where a guy treated me like crap, so now he's taken on the mantle of relationship advisor without my permission.* Emma's chest tightened as she tapped on the screen.

> Sean doesn't know when to stop

As she pressed the blue send button, she realized that had

always been her brother's issue. He'd kept working at that company even after red flags started to go up, kept fighting on the ice after the whistles blew, and kept holding the reins on relationships even after he'd been kicked in the chest. Kelty was good for him, but he'd lucked into that one. She was strong enough to stiff-arm him when needed, and he needed it often.

> If he gets that worked up when a guy talks to you, I don't want to see him when you're actually dating someone

Emma groaned. *Exactly, Tyler.*
But...

Maybe her problem was that she wasn't enough like Kelty. Instead of standing up to him tonight, she'd done what she always did. Gotten angry and stormed off. Why hadn't she stayed at the pub?

She tipped over a bottle of toner onto a cotton pad, then swiped it over her face. Walking out had given him exactly what he wanted—Emma far away from hockey players, his teammates, and... *far away from Tyler.*

An idea coalesced in her mind, and she nearly laughed out loud as she dropped the pad in the trash. *Keep it in your pants.* Ha!

She picked up her phone, blood rushing in her ears. Sean needed to know that she was a grown adult. She wouldn't storm off this time and let him think that one comment could keep her properly cowed.

Emma started a message to Tyler and deleted it. *How could she possibly phrase this and not come off like a crazy person?* The only option was to own it straight up.

> Maybe we should see what Sean does? It might be ugly, but I'm sick of him trying to control my relationships.

> You've probably figured out that words don't make much of an impact on him. It usually works best to slam him against the boards.
>
> Would you assist me with that Friday night?

Tyler started typing, then stopped. Emma watched the screen, her heart thumping in her chest. This wasn't a smart idea, but she didn't care at the moment. She needed to make her point, and this would do it beautifully.

> I don't usually pick fights with teammates before a game, but the idea of you gearing up to drop mitts has me intrigued

Emma grinned. *Such a flirt.* She started to sweat and bit the inside of her cheek. The worst he could do was say no, but based on the tidbits of information she'd gathered, she doubted he would.

> Not fighting. Just pissing him off a bit.
>
> I thought we could pretend to be together for a few minutes before the game. Make him think we're dating.
>
> Could be hilarious, and I'll come clean right after, so you won't have to do much. I'll tell him I asked you to do it.
>
> Hopefully that will get my point across and he'll lay off

Emma hesitated over the send button. What was Tyler going to think of this? She glanced at the time. Midnight.

A little voice whispered that this probably wasn't the best time to be running with vengeful ideas that galloped through her head, but she ignored it. She would get Sean's attention, and then they could have a real conversation about this. He would apologize, she would forgive him, and they'd move on. She tapped send.

> You want me to pretend to be your boyfriend in front of Sean before the game?

Emma stared at his message. Concise and to the point.

> Yes

> My cell is 416-622-1517. Send your address. I'll pick you up at seven

CHAPTER Six

EMMA DIPPED a small brush into a mixture of glycerin and water, then gently dabbed it onto the ice cubes in the glass. The faux condensation glistened under the studio lights, making the ice look as though it had just been pulled from the freezer. She glanced over at Lindsey, who was adjusting the camera settings, and Vaughn, meticulously arranging the backdrop that mimicked kitchen tile.

"Ugh, I can't believe our HOA is trying to force me to repaint my house," Vaughn grumbled as he fiddled with a prop. "Since when is grey outdated?"

"Because HOAs suck," Lindsey answered in a sing-song voice. "Okay, I think that filter works better." She took a few shots and scrutinized the camera display.

"Did you get your taxes submitted?" Emma asked.

Lindsey scoffed. "Of course I did. I definitely didn't binge the second season of The Office instead of filling out the last six mind-numbing forms."

"I swear you're drawing it out on purpose just so you can complain about it," Emma murmured, her attention only half on the conversation as she sprayed more mist onto the glass filled with locally brewed root beer to make it look freshly fizzed.

"You might be onto something," Lindsey agreed with a smirk. "What would I even talk about if every annoying chore in my life was finished?"

Emma yawned as she straightened, finally satisfied the glass looked as good as it was going to get.

Vaughn raised an eyebrow. "Out late last night?"

"It was a rager. So much tossing and turning. Night sweating." Emma shrugged. "I know you're envious, but not everyone can have the exhilarating life I lead."

"All I heard was night sweating. What were you thinking about?"

Emma laughed and shook her head, but her lip twitch gave her away.

Vaughn's eyes widened. "It's that guy, isn't it? The one you were texting Sunday."

"No, stop, there's no guy." Emma walked around the table to get a better view of the computer monitor as Lindsey snapped away. She pretended to be entranced with the images of the glass filled with caramel liquid, but Vaughn saw right through it.

He perched on the counter next to her and tapped his fingers on the laminated surface. "I need to see this pretty man. Immediately."

Emma blew out a breath but didn't take her eyes off the screen. "No, trust me. That won't be helpful to this conversation." Vaughn leaned in. "He's...good-looking."

"I assumed. Rob was smitten. But how good-looking are we talking? Henry Cavill?"

Emma frowned. "Mixed with a little Ryan Reynolds."

Lindsey turned from the camera. "I wasn't going to say this in front of your parents since they raised three of them, but we swore off hockey players, Emma. Remember?"

"You've never dated a hockey player."

Lindsey sighed. "I meant the royal 'we,' as in mostly you, but I didn't want you to feel singled out."

Fair. After Alex, they *had* sworn off hockey players. For good.

Emma turned and leaned on the counter. "He was messaging about the game. That's it." She wasn't ready to admit what she'd asked Tyler to do on Friday, not even to these two.

Listening to her twelve o'clock ideas had been, predictably, stupid. She'd thought about messaging Tyler that morning and telling him she shouldn't be allowed to have her phone past eleven but hadn't followed through. The only thing more embarrassing than asking someone to be your fake boyfriend for an hour was texting them to cancel your fake relationship.

She'd tell Lindsey and Vaughn the whole story after the fact. Maybe a year after. When it would be funny and not childish because it had happened in the past, and *she'd grown up so much since then.*

"I think we've got this one. Let's move on to the hot chocolate." Lindsey moved to switch out the filters on the lights.

Vaughn whipped out his phone. "Does Tyler have socials?"

Emma groaned. "He has a few pictures online." *She wished there were more than that.* After googling him last night when she crawled into bed, she'd only found one other picture from a Calgary Sun article back in January. It showed him wearing all his hockey gear on the ice, which wasn't exactly what she'd been hoping for.

"Last name?" Vaughn stared at his screen.

"Bowen."

Emma didn't know where Tyler had lived before moving here, and she couldn't very well text him to ask that. She definitely couldn't ask anyone on the team without arousing suspicion after what happened at the pub the other night.

Emma moved the white porcelain mug from the counter, careful not to slosh the creamy chocolate up the sides. Time to add some steam. She grabbed a tampon, microwaved it for a few seconds, and hid it behind the cup, allowing tendrils of steam to rise up convincingly.

Vaughn switched out the backdrop and added a stack of aesthetic books and a sprig of lavender.

"Nice touch." Emma winked at him.

"I bet that's what you wish Tyler said to you last night." Vaughn turned his phone around and dropped his jaw.

"Wait, let me see." Lindsey stepped around the tripod and gawked at Vaughn's phone screen. "Ummm, does he look like that in person?"

Emma slumped against the counter. "No. Even better."

Tyler sat back at the desk in his apartment and picked up the robust roast beef sandwich he'd just made himself. He stared at the search results on his screen after typing Emma's name into the search engine. Once he'd visited at least five websites, he decided he needed food for this venture.

Where to start. He didn't normally search up girls he met online. Actually, this may have only been the second time. The first being Serina in Toronto, who nearly begged him to look up her acting reel on YouTube.

He clicked on Emma's official website and stared at her laughing expression, focused just off-camera as if someone was standing there making snarky comments. *Three different laughs.* This was the look she'd given him when she'd discovered he knew what a Bieber Brew was.

He shifted in his chair and took another bite of his sandwich, then scrolled down to read her bio.

Hi! I'm Emma, a dedicated food stylist with a passion for culinary elegance. Merging the worlds of art and cuisine, I transform ordinary dishes into compelling stories that will elevate your brand. Every plate is a canvas, and with precision, creativity, and a keen eye for detail, I take pride in bringing each culinary creation to life.

. . .

He kept scrolling through her portfolio and scanned through the photos. Sunny windows with freshly baked breads, pizza on a wooden peel in front of a stone hearth, a steaming cup of coffee. Her work was good.

Tyler paused when a picture of Emma came up, her brow pulled together slightly as she adjusted an apple on top of a fruit bowl. Her dirty-blond hair was pulled back, and the white sleeveless top she wore made her green eyes pop.

He swiped over to another tab and opened her initial messages to him, then clicked on her profile. He'd looked at this before but hadn't dug much deeper than her first few posts. *This wasn't spying. Her profile was set to public.*

He scrolled down her page and took in photos of Emma with friends, one with Sean and an older couple that had to be their parents—Emma looked exactly like her mother. Then he hit a dead zone. No pictures posted, only articles and comments from friends. He checked the date stamp. December 2021.

Tyler frowned. No Christmas or New Year's photos. Nothing. He finished off the last of his sandwich and was about to scroll back further when his phone rang. The name 'Troy Bowen' flashed on the screen.

Tyler hit 'answer' and put the call on speakerphone. "Hey, what's up?" Tyler asked, trying to sound casual and not like he was fantasizing about a woman he barely knew as he looked at her pictures online.

"Ty, I need to go over some accounting adjustments with you," his father said, diving straight into business. *He hated when he called him Ty,* like they were close, which they weren't. He was sure his father thought they were, but only because he didn't know how to be close to anyone. If Tyler hadn't been able to watch his mother and see the difference between the two of them, he likely wouldn't have known there was another option.

Troy Bowen allowed people to skate over the surface of his life, but never let them crack the ice and fall in. His mother was the opposite. She always offered gaps and openings for people to dive deep and swim if they chose to. He wished he had chosen to more often.

They discussed numbers and strategies for a while, but when Tyler attempted to steer the conversation toward his father's recent medical appointments, he was met with the typical deflection and vague responses.

"Oh, you know doctors. Never wanting to commit." If that wasn't the pot calling the kettle.

"Right, well I'm here if you need me." He'd moved to Calgary to help him, not just with the renovation projects but with his life. The last time he had pancreatic cancer, he'd been bedridden for months during and after treatment. Troy had opted out of treatment this time, and Tyler couldn't blame him. Frankly, he was lucky to have survived the first time. Now he was in his sixties and the prognosis wasn't hopeful either way. Better not to waste your last years or months wasting away in a hospital bed.

The doctor had told them when Troy's body started to crash, it would be hard and fast. Seemed he would have to wait until then before Troy would be willing to ask for help.

"Everything's fine, Ty. Don't worry about it. See you for dinner Sunday, yes? Ok." Troy hung up before he could answer.

Dinner Sunday. He wished he'd tried harder to set up dinner another night so he wouldn't miss Sunday Supper at Sean's. He'd attended those with the team for the past few months now. How had he never noticed a picture of Emma when he'd been at the house?

Probably because he hadn't been looking. He'd only walked from the entryway into the kitchen and dining room, then down to the basement to play ping pong and air hockey. There was a family photo there, but Sean and all his siblings looked like they were still in grade school.

He stood and took his plate back to the kitchen. In some sick way, he knew this was his father trying to connect. Have him meet at a Michelin star restaurant with whatever woman he was trying to impress, then laugh and joke as if they'd done this for years.

He could expect comments about how the two of them were cut from the same cloth. Troy would ask about his love life, then clap him on the shoulder and say, *"Good man. Always keep your eyes open for the right woman and enjoy the others in the meantime."*

He'd wink at his date, presumably to assure her she was the right woman he spoke of, though of course she never was. This Sunday he was bringing Melanie. That was three dinners in a row for her. She'd lasted longer than most.

Tyler sat and leaned back in his chair, scrolling up and moving his mouse over Emma's smiling face in front of l'Arc du Triomphe. May of 2022 she'd been in Paris.

Suck that, André. He did know some French.

CHAPTER Seven

TYLER RAPPED his knuckles against the door, then didn't know where to put his hands. He checked for a camera. If it was there, it wasn't obvious. At least she wasn't watching him stand here awkwardly.

He didn't do this. Pick women up. He met them at a restaurant, bar, or the gym, and sometimes they rode back to his or her place together, but he never went to their place and picked them up.

He'd thought about parking on the curb and texting Emma to let her know he was there. But she'd given him her apartment number.

Ironic that this was the first time in years that he was standing in front of someone's door when he wouldn't be returning at the end of the night. *How many firsts was that with this girl?* And all in less than a week?

The door flung open and Emma looked up, bent over with one hand on the door handle and one tugging on the back of her leather ankle boot. "Sorry, this zipper has been stuck for weeks, and it—takes a second—" She stood and flipped her hair away from her face. "There. Ready."

The corner of Tyler's mouth crept up without his permission. "You sure?"

Emma scoffed. "What, I don't look ready?"

He scanned her flushed cheeks and glossy lips. She wore a charcoal grey thermal top under her open puffy coat, wide leg jeans that fell over her boots, and fingerless gloves. Why was the image of her fingers half covered the detail that made his throat go dry?

Tyler cleared his throat. "No, you look ready."

She quirked an eyebrow and motioned for him to get out of the doorway. He stepped back into the hall and watched as she slung her purse over her shoulder and locked up.

"It's a nice place." He shoved his hands into his pockets as they walked down the hall to the lift.

"I lucked into it. My friend Lindsey's ex used to work for the management company, so I heard about it before it was posted."

She was talking fast. She pressed the elevator call button twice. Nope, three times. He grinned. Emma was nervous.

"Who's Lindsey?" He willed the elevator to take its time. He was enjoying this vantage point. Watching her play with her hair while she waited, her eyes not sure where to look.

"She's one of my best friends. We met working together at the studio."

"The one on ninth?"

Emma glanced over her shoulders, her lips parted a few millimetres in surprise. "You remembered that?"

"It's by the Saddledome. Of course I remembered that."

She breathed a laugh, and something fluttered in his chest. "Yeah, that studio. We've worked there together with my other friend Vaughn for almost three years now."

Her two friends. She mentioned that the first time they talked. The elevator opened and they stepped in next to a guy with half his head shaved clutching a vape pen like it was a microphone. They stood in silence until the door opened again.

"I parked on the street." Tyler pointed to his truck just east of the front rotating door.

She scoffed. "Who did you bribe to get that spot? I usually end up parking underground."

"Oh, I sold my soul to the parking gods a long time ago. I lived in Toronto."

Emma laughed, and her breath lifted into the air in a misty cloud. "That's where you were before Calgary?"

He nodded, not sure if he should open her door for her. She put her hand on the handle, answering that question, and he hit the button. She opened it and hopped up into the seat as he walked around on the streetside and got in. The cab of the truck was still warm from his drive over.

"Should we have driven separately?" she asked, stiffening as Tyler hit the start button. "I could still go get my car."

He shrugged. "You can if you want, I didn't—"

"I just wondered if it would be weird, you know? You having to drive me home after—" Her throat worked and she whipped her head forward to stare out the window. "I mean after we pretend to be together, it might be awkward."

"I've driven plenty of women home in more awkward situations than that."

Emma's mouth pinched, and Tyler immediately regretted the words. They were true, but the look on her face made his chest feel like someone had dug a hole in it with a dessert spoon.

He exhaled. "Do you want—"

"It's fine, just drive."

He pulled away from the curb, the warmth in the cab replaced by an icy silence. The arena was twenty minutes away. This would be torture if they didn't talk about something. "So the photography studio. You must love working there if you've been there for three years."

Emma exhaled. "It's been the best. I used to have to scramble for new jobs, constantly networking and building up relationships with potential clients. Now I get an email in my inbox each week with a list of requests and the three of us choose which ones we want to take."

"Does the studio only do marketing photos?"

Emma nodded. "Not all product shoots, though. Sometimes Lindsey and Vaughn do branding photos, but I only help with the food and product styling."

This was better. Tyler relaxed in his seat. He knew how to make women feel comfortable. That had always come easy to him, probably because he'd watched his dad charm and schmooze since he was in diapers. He was grateful for the skill and hated himself each time he recognized he was using it.

"How did you get into food—"

"My turn to ask questions." Emma turned in her seat. "When did you start playing hockey?"

Tyler shifted his hands on the wheel. He was glad she was talking, less glad that she was interrogating him. "When I learned to walk."

"Same with my brothers, but you're better than them. Where did you go after peewee?"

He shot her a look. "You think I'm better?"

Emma rolled her eyes. "Answer the question, Bowen." There was a fierceness in her expression, but underneath, he spotted something softer. She was using his strategy. *Smart girl to go on the offence.*

"I played in competitive and feeder leagues, probably much like Sean." He glanced over, and Emma nodded. "Then I got signed to the Drifters—"

"You got signed? *In high school?*" she interrupted. "That's North Carolina, right? How long did you play for them?"

He laughed and put up a hand. "Can you let me finish the story?"

She closed her mouth and folded her hands in her lap. "Sorry. Continue."

He pulled to a stop at a red light and drew a deep breath. "I was drafted, but not officially signed. I played for the University of Toronto that year, waiting for my contract to come through. When it didn't, I played a second year with them." He paused, his chest tightening. The light turned green and he pulled forward.

In an instant, he was back in that apartment with his teammates eating fried chicken sandwiches and packing for their tournament in Windsor when his roommate Shears picked up the phone and handed it to him. He'd never heard his father's voice sound that way before or since.

"My mom died in a car accident and I ended up pulling out and staying there in Toronto. Finished my degree in computer science."

Emma was still. Nothing like a death to lighten the mood.

"I'm so sorry, Tyler."

He turned and smiled. "It was a long time ago."

"So you worked there in Toronto? Or somewhere else before moving here?"

Tyler turned left at the next light. "Stayed in Toronto. Worked for a few different banks, then a software company. I'm still working for them remotely, but when my dad moved out here he needed help with a few projects. He's renovating a few different properties, turning them into bed and breakfasts."

She cocked her head to the side. "You moved here for your dad?"

Tyler ran a hand through his hair. He knew what she was thinking. *A guy who's loyal and loves his family.* Normally he'd run with it. Use it to his advantage to get her back to his place. But *that* was already off the table with Emma since the only reason she was here with him was to prove a point to her brother—his hockey captain.

"I moved here because he needed help, and the money was good. He and I have never had a great relationship."

To his surprise, she didn't look disappointed, only curious. Emma leaned on the armrest. "Is it difficult working with him then?"

"I think you've used up your questions."

Her lip pushed out in a mock pout, and he laughed. "Fine. Yes, it's difficult. Now, how did you get into food styling?"

Emma filled the last few minutes to the Ice Centre explaining how she started at the University of Calgary studying marketing, then fell into food styling while on a summer internship.

Tyler pulled into the parking lot. Seven-twenty, not bad. Their game wasn't until eight-fifteen, but most of the guys arrived early to suit up and get on the ice at least a half hour before to warm up.

He parked in a spot near the back of the first row. When he reached to turn off the truck, Emma's hand shot out and landed on his arm. His muscles tensed as his stomach dropped through his seat.

She pulled back and swallowed hard. "Can we sit here and talk for a second? Before we go in there?"

Emma's heart raced as Tyler unclicked his seatbelt and turned toward her. It had been doable to talk with him on the way over. Not easy, since the smell of his cologne was reminiscent of Cool Waters, which reminded her of every hot guy she'd pined after in the late nineties, but doable.

Now he was looking straight at her, and the console of his truck didn't seem appropriately wide enough. She pressed her back up against the passenger door and fiddled with the edge of her fingernail. "I didn't know—I mean, we're just going to stand there and pretend to be talking or something, right? You could put your arm around me just for a second—it can be subtle."

He blinked, slow like a cat and Emma's mouth went dry. "Subtle. You think that will make your point?"

Was it possible for her heart to explode? It happened to rabbits. They got too worked up and just died right there on the spot. She pulled at the collar of her coat, then turned to open her door. "Sorry, I think I'm getting overheated."

Tyler turned off the truck and opened his door, then stepped out into the parking lot and grabbed his bag, skates, and stick from the backseat. "It's fine. We can head in and hang out in the atrium. When Sean comes in, we'll give him a show." He slung the bag over his shoulder, pulling his athletic-fit Henley even tighter across his broad chest.

He nodded toward the Ice Centre and turned. Emma slammed the truck door closed and ran after him. "What kind of *show*, Tyler?"

He shrugged, his legs too long for her to keep up without nearly jogging. "We'll just see what happens."

See what happens? This felt like the exact wrong moment to fly by the seat of their pants. Her pulse shot up another few beats per minute. This was a terrible plan. They were going to be standing in the foyer where anyone could see them, not just Sean. She could have gone to Sunday Supper or something and forced him to talk with her after everyone left.

But that was just it. They'd talked about this before, and he always said he'd mind his own business, but then he made comments like "keep it in your pants" at the pub after the game.

"Emma?" Tyler stood holding the front door. She drew a deep breath and walked past him. He seemed totally fine with all this. More than fine. He was grinning at her.

"You think this is funny?" she hissed when he stopped next to her and dropped his bag.

Tyler tried to stifle a laugh and failed. "It is kind of funny. You look like you're going to throw up."

Emma pulled off her coat and draped it over the arm of the couch against the wall. "Unlike some people, I don't go around doing this with random guys."

Tyler propped up his stick and set his skates on top of his bag, then crossed his arms over his chest. Emma tried to keep her eyes from dropping to his pecs and failed. "Doing what?"

"You know. This."

"No, I don't know because it feels like you're accusing me of going around pretending to be in relationships with people on a regular basis."

Emma tucked her hair behind her ears. "Not pretending to be in a relationship, but you're *with* different people. Women—I'm not—" Tyler raised an eyebrow, and she groaned, turning to face the wall. "I'm sorry, I didn't mean—I'm just nervous."

Tyler's hand landed on her back. "In case you've forgotten, this was your idea. We don't have to do this. I'm happy to help you with Sean, but if you'd rather—"

Emma whipped back around, not thinking about the fact that Tyler's hand wouldn't move with her. She looked down at his hand now cupped over her bra. He yanked his hand back as her skin lit on fire.

"That probably would've convinced him," Tyler muttered, holding his hand out as if it had been accidentally peed on.

Emma ignored the sweat forming under her clothes and clenched her hands into fists. "We are going to do this. It's five minutes of our lives, and then I can talk with Sean after the game and I'll never text people after midnight again." Tyler wasn't looking at her. "Tyler—"

His arm curled around her waist like a snap bracelet and pulled her flush against his body. She'd barely processed her sudden change of location when Tyler tipped her chin up. Without a word, he slipped his fingers down the side of her neck and kissed her.

CHAPTER *Eight*

THIS WAS *when she would die*. It wasn't possible for a heart to pump this fast and not burst. It wasn't possible for a man to smell this good. To taste this good.

She gripped onto the sides of his waist and *holy mother*. His muscles flexed each time his lungs filled with air, his taut waist expanding under her half-covered fingers. *Why had she worn gloves?* She wanted to rip them off and press her palms into the contours of his hard stomach.

The scruff on his chin rubbed the soft skin of her cheek, and then, just like that, the moment was over. Tyler pulled back and opened his eyes, his hand still curved over the skin below the lobe of her ear.

Before Emma could speak, Tyler's eyes shifted. Emma turned and saw Sean stalking toward them from the front door. His expression was unreadable—stoney and cold—as he strode past and took the metal stairs two at a time down to the dressing room.

A pang of guilt hit Emma's gut. Why did she feel bad about this because Sean looked pissed? How many times in the last year had he done something to put that look on her face, and he'd never apologized?

Tyler dropped his hands and stepped back. His lips looked flushed and warm. When they turned up at the corners, she realized she was staring.

"Alright, then. Thank you for helping me with that. I hope you have a good game." The words came out more breathless than she'd anticipated.

Tyler picked up his equipment and headed for the stairs. "Thanks. I'll see you after for the *awkward* drive home."

"I'll catch Sean after the game. It might be a minute." She knew she should've taken her own car. The second Tyler had shown up, all six-foot-three of him standing in her doorway, she should've called an audible.

Tyler nodded. "I'll probably stop by the pub anyway, so no rush." He waved over his shoulder and started down the stairs. Emma looked up and locked eyes with the woman selling tickets. She winked and gave Emma a thumbs-up.

Emma took her seat next to Kelty on the bench as the game began. The sounds of skates slicing through the ice, sticks clashing, and the chatter of the crowd felt more abrasive than it had the other night. Probably because now it was distracting her from replaying that kiss.

Her hip still tingled where he'd held her, and his cologne still clung to the front of her shirt. She lifted it and breathed him in.

There weren't as many people at the arena for this game, and Tyler's fan club was noticeably absent. It made sense that tonight wouldn't be as well-attended—the Snowballs hadn't lost to Dr. Quinn Medicine Hattrick in years.

The puck hit the ice, and it only took a few minutes for Emma to recognize something was off. Sean's posture on the ice was all wrong. He never looked as relaxed as Tyler, but tonight he was so tight, he looked like he was about to fold over.

Kelty frowned. "What's wrong with Sean?"

Emma's lips drew into a line. *She had a hunch.* Sean skated like someone who'd just caught their partner cheating and found themselves in the middle of a smash room.

"He's going to hurt himself," Kelty muttered as Sean hit the boards and went down, then charged after the defenseman.

Fly intercepted the pass and sent the puck to Curtis who crossed it to Sean. Tyler flew down the ice, waiting for the pass, but it never came. Sean worked it away from the boards, then lost it as two defenders swarmed him.

Emma's stomach twisted. *He wasn't passing to Tyler.* Her nails dug into her jeans. What was wrong with him? He was so worked up about one kiss that he'd throw this game away by blackballing his best player?

Tyler glided around the back of the net and threw up his hands in exasperation as the buzzer went off at the end of the first period. He lifted his facemask and shouted something at Sean.

Emma stood up and clapped a hand over her mouth as Sean dug his skates into the ice and rocketed toward Tyler, who was skating backward toward the bench.

"What the hell is he—" Kelty started, then gasped as Sean slammed Tyler against the boards. His helmet went flying, and Sean took full advantage of his hit. He tore Tyler's jersey over his head to force him down to his level and started wailing on the perfect abs Emma had been admiring an hour ago.

"*Shit!*" Emma hissed, jumping over the benches until she stood next to the boards. "Sean Thompson, stop being a *CHILD!*" she shrieked across the ice. Tyler was punching Sean now. Blood ran down both their faces, and Emma started running.

The ref, who'd already left the ice, skated over and tore them apart, screaming something in their faces. Probably threatening to kick them out of the arena, and Sean, at least, deserved it.

Pressure built behind her eyes as she rounded the curve and started down the other side, approaching the back of their bench.

The Snowballs stood on the ice, leaning on the boards as the ref shoved Sean and Tyler to their bench and slammed the door.

"Sort it out or I'll upgrade it to game misconduct!" he yelled over his shoulder as he skated back to the scoring area. Someone's blood was streaked over the white stripes on his left arm.

Tyler leaned back, holding the bridge of his nose. Blood oozed over his lips and chin, and Emma couldn't tell where it was all coming from. Tears pricked the corners of her eyes. *This was her fault.* She shouldn't have dragged Tyler into this.

Emma looked at her hands. What was she supposed to do now? She'd run all the way over here and hadn't even brought her purse. There were at least a couple of Band-Aids in there.

Footsteps pounded behind her, and she whirled to find Kelty holding a first-aid kit. She cracked open the lid and stuffed a handful of gauze into Emma's hands. "You take Tyler, I'll help Sean."

Emma nodded and pushed through the door. She had to walk past Sean to reach Tyler at the end of the bench and kicked his skate as she passed. If he noticed, he didn't show it.

"Here, let me help," Emma murmured, tapping Tyler's hand. Blood soaked the front of his powder blue jersey. She pulled it back down over his pads with one hand and held a thick stack of gauze against his nostrils. *"I'm sorry."*

Tyler's eyes were already swelling. A tear slipped out over her cheek and she drew a deep breath, trying to keep her hand steady. She'd always hated hockey fights, but this one was personal.

"He's your *teammate*, Sean," she snapped in her brother's direction. Sean opened his mouth but Kelty grabbed his face and yanked it back to face her.

"Shut your mouth. Do you hear me? You will not say a damn word. Not tonight."

Emma loved that woman. She turned back to Tyler. "Are you okay?"

"Been through worse," he grunted, suppressing a wince as her hand shifted.

The gauze was already soaked through. "Here, hold this a second."

Tyler lifted his bloody fingers and did as she asked. She reached for more gauze in the first-aid kit and made another stack. After switching it out, she grabbed antiseptic spray and a bandage for the gash on his left eyebrow. Her fingers trembled as she dabbed it clean, sprayed it, then pressed it together and applied the bandage.

"I think the bleeding is slowing. Did you break anything?" Emma struggled to keep her voice steady as she cleaned the blood from his swollen knuckles.

"He didn't break anything," Sean muttered across the bench.

"Not. A damn. Word." Kelty put a bit of force into her next application of gauze, and Sean grunted.

Emma pushed closer to the bench between Tyler's legs so Country could grab a few water bottles.

"Second period's starting in three." Fly pushed his hair back from his forehead and repositioned his helmet.

"Hope they enjoy their power play," Emma muttered, shaking her head at the pile of bloody gauze on the bench.

Country slapped a hand on Fly's shoulder. "Let's go, Gramps. Five minutes, then Tyler will be—"

"Tyler *won't* be." Emma spun and knocked against Tyler's knees. "He can barely see."

"But—"

"Blame your captain!" Emma pointed accusingly at Sean. "You'll have to sub in Curtis and have him serve the five minutes. And I assume Sean got a misconduct?" Boyd nodded, adjusting one of his goalie pads.

"I just need a minute to make sure the bleeding—" Tyler started, then saw Emma's face. She bent over and started gathering the used gauze. *Rage cleaning.*

"C'est tiguidou." Andre laughed and waved him off. "Get cleaned up. We'll take this."

Tyler nodded and pushed up from the bench. Emma wasn't going to embarrass him by asking if he needed help washing up, even though she wanted to. Hockey players didn't react kindly to being babied, even when they acted like toddlers.

She bundled the mound of gauze in her hands. "I'll wait for you up top."

Tyler insisted he didn't need to go to Urgent Care. Since his nose didn't look crooked, Emma gave up on that point and typed the address he gave her into the GPS. She didn't trust him to give her good directions.

He lay back in the passenger seat with his eyes closed. "It's not as bad as it looks." Tyler sounded like he had a raging head cold.

"Would you seriously have gone back on the ice?"

He shrugged. Of course he would have. She remembered a tournament where Carter ended up needing stitches along his hairline after playing two overtime periods past a fight.

She offered to carry his gear inside, but he wouldn't let her. Instead, she took his keys and walked up the steps to open the door. Brett wasn't home from the game yet. She doubted anyone had gone to One Place, but they all still had to clean up. Tyler, since he'd left the game early, was ready to go when the buzzer went off.

Tyler dropped his gear next to the boot rack and stretched out on the couch.

"Do you have an ice pack?" Emma asked, searching the freezer.

"There might be one in the door."

Emma didn't see one but grabbed a bag of frozen corn. She double-wrapped it with a paper towel, walked to the couch, and kneeled next to him. Tyler took the bag and gingerly placed it over the bridge of his nose.

The swelling was bad, but now that he'd showered, he really only had the one cut over his brow. Everything else was bruising.

"Do you want painkillers?"

Tyler nodded. "There should be something in my bathroom medicine cabinet."

Emma leaned over him and brushed his hair away from the bandage over his eye. "I don't know which room is yours."

Tyler's breathing changed, and Emma pulled her fingers back. *Why had she just touched him like that?* "First door on the right."

She pushed up from the floor and walked down the hall. Her pulse quickened as she pushed the door open and walked into the darkened room. *No snooping, just go to the bathroom and get him some ibuprofen.* She flicked on the light. His room was tidy. A pair of jeans hung over the end of the bed, and his comforter was slightly mussed near his pillow.

She forced herself to walk to the bathroom and not imagine him taking those jeans off. The bathroom was just as neat, his toiletries stacked behind the sink. Emma opened the medicine cabinet and spotted the white bottle, but as she reached for it, she paused. A beaded bracelet sat on the shelf next to his razor. Silver and turquoise. Not masculine in the least.

She grabbed the bottle and closed the mirror, then turned off the lights as she walked back to the kitchen. So, he had a woman's bracelet in his bathroom. That was consistent with what she knew about Tyler, and she had no claim on him. So why did it make her feel like she'd swallowed a handful of rocks?

It took her three tries to find the glasses, but she pulled one down and was filling it with water when her phone rang. Setting the glass down, she pulled it from her back pocket.

Her nostrils flared. Sean's name rolled across the display. She didn't want to answer, but Sean never called. If something was wrong, she'd regret not talking to him.

Emma pressed the green button. "Yes?"

"Hey."

She didn't answer right away. "Did you and Kelty get home okay?" *I'm mostly asking about Kelty,* she wanted to add, but didn't.

"Yep. You?"

"I'm at Tyler's." She dared him to comment. She twisted the cap off the ibuprofen and poured out two pills, then tucked her phone between her head and shoulder and walked the water and medicine to the coffee table.

"Look, Em, I shouldn't have reacted that way."

"You think?" Emma scoffed. Tyler put out his hand and she dropped the pills into his hand. "You lost the game, Sean, and hurt your best player."

Sean exhaled. "I get it. I'm an ass." He had that right. "I just—I don't understand why you're doing this to yourself again."

Tyler winced as he sat up, and she handed him the glass of water.

"I'm not doing anything to myself, Sean. Tyler and I aren't together. I was trying to make a point." Silence. Emma continued, "You can't keep being my guard dog. Eventually, I am going to meet someone and—"

"Not like him! Emma, you have to see this pattern. It's like your radar is broken. Instead of lighting up when someone stable comes around, you have damn stars in your eyes the second you see a fu—"

"Just stop, okay? I'm not as naive as you think." Emma's cheeks flushed when she saw Tyler was watching her face. She stood and turned from the couch.

"So you're not into him?"

"I—that's not the point! It doesn't matter who I'm into or whether I make stupid dating decisions. It's not your job to save me from it! I don't need a gatekeeper, I just—" Emma ran a hand through her hair. "I'm sorry I messed with you, Sean. I was just so sick of you making it abundantly clear you don't think I'm capable of taking care of myself."

Another pause. Then Sean said, "I don't want anyone to ever treat you like that again." Emma bit the inside of her cheek. "Tyler's always with someone new. They never stick around long. If that's what you want—"

"You know that's not what I want." She wanted what he and Kelty had. Someone who would tell her to shut her damn mouth, then take her home and hold her as they fell asleep together.

"I'm sorry." Sean didn't say what for, but Emma stood there, gobsmacked. She'd never heard those words out of her brother's mouth.

"Is Kelty standing there forcing you to apologize?"

"Absolutely."

Emma laughed. "Well, tell her you need to apologize to Tyler and the team."

Sean scoffed. "Already on it."

Of course she was. "Goodnight, Sean."

"Goodnight, Ems."

Emma hit the button on the side of her phone and slipped it into the back pocket of her wide-leg jeans. She turned to see Tyler watching her through swollen eyes. Her cheeks flushed as she flashed back over the words she'd said to Sean, completely forgetting that Tyler—though injured—was still awake and lying on the couch behind her.

Tyler was the first to speak. "Maybe you should've chosen someone else to make your point. Would've gone over better."

Emma sat down on the end of the coffee table. "If only Fly would've dropped his driver's licence."

Tyler chuckled then put a hand over his stomach. "Don't make me laugh."

Emma winced. "How bad is it?"

Tyler flicked up his shirt, and Emma cursed under her breath.

Her eyes traced the lines of his muscles, interrupted by bruises blooming like storm clouds across his skin.

Tyler dropped the fabric and replaced the ice pack over his eyes. "Emma, what Sean said—"

"You heard that?"

"Sean's voice carries."

Emma pursed her lips. That it did. When she was a kid and he got up on Saturdays for early hockey practice, his was the voice that always woke her up. Not Carter's, even though he was older. It might've also had something to do with the fact that Sean couldn't keep track of his skates.

"You don't need to explain anything to me, okay? I'm not going to judge you for being a beautiful man whore." *Did she just tell him he was beautiful?*

Tyler laughed again, wheezing as he tried to keep his muscles from contracting. "Don't make me laugh."

"It's hard. I happen to be hilarious." Emma stood and surveyed the room. "Can I do anything else? Do you need a knee pillow or something?"

Tyler peered at her from over the paper towels. "A knee pillow?"

"Yeah, you know those things they put under your knees when you get a massage. It's—" She exhaled when she saw Tyler's grin. "Never mind. No knee pillows." Emma turned and pulled her puffy coat from the back of a chair, then slung her purse over her shoulder. She reached the door and froze.

She'd driven Tyler's truck here, which meant she had no way home. She could call a rideshare.

"Take the truck," Tyler mumbled. "I'm not going anywhere tomorrow anyway."

"But what if you need it?" Her heart pumped faster. She didn't want to take his truck, and *she wanted to take his truck.* It felt the same as accidentally leaving a sweater in a guy's apartment.

Emma didn't know how she felt about that. Her body knew

how it felt, and that was the problem. Sean, even if he *was* being an ass, was correct about one thing. She did light up around guys like Tyler. Then again, most women did, so at least she wasn't alone in her idiocy. Somehow that thought wasn't any more comforting.

She needed to rise above her lizard brain shouting, *Did you see those biceps? He's big and strong! He'll protect you and fertilize your eggs!* and check this off the list. Pretend to date Tyler Bowen and enjoy one of the most heart-stopping kisses of her life? Check.

But . . . she did owe him. He was sporting black eyes, a swollen, bloody nose, and watercolour abs because of her. If she took the truck, she could fill it up with gas, wash and sanitize his gear, and drop it off in the morning. She wouldn't even have to see his face.

Emma picked the keys up from the table. "I'll bring it back first thing."

CHAPTER Nine

TYLER AWOKE WITH A START. His body was sinking into something, and when he tried to push himself out, sharp pain exploded through his midsection. *Right.* He was on the couch.

The muffled echo of last night's events reverberated through his mind, compounded by the dull throbbing in his face. He opened his eyes, relieved to have his full range of vision. Most of the swelling must have gone down overnight with the help of the meds Emma had given him.

Emma. She'd been here last night. She'd driven him home, then he'd told her to take the truck. He rolled to the side and pulled his phone out of the pocket of his jeans. Seven-thirty in the morning. Saturday. He had over thirty missed messages, including a text from Sean, but he wasn't in the mood to read that. He wasn't in the mood to read any of them.

Tyler set the phone on the table and felt along his face. Tender but not terrible. He pushed himself to a sitting position, holding his breath at the ache along his ribs. The morning light streamed through the gaps in the drawn curtains, casting long slivers of sunshine onto the wooden floor.

With stilted breath, Tyler made his way to the kitchen. He was pissed that Sean had started something during the game but more pissed that they lost. When Emma had suggested this plan, he knew there was a chance Sean would lose his shit. Sean wasn't an enforcer, but he was pretty damn close, and if he were going to protect anyone, it would be his own family. Tyler had to respect that.

He pulled out a skillet and placed it on the stove with a clang as pain flared across his side. He flinched, hoping Brett either wasn't home or was a heavy sleeper. Normally he was up before Tyler ever was on the weekends.

He cracked a few eggs and whisked them up, throwing in a pinch of salt and some diced vegetables he'd left in the fridge. As the eggs cooked, Tyler popped two pieces of bread in the toaster.

When it was ready, he spread butter over the crusted surface, scooped the eggs onto his plate, and sat down at the table. He didn't realize how hungry he was until the first bite hit his tongue. Had he eaten anything after the game last night? Normally he would've ordered a Reuben at One Place, but they'd come straight back after the game.

He devoured the food, then cleared his plate and rinsed it. The warm water ran over his hands, soothing his sore knuckles. After his bruises healed in a few days, he should schedule a massage.

That thought made him smile. What had Emma called it last night, a knee pillow? She'd been talking about a bolster, but he didn't want to correct her. She'd been too adorable trying to explain.

He paused for a moment, looking at his reflection in the window above the sink. His father wasn't going to be thrilled with him showing up like this at dinner tomorrow. Tyler was drying his hands on a dishtowel when he heard feet scuffling in the hall. Brett emerged from the hallway, hair tousled and eyes heavy with sleep.

"Bud, you look as bad as I feel." Brett rubbed his eyes as he squinted against the morning light pouring through the window.

Tyler leaned back against the counter. "Looks like I'm not the only one that came home with a mark." Brett slapped a hand over the circular bruise on his neck. "That one from Sean too?"

Brett snorted. "He wishes." He sat heavily in the chair and rubbed his eyes. "Glad you're okay. You were dead when I came in at two."

"At One Place?"

"No, we went to Dusty Rose after a few drinks." He looked up and waggled an eyebrow. "Ginger asked for you, eh."

Tyler shook his head. "Relentless."

Brett laughed. "Yeah, go cry in your bag of panties." He slapped his hand on the table and stood back up. "I'm heading back to bed. Just wanted to check in. You good?"

Tyler nodded. "Yeah, I'll be fine. Thanks. Get some rest."

As Brett shuffled back to his room, Tyler brushed the crumbs from the table into his palm and dropped them into the sink. He mulled over Brett's comment, annoyed that it bothered him. It only rankled because of what Sean had said the night before.

He wasn't awful to women. Yes, he spent time with a lot of them, but he didn't ever lead them on. Didn't pretend he was giving them something more than he was. *He wasn't like his father.*

Tyler turned the corner and strode toward his bedroom when a tentative knock sounded at the door. He paused, wondering if he'd misheard, but it came a second time. *Who would be knocking at the door at eight in the morning on a Saturday?*

He walked lightly over the floorboards, then hunched to look through the peephole. Emma stood on the step with a toque and scarf, shifting her weight from one foot to the other. Tyler's breath hitched in his throat, and his chest warmed. *She was just bringing back his truck.*

He opened the door. "Hey."

Emma smiled and couldn't keep her eyes on his face. "Hey, I brought you this." She dropped his hockey bag on the landing between them.

Tyler glanced up at his truck sitting next to the curb. "Did you wash that?"

"The truck or the gear?"

"Truck." He looked back to find her eyes trained on the hockey bag. "Emma, you didn't—"

She wrung her hands. "I washed both. I have brothers, remember? I know how to sanitize, and I wanted to do something to apologize."

Tyler leaned against the doorframe, his eyes as wide as he could make them with the residual swelling. She'd opened his sweaty hockey bag and— He exhaled through his teeth. He'd thrown his bloody jersey in there and his compression shorts with his cup.

His neck flushed. At least he hadn't played the whole game so it wouldn't have been as rank as usual. "Apologies don't typically require you to dive into the third corner of microbial hell."

Emma laughed and kicked at the thin sheet of ice cracking on the edge of the porch. *That was laugh number one.* She took a step forward, and his heart kicked before he realized she was handing him his keys. "I should probably go. I'm really sorry about all this. If there's anything I can do to make it up to you, just let me know."

He closed his fingers over the keys as she turned to the steps. "How are you getting home?"

She pointed to a blue sedan idling a few cars behind his truck. "Lindsey to the rescue."

Tyler nodded, but as he took a step back to close the door, his ribs felt like they'd shrunk in the wash. This wasn't from the bruises. How many times had he walked a girl out and watched her walk down the steps like this? Never once had he dreaded closing the door.

"What about a do-over?" he blurted after her.

Emma stopped and had to grab the handle on the stairs to keep from slipping. She looked back. "What do you mean?"

He took a step out onto the frozen porch. "I'm just saying,

your fake date kind of sucked. For me, at least. You asked if there was anything you could do, and I actually have a thing I could use help with tomorrow."

Her eyes narrowed. "A thing?"

He ran a hand through his bedhead and ignored the ice under his toes. "I have to go out to dinner with my dad and his girlfriend. You wanted to make a point with Sean, and I need to make a point with him."

She ascended a step. "What kind of point?"

"You asked the other night if I moved here for my dad. He and my mom were divorced when she died, and he's been married six other times."

Her jaw dropped. "Six?"

Tyler nodded. His feet were going numb. "He's convinced I'm exactly like him and likes to make that point every chance he gets. Says I like my freedom too much to settle down. He doesn't think I'm capable of holding a long-term relationship—"

"Let me guess, you're inheriting his kingdom, and you have to be married by the time you're thirty or you lose everything." She leaned against the porch column, her eyes dancing.

"I'm thirty-three."

She scoffed. "Weird age to bequeath a kingdom, but what do I know?"

Tyler laughed out loud. *Who was this girl?* "Yeah, something like that."

"So you want me to come to dinner and pretend to be your long-term girlfriend?"

"Something like th—"

"*Something* like that?"

"Yes. Exactly like that."

She grinned. "Just wanted to hear you say it. At least I'm not the only psycho."

"Always happy to keep you company on that front."

Emma chewed on her lower lip. "But won't it be worse when your dad sees I'm not in the picture anymore?"

Good point. Tyler leaned over the porch railing to take the pressure off his feet. "So come twice. Once now and then again in six weeks or so. Two free dinners."

"Six weeks? That will convince him you're in a long-term relationship?"

Tyler chuckled. "Three times longer than any relationships of mine he's witnessed."

Emma's eyes widened. "Seriously?" He held out his hands as his body started to shiver. Emma motioned at the hockey bag. "That's two favours, and I cleaned your fluids—"

"*Fluids?* Blood. Let's not get ahead of ourselves."

Emma blushed and pursed her lips. It made him want to kiss her again to force them to relax. "Don't you think doing something like this kind of proves your dad right?"

Tyler stiffened, then pushed off the railing and stepped back to the door, picking up his hockey bag. *Had she seriously washed his gear?* "I'm working on that, but I've only lived here a year—"

"And found plenty of candidates," she muttered. Tyler nodded slowly, and Emma stepped up to the landing. "I'm sorry, that wasn't polite."

Emma obviously wasn't the first to point out his blasé attitude toward dating. It was typically easy to brush the judgement off or pretend to wear his reputation like a badge of honour, which it wasn't. It was a survival skill. A crutch. One he didn't think he was capable of walking without. This time, her comment dug under his skin.

Tyler's jaw tensed. "It's fine, I shouldn't have—"

"I didn't say I wouldn't do it, I just—" Emma shook her head. "I'll go, but no more kissing." Her lip twitched, and she wouldn't meet his eyes.

"Got it." *Had the kiss been that bad?* He'd never had complaints before.

Emma finally looked up, her brow furrowed. "Can I ask, why me? I'm sure there's a line a kilometre long of girls who'd love to be your plus one. Twice in six weeks."

Tyler adjusted the strap on his shoulder. He'd had dinner with his father every few weeks since moving here, and never had he thought to bring someone along. *Why her?* "Because you're exactly the type of girl my dad wouldn't expect me to be with."

———

Emma's cheeks burned as she walked back to the car. She'd barely slept the night before and wasn't in a place to be philosophical about what Tyler had just said. *Exactly the kind of girl my dad wouldn't expect me to be with.* Because she was wearing yoga sweats and a puffy coat? Because she ate honey crullers for dinner?

Lindsey stared at her as she sat in the passenger seat. "I thought you were just dropping off his stuff."

"I was." Emma exhaled and unzipped her coat.

"That was quite the extended conversation on the porch. And you're right, his face looks like he tried to kiss a running blender."

"If it had a pulse, I'm sure he would've," Emma muttered.

Lindsey chortled and pulled away from the curb. "You like him, don't you?"

Emma stared at her. "No, I feel bad that my brother made him look like Picasso's rough draft." Her heartbeat pulsed in her fingertips.

"It's not your fault, Emma. You had nothing to do with it."

They drove in silence until Lindsey turned off Shaganappi and into the neighbourhood. Emma swallowed the twinge of guilt that bubbled up from her gut. She'd asked Lindsey to drive her but hadn't admitted the full details of the fight the night before. Telling her friends that she'd asked Tyler to pretend they were together to annoy her brother felt like peeling a sunburn that was still tender and raw.

"Thanks for the ride."

Lindsey put the car in park. "Do you want company today?"

Emma yawned. "No, I didn't sleep well. I'm going to crash." She waved and got out of the car, then strode through the front doors she'd walked through with Tyler the night before. His words tumbled around like her mind was trying to polish them and smooth their edges.

She knew what a guy like Tyler wanted. Those girls who wore toques with puff balls on top, their hair glossy and highlighted, their eyelashes curled so high they brushed their eyebrows. That's who he went home with. She was the organic, locally grown apple to their cinnamon apple pie with streusel topping.

Nobody craved the raw ingredients. Nobody fantasized about the apple.

Which was why she kept allowing herself to be cooked and mashed and mixed until she barely recognized herself, hoping that in the end, someone would see her as the main event. But she was exactly the kind of girl he couldn't see himself with. And yet she couldn't stop wanting to be kissed like that. She couldn't stop wanting to be *wanted* like that.

Emma pulled off her boots, hung her coat on the hooks, and spread herself on the couch like the bland applesauce she was, then tugged a blanket over her shoulders and fell asleep.

CHAPTER Ten

EMMA STOOD in front of the bedroom mirror, biting her lip as she examined her reflection. Her chestnut hair cascaded down her back in waves, and the loose button-up with the top buttons undone made her look professional . . . but kind of sexy.

For a hot second, she'd been tempted to transform herself into exactly the kind of girl Tyler would date, though she had none of the needed supplies, but she couldn't bring herself to do it. This wasn't about her. Tyler needed to make his point just like she'd needed to the other night, and since he was the one who would take the brunt of the consequences, she could swallow her pride for a few hours and be herself—with a little extra cleavage.

Every moment with him over the past few days played on repeat like the bad memes Lindsey refused to stop sending. His hand on her waist. His lips over hers. His smile peeking out under the bag of frozen corn. His voice asking her for a do-over.

This was her problem. She knew exactly who he was. She knew what she wanted, and yet she was still a stupid moth flying straight for the flame that would leave her empty and burned to a crisp.

Her phone buzzed on the bathroom counter, and she jumped.

Lindsey's face stretched across her screen, her red lips puckered into a juicy kiss.

"Hey, Linds! What's up?" This was good. She needed a distraction. Emma exited the bathroom and started folding her unused wardrobe strewn on the bed.

"Did you get the email?" Lindsey asked.

Emma frowned. "I haven't been on my phone—"

"I'll wait. Check it."

Emma put Lindsey on speakerphone and swiped to her email, her mind buzzing. What could've come through to make Lindsey this intense? A new contract? A complaint? Ugh, she hoped it wasn't another complaint. They'd shot for three different small businesses in the past month, and she knew one of them was going to come back based on their feedback during approvals. *Could you make the colours a bit more vibrant?* They were shooting baked bread. What did they want? Her to dust the crust with gold?

Emma found the email Lindsey must have been referencing sandwiched between *These summer tops are 'fire emoji'* and *Hottest dirty talk to make your man obsessed.* How did her phone always know?

"Got it. Opening." It was from Greg Mackintosh, which was strange. He was the owner of their photography studio. Normally their job menu came from Pam, the studio director. The text populated on her screen, and Emma began to read.

> *I hope this email finds you all well. As we've always been more than just colleagues—we've been a family—I wanted to share some personal news with you transparently and directly.*
>
> *For a few years now, Tina and I have been contemplating the idea of selling the studio space. Our desire was always to retire and move to Kelowna, which you already know.*

That tidbit was difficult to miss since Greg brought it up almost every time he stopped by to pick up supplies. They'd be in the middle of a product shoot, and she'd hear, "It's fifteen degrees warmer in Kelowna right now. Did you know that?" She kept reading.

> *Unfortunately, the commercial real estate market hasn't been in our favour, and we've been waiting for the right opportunity. Recently, we received an offer from a yoga studio interested in the space. After much consideration, we've decided to accept the offer and take this as our sign to embark on our new adventure . . .*

What. The. Hell. Emma began to scan. *Two weeks. Build out starting on Thursday. Contracts reassigned to Chinook Marketing—*

"You still there?" Lindsey's voice pulled her up to the surface.

"Yeah." Emma closed the app, turned off the speakerphone, and put the phone back to her ear. Lindsey's exhale hissed through the speaker as she stared at the swirls of blue in the floral painting that hung over her dresser.

"So. We're out of a job. He's giving us residuals, and there are two gigs on location in May that are still ours . . ."

Emma nodded, Lindsey's words like water trickling over clay soil. Her panicked thoughts clashed with questions, creating a clog in the pipeline between her ears and her brain. She was so shortsighted. Why had she relied fully on the studio to build her portfolio? Why hadn't she continued to network and build relationships—at least run a social media page?

Lindsey sighed. "I know this is a lot. I've had about an hour to process—"

"Have you told Vaughn?"

Lindsey groaned. "He's my next call. Unless you want to do it."

Emma looked at the clock next to her bed. Tyler was going to be here any minute. She rushed back into the bathroom and untucked the front of her shirt from her jeans. This day already called for more deodorant. "I have an appointment here in a few minutes. I can call him after."

"No, he needs to know now. What appointment?"

Emma swiped her armpits, then retucked her shirt. "I really need to go, Linds. Talk later?"

"Got it."

"We'll figure this out. I'll start sending emails—"

"I'm already searching for rentable studio space. Vaughn's parents still have that shed out back."

"Maybe this is the push he needs to let us convert it?"

"Exactly my thoughts. This appointment isn't for something serious, right? I didn't think your gynecologist's office was open on Sunday."

"Not serious. Promise. I'll call you tonight."

"You know you can always tell me if your ovaries are malfunctioning."

"You'll be the first to know." Emma hung up. Guilt niggled at her as she flew out the door and ran to the lift. Lindsey would be the first to know about anything important, but this wasn't important. This was a repayment of a fake dating debt, nothing more.

Tyler was walking toward the glass doors, getting more than a few looks from people on the sidewalk, when she stepped off the elevator. He wore a heather grey knit pullover and tan slacks that hugged him in all the right places. Emma groaned and hustled outside before he could reach for the door handle.

"I told you you didn't have to come in. It's not like this is a date." He knew it, and she knew it, and she only had to make sure her body knew it. She would say the words aloud as often as possible to ensure her lady parts got the message. *Especially when he smelled like that.*

Tyler blinked. "Good evening, Emma."

Her stomach swooped. His hair was still damp, curling around his ears, and the swelling was gone now. There was still bruising under his eyes, but somehow the blues and purples screamed *I'm pumped full of testosterone! When I'm not fighting, do you know what I like to use it for?*

Her biology was no better than a golden retriever staring at a frisbee. "Good evening, Tyler." She walked faster.

"Thanks for doing this," he said as they both settled into the truck. His smile was sheepish as he started the engine. "You were right, by the way."

Emma clutched her purse in her lap. "About what?"

He flipped a U-turn. "This is proving my dad's point."

Emma exhaled and relaxed into the seat. "Well, asking you to be my fake boyfriend was kind of proving Sean's, too."

"How so?"

"He thinks I make terrible decisions."

"Do you?"

"Clearly." Emma stared out the window at a corgi in leather booties and a red sweater peeing on the streetlight. The perfect metaphor for her life at the moment.

Tyler tapped his fingers on the wheel. "Are you alright? You seem a bit tense."

Emma didn't answer. She did not want to talk about the studio sale on top of everything else, and her mind was fixating. "Sean thinks I'm oblivious, but I'm not. It's not like I'm not trying." Tyler was silent next to her. She drew a heart in the condensation from her breath building up on the glass.

"Here." Tyler pulled a cup from the console and passed it to her.

Emma turned. "London Fog?"

"Hopefully you weren't lying when you said you liked it the other night."

"A cardinal sin. Never." *Though I lie about "appointments" to my best friends.* She took a sip. "How are your ribs?"

"Feels less like a shard of glass is puncturing my side every time I inhale."

"Hey, that's all a person can ask for."

Tyler chuckled. "Sean apologized, by the way. To the whole team."

Emma's jaw dropped. "Well." She couldn't think of anything else to say. Two apologies—regardless of whether they were motivated by Kelty's hot rage—was something.

"I apologized, too."

Emma frowned. "Why? You didn't—"

"For letting his little sister corrupt me."

Emma rolled her eyes and smacked his shoulder. "I'm a convent nun compared to you, Bowen. Any corruption in this relationship is flowing in one direction."

"You're saying we have a relationship?"

Emma laughed, all the pressure in her chest beginning to fizz like a bottle of champagne. "Save your flirting for Ginger, please."

"I don't *need* to flirt with Ginger."

"And therein, my dear sir, lies the problem." Emma lifted her hand in a flourish.

Tyler grinned. "Are you secretly obsessed with Arthurian literature?"

"Only if there's spice."

He blinked. "I don't think I want to know." Emma had to look away to keep from fixating on the smile lines crinkling next to his hazel eyes.

They drove in silence until Tyler pulled up to the curb down the block from a farm-to-table restaurant. There was an instant shift in his demeanour. His shoulders were stiff, his mouth drawn into a line as he glanced through the window and parked.

"This probably won't be fun," Tyler admitted, his expression unreadable.

"I gathered as much. Seems fair since *that* wasn't exactly fun either." Emma motioned at his face. "As long as I can eat roasted chicken and nobody challenges me to a duel, I'll be fine."

She'd looked at the menu ahead of time, and though there were plenty of tantalizing options, the half-chicken with fennel and rosemary was calling her name. Emma opened the door and dropped onto the walkway. *She hoped she'd be fine.* How long had it been since she'd met a guy's parents?

Tyler slipped his hand into hers as they strode up the block. *Right.* Not just dinner, she had to pretend to be with him. She breathed a sigh of relief, remembering she'd already set the boundary where her lips were concerned. The way her skin was lighting up under the feel of his palm and the brush of his fingers between hers confirmed that had been a wise and necessary decision.

They entered the restaurant, and the clink of glasses and folk music greeted them. The lighting was dim with exposed bulbs hanging in geometric light fixtures over each rustic, oiled tabletop.

The hostess pointed toward the back of the restaurant, and Emma spotted Tyler's dad immediately. He was shorter than Tyler, with greying hair, but the resemblance between the two men was uncanny.

"Ty, you walk into a beehive again?" his father laughed, pulling him into a hug and clapping him on the back.

Tyler mumbled something about hockey, and then Emma was pulled into the man's arms.

"I'm Troy, and you must be Emma?" Troy pulled back to look at her, his hands clamped onto her shoulders. His charismatic smile and warm hazel eyes mirrored Tyler's. She nodded. "It's a pleasure to finally meet you," Troy extended his hand with genuine warmth. "Tyler's told me so much about you."

Emma shot a glance at Tyler, but he didn't look at her. *Finally?* Tyler had asked her to this dinner yesterday. Troy was so smooth, he made elevator jazz seem garish.

"I'm flattered. I've heard quite a bit about you as well."

"Ah, well, I hope my son hasn't been filling your head with too many tall tales," he chuckled, leaning back in his seat and throwing his arm over the slender blond sitting next to him. She was stunning. Smooth skin with a perfect blush on her cheeks, arched eyebrows, and teeth so white, they almost looked pale blue.

She offered a hand to Emma. "I'm Melanie."

Emma took it. Her fingers felt like ice. *She needed to eat more carbs.* "Lovely to meet you."

"I was telling Mel how you met." Troy shook his head. "Seems like I should've started dropping my driver's licence in parking lots years ago, eh?"

Emma blinked. "You told him that?"

The corner of Tyler's mouth curled. "Of course."

"You know you can drop those off in the mailbox, and the postal workers will take care of it," Melanie offered, taking a sip of her wine.

Emma opened her mouth, but Tyler lifted his arm, sliding his hand over her collar and threading his fingers in her hair. "It's a good thing she didn't. The address on my licence wasn't correct."

She shivered and drew in a breath, trying to keep her cheeks from flaming like solar flares. "Social media for the win."

"Said no one in history." Troy winked. "No, I'm kidding, I love some aspects of social media. Especially when it brings in bookings."

Emma didn't want to move. Tyler's fingers traced across her scalp, sending tingles tiptoeing under her skin. At least Troy had brought up a safe subject. Men like him loved talking about themselves, and since her throat was responding as if she'd been the one to disrupt a swarm of bees, she needed him to monologue. "I'd love to hear how these property renovations started."

"Ah, that's a long story."

She hoped her smile didn't look forced. "Start from the beginning."

Her lemon water and salad arrived as Troy regaled them with tales of his various business ventures and the far-flung corners of the country they took him to. Her chicken arrived well before he ended with this renovation project in Calgary.

"Every city has a rich history, and if we don't care enough to preserve it, these buildings disappear."

"An act of pure altruism, eh?" Tyler took a bite of his steak.

Troy's eyes glittered with amusement. "It's not wrong to benefit from your sound business decisions." He dabbed his lips with his napkin.

"I think it's a gift that the two of you get to work together and that Tyler jumped right in after moving to Calgary."

Troy cocked his head to the side. "Jumped in?"

Emma chewed the tender chicken and swallowed. "I think it takes most people some time to get acclimated to a new place. Tyler's already killing it on his hockey team and is well-connected. It's impressive."

Troy chuckled. "Getting connected hasn't ever been our struggle, eh Ty?" Tyler's lip twitched as he reached for his water.

Emma put a hand on Tyler's knee under the table. "Have you been to one of his games?"

The easy smile on Troy's face slipped a little. "I've been extremely busy with work."

Emma nodded, but couldn't believe what she was hearing. *Tyler had been here for how long, and Troy hadn't seen him play?* With every comment out of Troy's mouth, Tyler retreated a little further into himself, and she hated it. Even if he hadn't fallen far from his father's tree on paper, something clashed within Tyler, and the energy rolled off him in waves.

"But enough about the Bowens," Troy continued. "Tell me about your work, Emma."

Tyler cleared his throat. "Emma does food styling, and product shoots through a photography studio downtown—"

"For the next two weeks," she muttered, then froze with her glass halfway to her lips. Tyler frowned, and she waved the comment off. "Sorry, I didn't mean to bring that up. I just found out things at work will be shifting a little, that's all."

She'd decided not to share anything about the studio because there hadn't been time for her to process or find solutions. There was nothing to tell besides the fact that she'd be out of a job, and she didn't want to make this dinner about her.

"Shifting how?" Tyler lifted a hand onto the back of her chair. The distance between their bodies seemed to be directly linked to her heart rate. Inversely proportional.

"The owners of the studio got an offer for the space, so they're selling. It just means I'll need to go back to working freelance."

The furrow between Tyler's brows deepened. "You've solely been there for a few years. Do you still have connections with other brands?"

He didn't miss much, did he? "Between the three of us, we'll pull some strings. It might take a little time to get our volume back up to what we're used to, but I'm not worried." Emma was terrified. A little time could be months to years, depending on the market, and she'd opted to purchase her apartment rather than rent. She had some savings, but not enough to cover a year's worth of mortgage payments.

"The three of you?" Melanie asked.

Emma drank the last of her water. "Two friends of mine. Photographers. We've worked together for years. Kind of a package deal at this point."

Melanie shared a look with Troy. He sat up and clasped his hands, setting them on the table between them. "The three of you do marketing work?"

She nodded. "Yes, food and product styling, commercial spots."

Troy considered this, swirling the last of his wine in the flared glass. "You know, Emma, I've been looking to build my marketing team for all three of my properties. I need content for our social media platforms, online menus, booking sites, and advertising. Do you think you'd be interested? As long as I like your portfolio, of course."

He reached into his jacket pocket, pulled out a business card, and extended it toward her. The gold embossed lettering shimmered in the warm light of the Edison bulb. "Consider this an open invitation." Troy flashed a charming smile. "I'd want you to be available full-time for the length of the project. I'm kind of a fast and furious guy." Tyler stiffened next to her. "Take some time to think about it, and send me your work and fee schedule. I have a feeling you'd make an excellent addition to the team."

Emma took the card from him, her thoughts buzzing. "Wow, I don't know what to say. Thank you for the offer. I'll submit that to you and talk with my partners."

"Do that, and don't dally. I want you to think about it but know that it doesn't take long for the Bowen men to get distracted. Keep our attention, Emma, and we'll get along just fine."

CHAPTER
Eleven

TYLER AND EMMA stepped out of the warm, bustling restaurant into the brisk Calgary night. Emma gently pulled her hand from his grasp as soon as they were out of eyeshot of the restaurant. His dad and Melanie had just ordered another bottle of wine, so they wouldn't be following.

The crisp night air nipped at their cheeks, and Tyler shoved his hands into his pockets. The streets were slick with a thin layer of frost, reflecting the dim glow of the streetlights above. Laughter echoed from a nearby pub, blending with the distant hum of traffic and the muted sounds of footsteps crunching on the icy pavement.

"Thanks for dinner." Emma shivered and wrapped her scarf around her neck.

"Did the chicken hold up? You had massively unrealistic expectations."

She scoffed. "Because I mentioned it once?"

"Obsessed."

Emma lifted her nose in the air. "It was delicious. Yours?"

Tyler had ordered the ribeye with mashed sweet potato and haricot verts. "Astounding." The steak had been overcooked and the beans a bit mushy.

"Liar. You can admit you wished you'd copied me."

He grinned as they approached his truck, their breath forming cumulus clouds with each exhale. Tyler unlocked the doors, and they both slid into the icy seats. Goosebumps prickled his skin as the cold leather made contact. Tyler flicked on their seat warmers and let the engine idle a few minutes before turning on the heater.

"Where are the properties you're working on?" Emma asked, her hands tucked under her thighs for warmth.

"I've only been to the one—the other two are being gutted, I think. Do you want to check it out?"

Emma's eyes lit up. "It's close?"

"Maybe eight minutes away?"

"That's a very specific estimate."

"I like to be accurate."

Emma pulled out her phone. "Starting a timer now."

Tyler took that as a challenge. He'd driven to the property from this street before, but never this exact spot. He pushed through a yellow light, then wondered if that would make up too much time.

"At six minutes and counting, Bowen."

One and a half minutes later, the truck tires crunched over gravel as Tyler pulled into the driveway of the old manor house.

"Admit it, Thompson. You're impressed."

She raised an eyebrow. If she was going to use his last name, he was going to use hers. She stopped her timer but didn't give him the satisfaction of a response. That alone told him he'd won.

The imposing brick facade cast a shadow across spotty snow drifts in the pale moonlight. He could see Emma's eyes widen with anticipation as they climbed out of the truck, her breath misting around her.

"Here." Tyler tossed her his Maple Leafs toque from the console. She turned it around.

"I don't think I'm allowed to wear this in this city."

Tyler pointed to his bruised face. "I'll protect you if you get jumped." He pulled on a striped toque, which he'd purchased at a gas station in Winnipeg when he was there for a tourney, and followed Emma along the paving stones.

"This place is incredible," she whispered as they approached the arching grand entrance. "What's the story?"

"From what Troy tells me, it was built in the early 1900s by an eccentric millionaire named Jasper Whittaker, who was obsessed with European architecture. Not quite as infatuated with it as you were with the chicken, but almost."

Emma smacked him and kept walking. "I see some Gothic, some Baroque."

"A little Victorian, too, I think. It was set to be torn down. Had some major foundation issues. Structurally, it's sound now."

"And the interior?"

"In progress. Some rooms are finished. There's an original claw tub on the third floor and a ballroom at the top."

"Shut up."

"I'm serious. Original paint on the ceiling as well."

Emma's eyes danced as she ran her fingers over the intricate carvings and stonework adorning the mansion's exterior. "Lindsey's head is going to explode, and Vaughn . . ." She stopped and pulled out her phone. "Do you care if I text them?" Tyler shook his head. She started to type, then stopped, pulling her lower lip between her teeth.

"Maybe I shouldn't." She looked up, and Tyler's heart stuttered. "They'll fall in love with it and if Troy doesn't like our portfolios—"

"He's going to love them."

Emma gave him a skeptical look. "You don't even know what my photos look like."

Tyler walked past her, his pulse quickening. "Yes I do, and I know he's going to love them."

Emma didn't follow him. "You've seen my work?" He

nodded, pretending to peer through the glass, even though the interior was pitch black. "How?"

"It's called the internet."

Emma's voice softened. "You looked up my website?"

I looked up a hell of a lot more than that. "Yep. Had to make sure I wasn't fake dating a terrible photographer. I have standards."

Emma grinned as she watched him, backlit by the streetlamp. "Well, in that case, maybe I'll send them that message."

Tyler kept walking, turning to catch his breath without her noticing. When he heard her footsteps rounding the corner, he pressed back against the wall and waited. This was a terrible idea, but he couldn't stop himself from doing it. It was too good.

Emma stepped past the wall, and Tyler launched himself forward, growling low in his throat. A blood-curdling scream filled the air as the back of Emma's hand slammed upward into his chin.

Tyler groaned and stumbled back as Emma panted in front of him.

"You *nutsack!*" she hissed, crouching over her knees.

Tyler righted himself and stared at her. "Nutsack?"

Emma refused to look up, holding onto the rim of the toque with both hands, pulling it down over her eyes.

Tyler erupted with laughter. Full guffaws that tore at his sore ribs, but he couldn't stop. He laughed until tears streamed down his face and he clutched at his midsection, leaning against the brick to keep from collapsing.

Emma stood, her arms folded in front of her chest. "You finished?"

"I don't know," he gasped. "Can you please say that again?"

Emma's lips twitched. "You don't deserve to hear that again."

"Who says 'nutsack'?"

Emma's sour expression cracked. "Someone with three brothers who used to hide in the basement for hours and make her pee herself when she braved the dark to get a jar of peaches from the storage room."

Tyler straightened, holding his cheeks and feigning sobriety. "That sounds... painful."

"Thank you for recognizing that. I'm sorry I tried to throat-punch you."

"You missed."

"Maybe your throat is in the wrong place."

Tyler's feet seemed to sink into the ground as his eyes ran over her face, flushed and alive in the moonlight. He wanted to kiss her. Two steps was all he needed. His hands itched to wrap around her hip, to feel the arch of her back. It had been just a few seconds at the arena, but that moment flickered to the forefront of his thoughts more often than he liked to admit.

Emma's phone buzzed, and she pulled it from her pocket. She smiled. "They're sending their portfolios to Troy now. I sent them his info."

"Did you already send yours?"

She nodded and looked up, opening her mouth and then thinking better of it.

"What?" Tyler asked, his heart still hammering in his chest.

"Do you... I mean, are you okay with this?"

"Okay with what?"

Emma motioned to the house. "With me working for your dad, being at your place of business, if he decides to hire us."

Tyler inhaled and nodded for them to walk back to the front of the house. "It's a good job. You'd be perfect for it."

The corner of her mouth lifted before she pulled it back down. "But—"

"Don't overthink it. You're still recovering from a traumatic experience."

She flashed him a look, and he had to touch her. His hand moved before he gave it permission, and he quickly pulled it high and ran his knuckles over the toque on her head.

Emma ducked away from him. "Okay, I know my hair isn't much, but it looks half decent when it isn't matted."

Tyler laughed and rounded the vehicle, slipping back behind the wheel. Emma tore off the toque and looked in the mirror to straighten her part.

Tyler hesitated before starting the engine, his fingers resting on the ignition as he glanced down at his phone.

"What is it?" Emma's voice in the dead air of the cab sent shivers down his spine.

He swallowed hard and stared at the text from Brett.

> Bud, heading to Cowboys if you want to join

His blood raced, everything inside him feeling like pop rocks fizzing against his tongue. He needed to do something to blow off steam.

"Tyler, is—"

"Do you want to go home or—?"

Emma watched him, and he could see the wheels turning in her head. "Or what?"

"Some of the guys from the team are heading to Cowboys. You want to go?"

She glanced down at her outfit. A button-up that cut low enough, he'd glanced at the swell of her breasts at least three times tonight. Dark jeans that hugged her hips and tucked into the space between her butt and her thighs. He'd noticed that, too.

"You look fine."

Emma glanced up with a look that said, *fine?*

Tyler started the truck. "I can drop you off at home if—"

"I'll come. Sounds fun."

CHAPTER
Twelve

EMMA TWISTED her hands in her lap, questioning her decision to go out with Tyler and the other Snowballs. For sure, Country and Brett would be there, probably André and Darcy. The only reason she'd said yes was that Kelty had mentioned on the family chat that she and Sean had tickets to see Josh Groban at the Saddledome tonight, so there was no risk of an awkward encounter there.

But why was she going? She had to head to the studio in the morning, not crazy early, but it was already close to ten o'clock. It was the look in Tyler's eyes when he'd asked if she wanted to go home. Something had shifted in him tonight, and she couldn't figure it out. It was like an itch in the centre of her back that she stretched for but couldn't quite reach.

Tyler turned onto Crowchild, and Emma felt like she'd dropped down a playground slide. *You look fine.* She'd seen him glancing over at the V in her shirt during dinner and that dark flicker in his eyes when he said it.

It was straight poison. And Emma wanted to bottle every last drop and drink it in.

The moment they entered the bar, thumping bass and infectious energy washed over her. They showed their IDs, Emma feigning surprise when Tyler had his in his wallet, and checked their coats. The dim lighting was punctuated by neon signs and the occasional flash of multi-coloured strobe lights from the dance floor. The guitar sang, and the drum beat pulsed through her veins, begging her feet to move.

"Emma!" Jess, Fly's girlfriend of over seven years hailed her, and Emma waved, glad for the distraction. At least she'd have one friend to dance with when Tyler inevitably went off with his teammates. They couldn't look like a couple here, even if Sean wasn't showing up.

As she made her way through the crowd, she spotted a couple of friends from a job she'd done in Okotoks. They'd spent a month together shooting an entire brand of organic dog food. She threw out her arms and greeted them with hugs.

She could do this. Tonight would be exactly what she needed.

Emma lost herself in the music, dancing and catching up with friends, avoiding the sweaty men who kept pressing up against her back. She did one shot with Jess, then Boot Scootin' Boogied until she felt dizzy.

After the line dance, she pushed through the crowd to the rail and sat up, pulling her hair into an elastic to let the sweat dry on her neck. That's when she saw him.

Tyler, surrounded by his teammates as they pumped their fists. She peered closer, trying to figure out what they were doing. For a brief moment, Tyler's eyes met hers across the crowded room.

Then there were four women in only their bras winding their hands through his hair and pulling him up onto the bar. The brunette wearing a belt buckle and neon pink lace stripped off his shirt and put her boot on his chest, pushing him down on his back.

The Snowballs cheered along with half the bar. A girl in a black satin push-up bra and a faux hawk with purple tips jumped behind the bar. *Did she work here?* She opened the fridge and pulled out an ice cube tray.

A blond giggled and traced her manicured nails over his arms, stretching them over his head. Faux hawk tipped over the tray onto a plate. Jell-O shots. Pink lace plucked three of them up and lined them up on top of Tyler's abs.

Bile rose in Emma's throat.

"Hey, are you okay?" Jess grabbed onto her leg, startling her.

"Y-yeah, I'm fine," she stammered. "I think I just need to get some air."

Jess nodded. "Fly wants to head out. I think we're going to make our way to the coat check."

Emma looked up to see the blond drop onto all fours on the bar over Tyler. Her stomach heaved.

"Emma—"

"I think I'm ready, too. Could I catch a ride home with you?"

Jess nodded, her brow furrowed. "Do you need to tell anyone—"

"A friend dropped me off." Emma jumped from the rail and grabbed Jess's hand, pulling her toward the exit.

They made their way through the crowded bar and waited nearly ten minutes for their coats since Fly lost his ticket. Emma's head throbbed as they stepped outside and the noise of laughter and music faded, replaced by the distant hum of traffic. Stupid. She shouldn't have come—she knew she shouldn't have come. Bars weren't her scene in the first place, *but bars with Tyler?*

Her ears felt like they were covered with cellophane. Emma pulled her coat tighter around herself as she followed Jess and Fly to the back corner of the lot.

"Emma, wait!" Tyler's voice called out from behind her. She whirled to find his shirtless figure illuminated by the dim glow of the streetlights.

Her heart raced, a mix of emotions flooding through her as she took in his still-bruised body, now slick with gelatin and at least one woman's saliva. He jogged toward her, weaving through the parked cars.

"Tyler, stop." Her voice wavered as she struggled to maintain her composure. "I don't think this is a good idea. I shouldn't have come tonight."

"Emma—" he began, but she held up a hand, flicking a glance over her shoulder to find Jess and Fly. They stood a few rows back, watching them. *Fantastic.*

"Go back inside. I've got a ride home with Jess."

Tyler ran his hands through his hair, his nipples pinching against the cold. She hated that she noticed. "I wasn't—"

"Oh, you definitely were." She laughed at the ridiculousness of the situation. "You don't owe me an explanation, okay? Thank you for the invitation, but I'm tired and Jess and Fly are heading out. I'll see you at work."

She shuddered, imagining having to see him ever again after tonight. The image of flashy bras and tongues travelling over his golden skin. Emma clenched her jaw. This was his life. This was what Tyler Bowen did on the weekend, and Sean knew it. That was why he'd warned her, and that was why she needed to get the hell out of this parking lot.

"Goodnight, Tyler." She turned, but footsteps sounded behind her.

"Emma, I can go back in and grab my shirt. I'll drive you home."

She whipped around and held out her hand. He was closer than she thought. "Can you even safely drive or should Fly call you an Uber?"

Tyler frowned. "You've had more to drink than I have."

"Because you know how much I had to drink?"

Tyler's jaw flexed. "Yeah. I do."

"How much, then?" Emma planted her hands on her hips.

"One shot with Jess."

Her cheeks flushed as she scoffed, "And you had less than that?"

"I haven't had a drink tonight. I don't drink. Haven't since my first year at Toronto." His voice was low, and Emma took a step back.

"What?" His words didn't compute.

Goosebumps covered his skin, and he rubbed his hands on his arms. "My coach didn't allow any substance use. After a couple of years, I got used to it. One night I went to the bar and felt like shit the next day, so I stopped. Never went back."

Emma pursed her lips. "So you did all that sober?" Her chest felt like it was filled with baking soda and vinegar. *Why was she so angry?* She needed sleep, and she needed to not be looking at Tyler's abs.

She turned a third time, but Tyler caught her elbow. She yanked her hand away, but he held onto her coat.

"Can you wait ten seconds and I'll drive you home?"

"Why did you really want me to come to dinner tonight?" she asked. He blinked, confused. "Your answer on Saturday morning, it wasn't a good one. That display on the bar in there says you clearly don't care about impressing your dad." Tyler's throat worked, but he didn't answer. "You helped me out, and I helped you. We're even."

Something flashed in Tyler's eyes as he dropped his hold on her puffy coat. "My dad has cancer, Emma."

The words hung in the air like an icy fog.

"Emma, you coming?" Jess called.

Tyler ran a hand over his face. "I'm sorry, I should've said something sooner."

Emma swallowed hard. She turned and waved at Jess and Fly. "Tyler's going to take me home!" Jess gave her a thumbs-up and jumped into the car. She turned back to Tyler.

"I'll go get my shirt." Tyler turned and jogged back toward the front door.

Emma hated that she watched.

CHAPTER
Thirteen

TYLER STEPPED ONTO THE ICE. The atmosphere at practice was palpably tense, a lingering residue from last week's fight. Soothed by last night's antics at the bar, but Sean hadn't been there. He was the sheep that needed to be brought back into the fold, and they didn't have loud music or Jell-O shots to facilitate that now.

Country and André were green around the gills. He didn't miss that feeling. He didn't miss worrying about what he had or hadn't done the night before, either. He remembered his conversation with Emma perfectly.

"*Should I come inside?*" *he asked.*

"*Nope. We can talk here.*" *Emma had pressed herself up against the passenger door.*

"*You look terrified. And cold.*"

Emma reached out and turned up the heat. "*I'm not terrified.*"

Tyler leaned onto the console. "*Then why—*"

"*Get back on your side, please.*"

He'd given her a questioning look, and she'd crossed her arms over her chest. "*Oh please! Don't pretend you don't know the effect you have on women, Tyler. You're attractive and it's late, and I'm emotionally unstable, and this console is necessary for my sanity.*"

He'd gawked at her then. Yes, he was aware of the effect he had on some women, but Emma had never acted like them. "You think I'm attractive?"

Emma groaned and planted the side of her face against the headrest. "Yes, Tyler. I find you attractive. Are you happy? Now can you please explain?"

Yes, he'd been happy. He'd been a damn labrador with its tongue lolling out and tail wagging to hear she found him attractive. So attractive, in fact, that in her weakened state, she couldn't be trusted to bring him up to her apartment.

He could still see Emma in the passenger seat, the greens and reds of the traffic lights passing over her face as they drove silently back to her place from Cowboys. He hadn't told anyone about Troy's diagnosis, not even the guys on the team, but now she knew.

"So that's why you moved here?" He thought she was going to get out the second he pulled up to the curb, but she'd paused, her fingers brushing the door handle.

"Did the panties match the bra?" Darcy called, smirking as he skated past.

Tyler jolted, then swatted his padded ass with his stick. Thankfully, it seemed Darcy had been the only one to notice Emma leaving with Jess and Fly last night. The rest of the guys inside assumed he'd left with the blond from the bar, and Tyler was happy to keep it that way.

His body felt stiff and bruised beneath his gear. Not surprising, since this was his first time out after the game against Hattrick. He'd loosen up once his muscles warmed.

Sean set up cones and they started practice drills. Tyler wove in and out of the cones, and though his lats complained, he sent shot after shot whizzing across the ice toward Boyd in the net, half of them hitting the back of the net with a satisfying thwack. He'd practise pocket shots later when Boyd wasn't in position. They never shot high in practice.

Darcy circled in a wide arc around the net. "Did you hear

that the goalie for Don's Cherrypickers tore his nutsack saving a goal last weekend? That's the kind of commitment I'm talking about."

The image of Emma jumping back and yelling *nutsack!* in the moonlight hit Tyler full force. He snorted, nearly choking on his spit. Then he remembered her flushed cheeks and his toque on her head. He stumbled and nearly took out a cone.

André shot the puck wide, and Boyd kicked out a leg. "My nutsack is flexible. Too supple to tear."

Curtis snorted, waiting for his pass. "My wife wants me to get waxed."

Ryan slapped his stick on the ice. "Isn't that why you're married? You can let the weeds grow free?"

"You get Emma home okay?" Fly sprayed shaved ice behind him as he stopped at the end of their practice line. Tyler's heart skipped a beat, and he glanced over at Sean sprinting through the cones.

He nodded once. "She's working for my dad. We had a work thing to discuss."

Fly wet his lips. "A work thing. Very specific."

Tyler exhaled, but Fly nudged him with his elbow.

"Emma's not a puck bunny, eh?"

"I didn't think—"

"Just telling you what's what." Fly nodded toward the cones. He was up. Tyler turned and dug his blades into the ice.

Fly wouldn't say anything to Sean, but he'd made himself clear. *Don't piss around.* Fly had been a young buck once. He'd played in the NHL for two years before his ACL shredded. He knew this game, on and off the ice.

"Shit, Suraj, where was that in the game?!" Mike's dark braid hung down the back of his jersey as he playfully knocked him into the boards. Suraj slapped Mike's helmet.

Gary skated toward the back of the line, recently having returned from his trip to Europe. He looked a bit slow on the ice.

"Too many baguettes?" Tyler teased as he passed. The dude

was a monster on defence. Another thing they could've used more of with Tyler and Sean bleeding on the bench.

Sean whistled for them to circle up. "First playoff game Friday night. Against Mill Hoodies, as you know. They've got Dirty D and he's a menace, so wingers, keep your heads on swivels."

Darcy, André, Mike, and Ryan nodded. Tyler didn't have the same visceral reaction to playing Edmonton as his teammates. He only had to imagine the Mill Hoodies were from Montreal and he was right there with them.

Sean continued, "Their goalie is a dandy, but don't underestimate him. He's left-handed, Bowen." Tyler nodded. *Left high pocket. Check.* "Butter balm your sack, Boyd, and we should be good." Snickers sounded around the ice as Boyd rubbed his glove over his groin.

They broke into teams for a scrimmage, and Tyler stopped thinking. He dropped into muscle memory, and his lingering bruises, his dad's diagnosis, and the look on Emma's face in the parking lot faded into the background.

When he finally stepped off the ice and clomped down the hall to the showers, Tyler's body hummed and his mind felt clearer than it had all weekend. He peeled off his sweat-soaked jersey and pads with a grimace.

Sean's torso didn't look much better than his own.

"At least we match." Tyler pulled out his bag and started throwing his gear in, lamenting that it no longer smelled like Emma's lemon soap.

Sean grunted and stripped off his shorts. Tyler followed him into the showers. The warm water cascaded over his sore muscles as he lathered shampoo into his hair, rinsing away the grime and sweat from practice.

"What's the final count on the pot?" Gary asked, rivulets of water forming in his beard.

"Last I heard it was fifteen."

Curtis flicked his wrist to snap his fingers together. "That's almost a grand each. Wasn't last year more like seven-fifty?"

"Trans Canada is feeling generous, eh?" Darcy flicked soap at André, landing on the silver cross hanging on a chain around his neck.

The name of the Provincial cup changed each year depending on who sponsored it, but to them it was always the Rose. Had a better ring to it. The Snowballs had won it twice in the past five years, and while Tyler wasn't motivated by the money, he wasn't going to be the reason that trophy left the display case upstairs.

Tyler dried off and got dressed, then grabbed his gear and headed out to the hall. He was going to need more than a few full nights of sleep and ibuprofen to be in prime condition for Friday. He'd book a massage for Saturday morning preemptively.

"Looking good out there," Sean barked behind him. Tyler took the stairs slowly to let him catch up.

"Good practice, Cap."

Sean climbed next to him. "Didn't fuddle things up too bad then?"

Tyler clapped him on the shoulder with his free hand. They didn't say anything else as they walked out the front doors. The air bit against his skin, and Tyler tucked his chin into the top of his puffy vest. The stars overhead glittered against the charcoal sky, while the faint buzz of streetlights mingled with laughter wafting from One Place.

"Tyler?" He turned to see Ginger sitting on one of the benches, bundled up against the cold. "Hey." She had on a short skirt and sheer leggings.

Sean glanced between the two of them. "Don't stay out too late, Bowen."

Tyler's throat tightened as Sean strode to his car. "Hey, Ginger. You're not working at Dusty tonight?"

"I was in the neighbourhood. Thought we could chat?"

Tyler's heart rate quickened. Normally he'd pretend this was innocent. Give her the satisfaction of thinking she'd come up with a reasonable explanation for why she was freezing outside of the Ice Arena, then act surprised when she ended up between his sheets.

But he didn't feel normal tonight.

Ginger shifted on her heels. "Maybe we could walk to your truck? It's nippy out here."

Tyler nodded once and started walking.

Emma entered the bustling studio on Thursday, her heart pounding with nervous energy. Lindsey and Vaughn were already well into packing their photography equipment, the metallic clink of tripods mingling with the rustle and zips of protective bags.

"Do you think Troy Bowen has his hands in every part of this project?" Lindsey asked, her auburn hair bouncing as she secured a camera lens in its case. "I mean, the pay is incredible, but if he micromanages me . . . this is a full quarter we're committing to."

Emma set down her empty boxes and purse and began wrestling with a backdrop. "We only signed for the first property. If it's soul-sucking, we can bow out after a month or so."

"Agreed." Vaughn stacked his gluten-free energy bars into his backpack with precision. "I'm intrigued by the interior shoots, Linds. I think we'll come up with something breathtaking."

"Absolutely." Emma had no doubt they would, but her thoughts wouldn't stay planted on the bed and breakfast. All morning she'd been reliving the conversation in Tyler's truck Sunday night. His hazel eyes soft and vulnerable. His cologne mixed with the sweet and acrid scent of fruity liquor.

"That's why I asked you to come to dinner. I don't want to be like my dad, Emma. But I don't have much time left to figure it out. At least not when he can see it."

She'd listened as he filled her in on his dad's pancreatic cancer diagnosis ten years earlier. How he'd been declared cancer free, but now was in relapse. Refusing treatment since the odds were low he'd do more than languish in a hospital bed for months and die anyway.

Tyler described the end of his parents' marriage, how Troy had cheated on his mom at least twice that he knew about, and how he promised himself he'd never do that to a woman. Emma read between the lines. *I'll never get close to someone if I might hurt them.*

Though she hadn't admitted it in the cab, her heart mirrored his. *I'll never get close to someone if they might hurt me,* and as he spoke, a realization had snapped into place.

That's why she was drawn to men like Tyler. If she picked up a snake and got bit, she could never blame herself for deserving it. It was their fault, not hers. Her relationship with Alex broke down because he was a douchebag, not because Emma wasn't loveable.

Not because she couldn't make someone happy.

Not because she wasn't enough.

Tyler had tried to walk her inside, but she'd asked him not to. She didn't want him to see the tears welling in her eyes and think they were his fault. They weren't.

"Earth to Emma!" Lindsey snapped her fingers in front of Emma's face, bringing her back to the studio. "You okay there?"

"Uh, yeah," Emma stammered, blushing. "This is just a big change."

"Hey," Vaughn crooned, slinging an arm around her shoulders. "We're all in this together. If this doesn't work out, we'll find something that does. I already have emails in to Crowe and Black. A couple of others, too."

If this doesn't work out. She needed to text Tyler. Ever since Sunday night, she'd waffled back and forth about what to do at work. Tyler hadn't asked her to keep their ruse going, but how could she not want to help after hearing his story?

It would hurt. She knew that already. The way her body had wound like a spring seeing Tyler under that blond at the bar laid the truth bare in front of her face. She had feelings for him, and allowing him to touch her—kiss her—for a month was only going to make it worse, regardless of how many times she told herself it wasn't real.

She would hope it was. She would want him to be something he wasn't. Her lizard brain wouldn't get the memo once his hands were on her skin.

"We need a picture," Lindsey announced triumphantly, snapping shut the last case. She set her iPhone against the built-in cabinets and hustled to stand next to Emma and Vaughn. Emma wrapped her arms around her friends and smiled, then let Vaughn stack the boxes in her arms and open the door.

"Tomorrow." He kissed her cheek.

Emma smiled and waved goodbye with the only three fingers that weren't load-bearing, then loaded her car and drove home.

Emma parked, then trudged up the stairs to her apartment with the boxes in her arms. She fumbled with her keys, trying to find the right one without dropping everything, and managed to unlock the door before her hold slipped. With a sigh of relief, she pushed the door open with her boot and carried the boxes inside.

She set them down in the living room, wincing as her back protested. Emma arched and stretched her arms over her head. She wasn't even thirty, which meant back pain wasn't allowed.

She stalked to the kitchen, opened the refrigerator, grabbed a pre-packaged salad, and collapsed onto the couch. Flipping on the TV, she scrolled through her options before settling on a recorded episode of CTV's version of the Bachelor. Trash TV was her guilty pleasure after work, and tonight she needed it more than usual. *Please, Francesca, tell me how crushed your heart is because Billy didn't take you home after your private date.*

Her phone buzzed as she picked at her salad. She set down

her fork, then nearly choked on a cherry tomato. A message from Tyler.

> Hey, got the contract from Troy earlier today.
> First day tomorrow?

First day tomorrow. Emma's chest felt like it was the bottle cap holding in the kombucha Vaughn had left fermenting too long in the studio fridge. She gave his comment a thumbs-up.

> We're packed up and ready to go

Francesca whined to the camera. *"It just hurts, you know? To be here by myself and know he's with her?"* Emma took another forkful of greens.

> I'll be there to help with any clean up. The
> kitchen isn't quite functional from what I hear

> Thanks. I think we'll start with desserts since
> they can be made off-site

Her thumbs hovered over the keyboard. She needed to bring it up, but they hadn't talked since Sunday. Now it all felt awkward. Emma chewed her lip, considering her options.

> Does Troy still think we're together?

She typed it out and held her breath. There was a chance that Tyler had already broken up with her between Sunday and now. No point worrying about it if so.

> Yes. Haven't seen him in a couple of days. I can
> break the news if he stops by tomorrow

> Don't

She texted back, surprising herself with her own decisiveness.

> We can fake it, but we need to lay down some ground rules

Air hissed through her teeth like a slow leaking balloon. Emma knew exactly what her family would think about this. But, based on Tyler's message, it didn't sound like Troy was on property all that often, which meant it wouldn't be every second of the day. If they could spell out boundaries, it wouldn't have to impact her life much.

Spending time with Tyler at work would be far easier than sitting alone with him in his truck, which she would have to ensure didn't happen again. She would see him at work and consider interacting with him part of her job description. If Troy only had a few weeks or months left, this was Tyler's last chance to show up the way he wanted to.

Emma didn't owe him anything, she knew that, but Tyler had stepped in with Sean when she'd asked him to—when they barely knew each other. He hadn't planned on her working for Troy, and she was the one benefitting there. It was only a few weeks, and then she could mop up the emotional wreckage as needed. That was a skillset she already had.

Tyler hadn't responded, and Emma second-guessed herself. Maybe Tyler didn't want to do this? She'd feel like an idiot *asking* to fake date him if he'd already written it off. Maybe she needed to make it clear she didn't want this, but was willing to—

His message popped up.

> I love rules

Emma grinned.

> Nobody loves rules

False

> Fine, Bowen. Name some rules you love

No icing. No offsides

Emma snorted. Hockey rules. Perfect.

> Great start.
>
> No offsides. You don't come into my work space unless I invite you.
>
> No delay of game. If I'm working, you can't distract me

How would I distract you?

So. Many. Ways. She ignored the question.

> No face offs

Emma snorted. Let him chew on that for a minute.

Then how do we start the game?

Emma laughed out loud.

> Touching only when necessary. If Troy isn't there, hands off

I wouldn't be offside anyway

> Exactly

Kissing?

Emma sucked in a breath. *No kissing* was her gut reaction, but that wasn't practical. Tyler was touchy, and his dad wasn't going to believe they were into each other if he didn't at least see a few. Her stomach swooped.

> Once a week. Max. I give penalties

The screen said *typing*. She waited, ignoring the dramatic music on the TV.

> One word from you and I'll tell Troy it didn't work out

> Which word? 'Halt' and 'desist' are both good ones

> Although adding 'good sir' would feel more final, you know?

> Goodnight E

> Goodnight T

CHAPTER
Fourteen

EMMA WALKED UP to the steps of the property, taken aback by the chaos that greeted her. Men in hard hats swarmed the exterior of the house, and the front door hung open for workers to come and go. The property was a beautiful testament to history, with its high ceilings, intricate crown moulding, and ornate chandeliers.

Troy had been adamant about preserving the architectural integrity of the place, ensuring that every renovation honoured and enhanced its original character. *He'd said, there's no point in leaving an old building standing if you aren't going to pay homage to its roots. May as well knock it down otherwise.* Emma respected that.

She walked through the front sitting room, but barely had time to glance up the dust-and-drop-sheet-covered stairwell before Lindsey popped into the hall. "Welcome to our humble abode!"

Emma grinned. "You got here early."

Lindsey motioned for Emma to follow her into the kitchen. The cabinets were installed and the tiling was done, though still a mess. Dust motes danced in the morning light through the kitchen window, and the smell of freshly cut wood filled the air as a saw whined from upstairs.

"That light, though," Emma murmured. She touched an original stained glass panel inset in the wall between the kitchen and the sitting room.

"Oh, I know." Lindsey tossed her a damp rag. Vaughn was already hunched over the countertops, scrubbing away at grout with religious fervour.

They'd been forced into a half day since the sink had been unexpectedly installed early that morning. They couldn't shoot, but could prep for a dessert shoot the next morning.

Emma dropped her purse onto a stool and settled into the rhythm of scrubbing. Once they'd removed the first layer of silt, they switched to microfiber and polishing cloths. By two o'clock, the tiles were gleaming and Lindsey already had one light mounted.

"I'll go get the stuff from my car." She rinsed her rags and laid them on the edge of the sink to dry. When she walked back into the sitting room, her heart skipped a beat. When had Tyler arrived? He'd set up a makeshift office with his laptop and seemed lost in thought as his fingers clacked on the keys. He glanced up, then back at his screen. "How are things?"

Emma shrugged nonchalantly, avoiding eye contact. "Fine." She continued walking out the door, down the steps, then pulled the boxes from her car. When Tyler saw her coming, he left his standing desk and took two boxes from the top of her pile.

"You don't need to do that."

He lowered his voice. "What are fake boyfriends for?"

Emma's mouth lifted as they walked into the kitchen. "Where do you want these filters?"

Lindsey pointed to a stack of boxes already in the corner by the broom closet.

"The tile looks great in here," Tyler commented.

Vaughn looked between him and Emma. "Of course it does."

Tyler grinned, amused, and Emma waved him back out into the sitting area.

"The pastry chef will bring in desserts first thing tomorrow morning. She's making them fresh, but there will be sweating in the transfer, I'm sure." Emma opened the fridge to make sure they weren't there already.

"I thought I'd shoot that window if we have time after setup." Lindsey grabbed a polishing cloth and ran it over the mottled glass.

Emma narrowed her eyes. Now that she knew he was there, she could see Tyler in the other room, his head shifting in front of his computer screen. *How would I distract you?*

She turned away and wiped the sweat from her forehead. "Sounds like a plan."

They all worked together to finish setting up equipment and used the cupboards to lay out lenses and filters for the next morning. By the time Emma grabbed her purse and headed toward the front door, Tyler was already gone.

She glanced at her phone. Almost five. The Snowballs had their first playoff game tonight, and she was definitely going to be there. She may get away with not going to all the regular season games, but Sean and her parents would kill her if she wasn't there for this.

The game was at seven-fifteen, and her parents were having dinner beforehand at Moxies. Since she had the morning off, she was more than prepared. Her gloves and toque were already in the passenger seat, so Emma flipped around and drove straight to the restaurant.

After entering Moxies, she opened her coat and took in the contemporary décor. The warm lighting reflected off the wood furnishings, making the dining room feel cozy in the nearly-gone light streaming in from outside.

Sharla and Rob were already in a large booth with Kelty at the back, and they waved her over.

"Big night!" Her mother stood and gave her a hug. She wore a light blue sweater, and Emma spotted something white and fluffy sticking out of the top of her purse.

"Did you make snowballs, Mom?"

Sharla's eyes lit up as she sat back down. "I already showed Kelty, but I'll show you, too." She pulled the pom-poms from the bag and they floofed out like new pillows released from their packaging.

"Those are something." Emma laughed as her dad ran a hand over his bald head.

"She wouldn't be dissuaded," he muttered.

Sharla held the balls out and struck a pose with a wide grin on her face. "I'm just so excited for my boys. Had to do something special."

"Rob, I heard she tried to put face paint on you." Kelty took a sip of her pop.

He put his elbows on the table. "Tried to paint my entire scalp."

Emma laughed and sat down on the bench next to him. "If that wouldn't motivate a team . . ."

"Exactly, Emma. That's what I told him." Kelty clicked her tongue and picked up her menu.

The ambient hum of conversation made Emma almost sleepy as she settled into the bench and scanned the entrees.

Her mother sighed. "I can't believe the Snowballs made it to the playoffs for the third year in a row."

"Well, Sharla, they're the best team in the province," Rob grunted.

"I'm aware. It's just a big accomplishment."

Emma thought about Tyler, how he wished he'd gone pro and missed his chance. The Elite league, though well-regarded and competitive, wasn't close to the NHL. Did he feel like this was celebration worthy?

"Sean's always been dedicated . . ." her mother was saying. Emma settled on a quinoa power bowl and set down her menu, struggling to keep her mind from conjuring images of Tyler standing at his desk, his eyes focused on the computer screen.

"What's everyone thinking of ordering?" her dad asked.

"I've heard great things about their honey garlic sirloin," Kelty answered.

Sharla pointed at the middle of the menu. "I'm in the mood for their classic chicken burger. And a Caesar salad on the side."

"Make that two chicken burgers."

Emma grinned. "You two have been married too long. Quinoa bowl for me."

"Is that how you say that?" Rob squinted at the word.

Their server brought drinks and took their orders, then her dad insisted she fill them in on the new job. Kelty's eyebrow raised when she heard it was Tyler's dad who'd offered her the job, but she didn't comment.

Emma was grateful when their food arrived and she could focus on eating. Focus was a strong word. She felt like she was on a merry-go-round with her brother grabbing the handles and taking off at a sprint.

She'd been lucky today. Troy hadn't come to the house, but would he come tomorrow? When would Tyler touch her—how would he touch her? When would he steal a kiss?

Once they'd finished their meal, Rob signalled for the check while Sharla and Kelty freshened up. "You doing okay, honey?"

"Hmm?"

Rob turned in the booth. "You seem distracted."

Emma shrugged. "New job. Just a lot on my mind."

He nodded. "I know how that goes. If you need anything, you know we're there for you."

"Of course, Dad." She rubbed his shoulder.

"You coming to Sunday supper?"

Emma shrugged. "Not sure yet."

"We miss you being there, you know."

She leaned forward and kissed his cheek. "Love you, Dad. Thanks for dinner."

Emma had to park at the back of the Ice Centre parking lot. Fans in jerseys and scarves, blue for the Snowballs and purple for Edmonton, streamed in through the doors. The chill in the air was electric as Emma stepped inside and stomped the ice melt off her boots. She rushed down the stairs and found a spot in the stands, assuming she'd beaten Kelty and her parents there.

She'd guessed correctly. They filtered in a few minutes later and she waved them over to the spot she'd saved with her purse and coat spread out over the bench.

"Can you believe this crowd?" Kelty asked, gesturing to the packed stands. "I don't think I've ever seen it this full."

"I'm surprised at how much purple there is." Not that Edmonton was a far drive, but for an Elite league game, it was a commitment.

"Maybe they think they actually have a chance." Kelty winked and sat down beside her, tucking her first-aid kit under the bench.

"Refilled?"

Kelty rolled her eyes. "Hopefully we won't need it. But yes."

Emma pulled out her phone and shot a text wishing Sean good luck. She scrolled down to her texts with Tyler last weekend. It wasn't strange for her to text him the same thing was it? She thought back to Merle at Co-op. *Downright neighbourly*, that was all.

Emma sent the text and slipped her phone back into her purse.

As the teams took to the ice, the tension among the players was palpable. Emma could see Sean's intense focus on his teammates, the weight of responsibility evident in his serious expression. Then there was Tyler—strong and confident—gliding across the ice. She watched him shamelessly as he warmed up, changing the direction of her head every once in a while so Kelty wouldn't catch on.

"Let's go, Snowballs!" Kelty shouted as Sean moved to centre ice. "We've got this!"

The game was nothing short of intense. One player on Mills was nearly impossible to shut down. He scored twice in the first period, but the Snowballs' wingers adjusted, keeping him at bay in the second.

Sean and Tyler were equally as dangerous on the other end of the ice. Tyler scored once off a pass from Sean, then assisted Country with a chip shot right before the start of the third period.

They battled it out after the break, but the score remained tied as the clock ticked down to its final seconds. Edmonton's number twenty-four charged the net, but Ryan caught the puck with the end of his stick just before he took a shot.

The shrill sound of the buzzer signalled the end of regulation play, and the arena erupted in a cacophony of excitement and nervous energy. Overtime.

"Can you believe this?" Kelty shouted over the din, her eyes wide. "I think I might actually have a heart attack!"

"Seriously," Emma agreed, gripping the edge of her seat. This wasn't how the game was supposed to go. The Snowballs had expected an easy win, based on the family chat, but Mills Hoodie looked strong.

She watched as Tyler skated to the bench and gulped from his water bottle. He would definitely be one of the players taking the ice for the extra three-on-three period. She thought of the still-fading bruises around his eyes and wondered what his ribs looked like.

Guilt settled over her. If he and Sean both weren't a hundred percent and they lost this game because of it? Emma needed to pee something fierce, but she couldn't tear herself from the bench.

C'mon, Tyler. C'mon, Sean. Three players on each team took the ice. Neither team had been on a power play at the end of the third. There had only been a few penalties, but now that both teams were worn down, they'd probably start to get sloppy.

Emma stood up as Tyler left the bench. She raised her hand

and waved, flicking both her thumbs in the air. He smiled, then put on his helmet. Kelty looked over as she sat down, and Emma blushed.

"Sean didn't see me, but at least Tyler did." Kelty seemed convinced that her encouragement was for the team, not for one player individually.

That helped Emma believe it, too.

The crowd rose to their feet as the puck dropped. The Snowballs dug deep, fueled by the surging electric atmosphere around them. *So much empty ice.*

Sean, Tyler, and Country wove around each other in an orchestrated dance, attacking the net, then dropping back to defend and keep Boyd from facing number twenty-four solo. Brett subbed for Country, then Darcy for Sean.

Tyler never went off the ice and never slowed. "Come on, Tyler!" Emma couldn't help but scream. *What were fake girlfriends for?*

A puck bounced off the boards, and Darcy swooped in to seize control. He deftly maneuvered the puck, deking out a purple jersey, then passing to Brett stationed near the left boards.

Tape to tape. Brett pivoted to face the offensive zone. His eyes scanned the ice, weighing his options as Edmonton closed in. He made a quick pass back to Darcy, trying to open up some space. Darcy faked a pass to Tyler, sprinting toward the net, then dropped the pass to Brett, who had circled back to centre.

Emma squealed. *The defence misread the play, distracted by Tyler.* Brett capitalized, rushing forward and firing off a slapshot. The goaltender dropped to block, and Emma squeezed Kelty's hand.

A metal clang pierced the air as the puck hit the post. The crowd groaned, then gasped as Tyler caught the ricochet. Without missing a beat, Tyler faked to his backhand, pulling the goaltender out of position, and then shifted to his forehand.

With a swift flick of his wrists, Tyler shot the puck into the top left corner. The arena erupted as the siren wailed.

Tyler was mobbed by Brett and Darcy, then the rest of the team, as time ran out on the OT clock.

"Well, I need a Xanax." Her dad clutched at his heart and Emma and her mom sandwiched him in a hug. Emma turned to Kelty and threw her arms around her.

"You're all coming to One Place, right?" Kelty begged, her voice hoarse from cheering.

"Oh, this is too much excitement for one night." Sharla laughed, looping her scarf around her neck. "You girls have fun, and we'll see you Sunday."

Rob shot Emma a look dripping in expectation. While her parents waited to step into the aisle, she glanced toward the blue jerseys. She caught sight of Tyler's triumphant smile as he dropped his helmet and mitts. Warmth bubbled inside her.

"Ready?" Kelty grabbed her hand, and they flowed with the crowd toward the pub.

CHAPTER
Fifteen

ONE PLACE WAS a hive of activity when they arrived. Jubilant fans packed every available inch and were raising their glasses in toast after toast to the Snowballs players filtering in. The laughter and energy were infectious, and Emma couldn't help but get swept up in it.

Jess waved Emma and Kelty over to join her. Emma checked her phone as they sat. Vaughn and Lindsey were supposed to meet them here after the game. While they weren't excited for hockey games, they adored celebrating afterwards.

Vaughn had texted twenty minutes ago saying they were on their way. They should be walking in any minute. She was about to slip her phone back in her pocket when a message popped up from Tyler in response to her good luck wishes earlier.

> Thanks, I needed that

She grinned.

> No you didn't

> Why are you smiling?

Emma dropped her phone to her lap and looked up, her eyes wide as if she'd just been caught with her hand in the cookie jar. Tyler stood in the doorway next to Brett with a smug look on his face. It didn't last long as fans bid for their attention. It would take them a while to make their way back here, which gave her time to calm her heart rate.

She jumped into conversation with Kelty and Jess, and by the time she looked up again, all the warmth she'd felt seeped out of her. Tyler was nearing their table with Ginger from the Dusty Rose draped possessively over his arm. *Her crop top and leather pants seemed like a perfect choice for a hockey game in March.*

"Hey, are you okay?" Kelty asked, noticing the sudden shift in Emma's demeanour.

"Um, yeah, fine," Emma lied. *She was an idiot.* Smiling like a goon while Tyler was walking in to meet another woman? Ugh. What was wrong with her?

She glanced back to find Ginger flicking her hair over her shoulder. Hadn't Tyler sat in his truck less than a week ago and told her how much he didn't want to be his dad? How he wanted to be different? And yet here he was keeping the same company, probably ready to strip and let her lick shots off of his chest.

"I'm sorry, but why aren't we singing karaoke yet?"

Emma looked up and sighed in relief. "You made it!" She threw herself at Vaughn, then pulled Lindsey into a group hug before she could take off her coat.

"Seriously, though." Vaughn pushed toward the bar and leaned over to talk to Pat. She laughed and reached under the counter, then handed him two microphones. Vaughn snapped his fingers and pointed to the small stage in the corner.

Emma's heart started to race. One Place was packed, and she was more the type to sing to two old cowboys passed out in a booth after everyone else left for the night. But then she saw Tyler and Ginger moving her way and bolted from the table.

She would have fun tonight, damn it. If Tyler wanted to play his games and stay in his box of short, meaningless relationships, fine. *Fine.* But she wasn't going to pretend that something better didn't exist. That people couldn't have fun and hope to fall in love *for real.* So to hell with it. To hell with his flirty messages, his heart-to-hearts that obviously meant nothing, and *girls licking his washboard abs.*

"What song do you want, babe?" Vaughn asked, flipping through the black book.

"I've Got Better Things To Do. Terri Clark." A down-home Alberta girl who knew what she wanted and wasn't ashamed to say it.

As she stepped onto the small stage, Emma felt a surge of adrenaline course through her veins. The music started, and she grabbed the microphone. She belted out the lyrics, trading lines with Vaughn and harmonizing on the angry chorus.

Tyler was watching her, and she ate it up, making eyes with anyone *but* him. She bowed to raucous applause, then handed the mic off to a girl sitting next to Darcy and sat back at her table.

Emma ate. She laughed. She congratulated Sean. And she did *not* talk to Tyler. An hour or so later when it looked like he might make his way to her end of the table, she grabbed Lindsey's hand and smacked her other palm on Vaughn's knee.

"Ready?"

She pulled on her coat and waltzed out of One Place without looking back.

Tyler left the pub not long after Emma and her friends took off. His body had screamed for a hot bath and sleep. It had been complaining since they walked into One Place, but he couldn't tear himself away. Not with Emma putting on such a show. *What kind of show, Tyler?* She'd been all nervous and adorable in his truck that night before practice. Now the student had become the teacher.

Ginger was relentless. Even after the other night when he insisted on dropping her off at home instead of bringing her back to his place, she wasn't getting the hint. She was friends with Darcy, which explained why she kept showing up after practice and games, but that also meant that letting her down hard was going to be messy. Especially since the guys ended up at Dusty Rose at least once every couple of weeks.

He tried to put all of it out of his head over the weekend. The massage he booked Saturday morning was borderline celestial, and after sleeping in on Sunday and going for a light jog followed by a quick pump at the gym, he almost felt like his old self.

But today it was back to reality. His heart hammered as he pulled up to the property first thing Monday morning. There was less construction today since one of the crews wouldn't be there until Wednesday to finish off the drywall upstairs.

The landscapers would be able to start in a couple of weeks now that the soil was warming up. Right on track for their community open house scheduled the first weekend in May.

Emma's car was parked up the street. The sight of her singing country songs next to Vaughn at the pub had hounded him all weekend. His mouth went dry every time he thought of her shirt hitching up above the waistband of her black jeans when she danced, or the way she threw back her head and laughed at something Jess or Lindsey said and exposed the smooth skin of her throat.

He wanted her, and the more he tried to fight it, the more torturous that realization became. He'd been tempted to bring Ginger home just to blow off some steam, but everything about that felt wrong. He'd never been with a woman wishing he was with someone else—he'd never ached for someone this badly and not done something about it.

"Morning." Paolo, their pastry chef, stalked up the walk in a wool coat with his close-cropped salt and pepper hair sticking up in the back. He carried a covered tray in his hands.

"I'll get that." Tyler pulled open the door for him.

"Grazie." Paolo went straight to the kitchen where Tyler assumed Emma was. It took everything in him to stop in the sitting area and set up his laptop. She hadn't said a word to him Saturday night. Hadn't even waved goodbye. That, after she'd been hollering from the stands before overtime.

He'd thought that excitement was for him, but maybe she was caught up in the excitement of an extra period. Maybe she'd texted everyone on the team good luck. No. He'd seen her face reading his texts at One Place.

Tyler ran a hand over his face and logged in. More risk assessment this morning for a new client out of Windsor. Then penetration testing for a bank in Sioux St. Marie. *He wished he was penetration testing a different client, but he had no control over that.* His eyes flicked to the stained glass window, but there wasn't enough light coming through for him to make out any shapes in the kitchen.

Emma's laughter floated into the sitting area, and Tyler adjusted his pants. He put in his headphones and searched up a playlist of Canadian punk bands from the nineties. If anything could kill a hard-on, it was remembering he once wore a chain that connected his wallet to his belt loop.

It worked. Mostly. Until about ten in the morning when the laughter and the husky voice of Diana Krall became intrusive. Was this what photo shoots sounded like? If so, he'd chosen the wrong career.

He plucked out his earbuds, stalked across the room, and leaned through the open door. Emma, dressed in navy slacks and a pale-pink, long-sleeved top giggled as Vaughn held her in a traditional waltz position, crooning the words of the song at full volume. Her chestnut hair was piled on top of her head with a clip, tendrils that had broken loose framing her face.

Vaughn stepped back and lifted his hand, twirling her, then pulling her back with a hand on her waist.

Tyler's chest felt like an air compressor tank. He put two

hands on the door frame and gripped. Hard. "Is this what we're paying you for?"

Emma jumped, a hand flying to her chest. "Can you stop scaring me, please?"

Lindsey ran to the speaker and turned the music down. "This is a common problem?"

Emma flashed him a look as she caught her breath. "First of all, *you're* not paying us for anything, and second . . ." She turned and pulled the tray he'd seen Paolo carry in from the counter. "This is what you're paying us for." She pulled off the lid.

Tyler stepped into the kitchen and inspected the flourless chocolate cake and something that looked like it would have the word "glacé" in its title. "Paolo made those."

"And we're shooting them. Just waiting for them to settle in."

"Settle in?"

She put a hand on her hip. "They need to be comfortable for their photo shoot."

Footsteps sounded behind him. Tyler turned, expecting to see one of the other contractors, but Troy entered the room.

"Hey, look at those beauts." He strode forward and leaned over the counter, inspecting the gold leaf on the dark chocolate. "Paolo's a magician, isn't he?"

Emma straightened. "Can't wait to shoot these today. Should have the dessert menu finished by the end of the week."

"Then hopefully the gas will be hooked up, eh?" Troy turned and put a hand on the industrial stovetop. "Still plenty of time. Do you have everything you need?"

Lindsey nodded. "Giving the sun a bit more time to grace us with its presence and then we'll get going."

"Excellent. Ty, how goes it?"

Tyler rounded the island and opened the fridge, pulling out a bottle of water. "Just came in for a drink and to say good morning to Emma." He set the bottle on the counter, his heart pumping hard enough to fill a tire. Emma's eyes widened as he curled his hand over her hip and pulled her against him. This was perfectly within her rules, and by the look on her face, she knew it.

"Next time you all have a dance party, let me know. I'm the only one who gets to twirl Emma in this kitchen." He brushed the waves of hair from the side of her face and caught her lips between his before she could suck in a full breath. Her lips were slightly parted, and he couldn't help himself. She tasted like berry lip balm and morning coffee as he slipped his tongue past her teeth.

Her hands tightened on his waist as she relaxed into him, then quickly pushed back, out of breath. "Tyler, I'm at work." Her voice was breathless, her lips and cheeks flushed.

Troy barked a laugh. "Since when has that ever stopped the Bowen men?"

Tyler stiffened. Emma pulled her hands from his waist and took a step back, pursing her lips and rubbing to redistribute her lip product. "Good morning, Tyler."

"Good morning, Emma." He picked up his bottle of water and exited the room.

CHAPTER
Sixteen

THE FLUORESCENT LIGHTS cast a warm glow on Emma's face as she waved the heat gun over the chocolate torte. When it was glossy again, she moved out of the way. "Okay, I think we're ready for the close-up."

Lindsey balanced her elbows on the counter and levelled the camera. "So we're really not going to talk about what just happened?"

The camera clicked, and Lindsey tucked her hair behind her ear.

Emma swallowed hard and leaned against the counter behind her. "Nothing to talk about," Emma shrugged, trying to sound dismissive. "We're just doing this for his dad."

"Doing what, exactly?" Lindsey asked.

Emma blew out a breath. "Pretending to be together."

"And in all the time we were packing up the studio or prepping for shoots, you didn't feel like fake dating your brother's teammate was fodder for conversation?" Vaughn looked positively scathed, and Emma couldn't help but laugh.

"I'm sorry, okay? I felt like an idiot."

"She told me about finding his licence," Lindsey murmured behind the camera, clicking away. "And the fight."

Vaughn nodded. "How easy would it have been to explain how those things were tied together?" He pursed his lips and mimed tying a bow in the air.

Emma let out an exasperated sigh. "It's nothing! I got him beat up by my brother, and then I went on what I thought was one date that turned into us working together. Shouldn't you just be grateful I got this gig in the first place?"

Vaughn scoffed. "Mm-hmm, honey, those things are not mutually exclusive. We can be grateful and traumatized by your dirty secrets." He swiveled the light on top of the tripod while Lindsey fiddled with her camera settings.

Emma apologized at least three more times that afternoon and gave them as many details as she could without making it sound like she cared about the way Tyler looked when he picked her up for the game or how he stood on his porch in bare feet when she returned his truck.

After that day, she responded with one-or-two-word answers when they asked about Tyler, and pretty soon, they stopped asking altogether. For the following two weeks, Emma threw herself into work, determined to avoid Tyler as much as possible to avoid any more interrogation.

But mostly to avoid the soup of emotions that bubbled to the surface every time he was close. That kiss. It had opened a floodgate she didn't know she'd built. *Grateful and traumatized.* She desperately wanted more of his lips on hers, but feeling him that close—experiencing what that broke open in her—sent fear and self-doubt tumbling through her.

This wasn't real, and for all the work she thought she'd done since Alex, she was still a delicate wine glass teetering on the edge of a table, just waiting to be shattered again. She couldn't let herself get invested, and certainly not with someone who she knew wouldn't treat her heart carefully.

So she laboured over every detail in their menu shoots, transforming ordinary dishes into tantalizing works of art. At home, she spent hours researching businesses in the area beyond their normal network and sent countless emails to potential clients, hoping to secure new projects for when their current gig ended.

She updated her website, and when that was finished, Emma turned to deep cleaning her apartment. The sound of the vacuum and sight of bags full of donation items drowned out any thoughts of Tyler.

At the property, she found reasons to disappear over lunch, to leave the room when she saw his silhouette moving through the stained glass, and she left with her phone against her ear a few minutes before or after he started packing up for the day. She fake talked with so many people, she lost track.

Emma went to two more playoff games, but never went to the pub after. Sean and her parents didn't question it since she'd made a big deal about her stressful work schedule, and nobody else on the team missed her.

Because she knew how much Sunday Supper meant, to her mom especially, she stopped in but arrived early and left before most of the team even showed up. One time, Tyler walked in as she was putting on her boots. That had been a close call, but she'd successfully rushed past him, telling him an alarm was going off at her apartment building.

It was Friday again, and Emma found herself back in the now fully functional kitchen styling salads for the menu. The lettuce looked crisp, the tomatoes glossy, but as she studied Lindsey's display, something wasn't sitting right.

"It's the background," she murmured. "I need more texture."

"Ooh, Troy told me there were some antiques in the storage room downstairs," Lindsey suggested, switching out her lens.

"Excellent." Emma made her way toward the staircase. The refinished wood floors creaked beneath her feet as she descended. She took her time, absorbing this new part of the house. The stairs were narrow, and the wallpaper, faded with age, displayed a pattern of delicate flowers that stretched along the hallway. Wallpaper was making a comeback now, and she'd seen a similar pattern advertised in a Restoration Hardware shoot. This would show well on the website.

As she entered the storage room, Emma felt as though she'd walked into another era. Antique furniture lined the walls, mixed in with construction equipment and storage supplies. First-aid and cleaning supplies, old vases. Her fingers traced the edge of an ornate mirror in a tarnished frame as she breathed in the smell of dust and aged wood.

Her eyes landed on the woven baskets stacked on the top shelf. Perfect. She turned and shuffled to the back of the cramped room, then stretched her hands up. There was no way she was going to be able to reach them, even on her tiptoes.

She pulled out her phone and sent Lindsey a quick text.

> Can you ask Vaughn to bring down the step stool? Too short

Emma waited, feeling a bit uneasy staring at the dangling bare light bulb. She fiddled with a strand of hair as she tried not to bump into the shelves and get dust on her pants, then breathed a sigh of relief when footsteps sounded on the stairs. Emma watched the door, waiting for Vaughn to appear.

Her breath caught when instead, Tyler ducked in, his muscular frame filling the Hobbit doorway. Warning sirens blared in her head as her anatomy reacted instantly to his proximity. Heat flushed her cheeks, and it felt like tiny fireworks were bursting beneath her skin.

"Tyler."

He exhaled. "Well that's a relief. I wondered if you still remembered my name."

Emma scoffed, looking anywhere but directly at him. The sound of his deep voice contained in such a small space sent shivers down her spine. His polo shirt hugged his chest and his mussed, dark hair curled over his ears.

Emma had to try twice to plant her hand on her hip. "Did

you come down for a vase?" She pointed at the shelf. "I can see how that would be helpful for internet . . . searching. Or whatever it is you're doing today."

"Internet searching. Tons of it." Tyler stepped around a box that looked like it held a light fixture. He had searched her on the internet once. Her heart rate clicked up a notch. "Lindsey told me you needed help reaching something."

Lindsey, the traitor. She knew how hard Emma was trying to avoid being in the same room with Tyler. This was worse than when Faith teamed up with the Mayor on Buffy the Vampire Slayer. Lindsey was dead to her.

"I texted to have Vaughn bring down the step stool." Emma's voice wobbled, and she coughed so he could believe it was the dust in her lungs.

"I'm better than a step stool."

"Cockier too?"

The corner of Tyler's mouth lifted. "Where have you been after the games lately?" He moved a piece of an old lamp post to a more stable position, then stopped in front of her.

Emma's heart played its own drum solo. "I've been slammed. Work. Taking care of things at my apartment." She pointed up at the baskets.

Tyler frowned, then leaned next to her and reached up to pull the stack off the top shelf. As his arm retracted, the sound of his exhale and the scent of his cologne made her heady.

"If Troy's overworking you, you could've said something." Tyler stood barely a ruler's length from her.

"I'm surprised you even noticed I wasn't there." Emma reached for the baskets, but Tyler moved them to the side.

"Why wouldn't I notice you weren't there?"

Emma's eyes flashed. "Seems like you typically have plenty of company at One Place." She reached again, and this time Tyler stretched his arm further.

"What kind of company?"

Emma exhaled in annoyance. "Can you please just hand me the baskets? I'm in the middle of a shoot—"

"Why are you avoiding me? You haven't said two words to me in—"

Emma lunged for the baskets, and Tyler flinched, dropping the stack and knocking his forearm into the shelf. An avalanche of items rained down on them—small boxes, an antique clock, and various other trinkets that had been stashed in this forgotten corner of the house. A small, decorative metal box clipped Emma's exposed shoulder as it plummeted to the ground.

"Holy shit. Emma, are you okay?" Tyler scrambled up to stand and grabbed her, pinning her arms to her sides.

Emma steadied herself and nodded. "Yeah." She took stock to make sure that was a true statement. Her head felt a bit fuzzy, but other than that—

"No, you're not okay, you're bleeding." Tyler twisted her to the side and brushed her hair off her exposed shoulder. This sleeveless turtleneck wasn't exactly practical, but her arms looked amazing in it. That would teach her for being vain.

"It doesn't hur—"

Tyler let out a string of curses under his breath and kicked the boxes to the side as he reached for the first-aid supplies next to the door. "I'm so sorry." He ripped open a package of sterile gauze and held it to her skin.

Emma winced. "Tyler, I promise, it's not a big deal."

His fingers moved against her skin as he shifted his hand, and each bone in her spine tingled like plucked harp strings. He lifted her hand to hold it in place while he found a bandage.

"It is a big deal because I was being an ass."

"I'm not arguing that point." Emma tried to look over her shoulder to see how bad it was. When her vision doubled from his close proximity, she turned and looked at her reflection in the antique mirror.

"It's not bad," she scoffed.

"Please tell me you're up to date on your tetanus shot." Tyler opened the bandage. "At least this is antibacterial."

"Thank you, Dr. Bowen," Emma remarked dryly.

"The shot?" Tyler gave her a look.

Emma pulled away the gauze. "I don't know, probably? Are we back to requiring vaccination records?" That finally forced a smile out of him. He smoothed the bandage over her skin, and the heat from his body warmed the chilled skin on her arm.

"I'm sorry. I shouldn't have held the baskets hostage." His voice rumbled next to her ear.

"They didn't deserve that. They were innocent bystanders." She glanced down at the baskets strewn across the floor, but didn't move to pick them up. Tyler's hand brushed over the bandage again, as if convincing himself it was sealed to her skin.

She looked up into his hazel eyes, and the dusty air grew thick. "Tyler—"

His hand lingered, and she forgot what she'd been about to say. When it dropped from her cut and trailed over the back of her knit top, she forgot how to think.

Her shoulders curved as her eyes shut without permission. Air whooshed from her lungs. *She couldn't breathe.* Tyler's scent was everywhere, his warmth everywhere, his touch . . .

Colours spilled across the backs of her eyelids as Tyler's lips brushed against hers. He kissed the corner of her mouth, then wet his lips, flicking his tongue against her skin. She sighed— audibly—remembering the way he'd kissed her in the kitchen. Hungry and possessive. *It had been for show, but—*

Tyler's hands tightened around her, and his body made an impression against her. Hard granite against soft clay. For two weeks she'd convinced herself that she'd stamped these feelings out, but this was oxygen over coals. She was a can of Coke, dropped and shaken, then put back in the cooler lying in wait until some unsuspecting victim popped the tab.

Emma slammed her hands into Tyler's chest, gasping. Tyler's eyes seemed to drink in the shadows from every corner of the room. He blinked, heavy-lidded, and she pushed past him, not even thinking about picking up the items that dropped from the shelves.

"That was against the rules," she hissed, then jammed the baskets into her arms and slipped out of the room.

When it was finally time to pack up and leave, Emma couldn't get out of the house fast enough. She knew Lindsey and Vaughn noticed her mood, but her anger was too molten hot to talk about it. If she tried, she was either going to yell at someone or start sobbing, she didn't know which, but it wasn't worth the risk either way.

She pulled on her coat, slung her purse over her shoulder and stomped toward the front door.

"Emma, wait!" Tyler called after her as she pushed through the front door and hurried toward her car. She refused to stop, clenching her jaw and fumbling with her keys. "Can we talk for a sec—"

"Please, Tyler!" she choked out, not turning to face him. She pressed the button and the car door opened just as Troy stepped onto the street with a wide smile. He held up two tickets in his hand.

"Did I almost miss you?" Troy glanced down at his watch and chuckled. "Nope, I'm just late, but I'm glad you're here because I have a surprise for you."

Emma stood frozen, trying to force her face into a pleasant expression. Tyler ran a hand through his hair, and either Troy was oblivious to the tension between them or he didn't care.

"Rinkside tickets at the Blizzard game tonight, and I wanted to treat you both to dinner beforehand with Gina."

What?! Gina was the real estate agent. Emma only knew that because of the two times they'd talked in passing and the one memorable time when she'd seen Troy kissing her neck in the side yard when they were supposed to be discussing zoning permits.

Emma's brain started to short-circuit. The thought of spending an entire evening with Tyler made her want to walk over the broken glass that probably still littered the storage room floor, but going to see Calgary play *rinkside?* She could almost feel the angel and devil taking up residence on opposite shoulders.

Emma drew a deep breath. Troy was her boss, and this was kind. Sort of. More importantly, Gina had a thousand relationships with high-spenders in this city that she'd love to tap into. She'd tried to think of a way to milk that connection and hadn't found the right avenue yet.

Tyler shoved his hands in his pockets and waited for Emma to respond.

She was *not* doing this for him. "What time should we meet you?"

Troy clapped his hands together, delighted. "No need to meet anywhere, I'll pick you both up at six-thirty."

Emma nodded. That gave her forty-five minutes to get home and change. "Perfect."

CHAPTER
Seventeen

TYLER SPRAWLED across the back seat of the car his father had sent to pick him up. He'd thought it was strange that Troy was going to pick them up personally. This made a hell of a lot more sense, but he could guess what Emma's reaction would be when she saw it was only the two of them in the back of a luxury car. At least the seats reclined and there was still a centre console. She seemed to feel safe with those. He pulled it down between the seats and clicked it into place.

His stomach lurched as the car pulled up to Emma's apartment building. Emma stood waiting outside her apartment texting someone on her phone. Tyler momentarily forgot to breathe.

She wore a little black dress that hugged her athletic figure and hit mid-thigh. Her legs stretched toward the sidewalk. *Bare.* There was a Chinook, but it couldn't be warm enough that she wasn't shivering out there.

The warm wind tossed her loose curls around her face, and she shifted her weight on her peekaboo heels. She had a coat on, at least.

The partition lowered. "Excuse me, sir, but does the other party know we've arrived?"

Tyler blinked. *Right.* Emma had no idea what car would be showing up. Tyler pushed the door open and stepped out on the sidewalk, suddenly self-conscious of his grey v-neck and lined suede jacket.

Emma's eyes widened when she recognized him. She started toward him, and he couldn't feign nonchalance if he tried. Her eyes were darker, smoky, offset by the light shade of pink on her lips. A sleek bag was slung over her shoulders, not her normal purse.

She peered toward the passenger window and found it empty. "No Gina?" Emma looked disappointed.

"Uh, no," Tyler stammered, running a hand through his hair. "I mean, yes. At the restaurant. My dad sent a car for us."

A small frown creased her forehead. Tyler walked around to the street and got in on the other side, leaving the door open for her. Tension settled around them like a thick blanket as they slid onto the plush leather seats.

The driver pulled away from the curb, and each second of silence between them felt like the clang of a grandfather clock.

"Do you need water?" Tyler opened a mini fridge near the floor.

"No, I'm good." She looked out the window, her hands clasped in her lap. This was going to be torture.

"Look, Emma, about what happened—"

"I don't want to talk about it." Her words were clipped, her tone cool and distant. "I'm here to network, that's it."

Tyler clenched his jaw and rubbed his hand over his chest, as if that would ease the pressure there. *She wouldn't turn her face from the damn window.* "Then I'll do the talking. I'm sorry for—"

"You already apologized."

"I apologized for keeping the baskets, but not for breaking the rules, so *I'm sorry.* Again"

Emma didn't answer. The collar of her wool coat was flipped up on one side, and he wanted to reach out and fix it. He was so focused on holding his hands in place, he couldn't keep his thoughts from spewing out.

"I missed you," he whispered. "I texted and never heard back, and every time I tried to talk to you—" His throat tightened, and he swallowed. *What the hell was wrong with him?* It felt like every one of his ribs was curling inward and pinching his lungs.

He unzipped his sweater. "Then you were standing there in that hell-hole of a closet with your hair all . . . and that sweater —" Tyler squeezed his eyes shut, and when he opened them, Emma had turned from the window.

She pinned him with a steely gaze. "Are you saying you find me attractive, Bowen?"

Tyler coughed a laugh and reached for his bottle of water already sitting in the cupholder. Relief flooded through him. He didn't for one second believe she'd forgiven him, but this was something. "Don't pretend you don't know the effect you have on *men*, Emma."

Her lips twitched, recognizing her own words from that night they'd sat in his truck outside her apartment building.

Tyler's stomach lurched. *Holy. Hell.* Had he ever paid that much attention to someone? He barely remembered what he had for breakfast on any given day, but when it came to Emma, he had every minute detail seared into his head.

He'd kissed her in the storage room not because he found her *attractive*, but because he *needed to*. Because if he didn't touch her, his body was going to split at the seams and smoulder.

Did he—? Was this—?

Tyler took another long swig from his water and reclined, staring at the upholstered ceiling. *Shit.* Blood rushed in his ears thinking about practice the night before.

Sean handed him his mitt in the dressing room as he was getting dressed. "You left this. After the game."

Tyler dropped his hockey bag. "I was just about to run out to my truck. Thanks, man."

Sean turned, then hesitated. "I went to stop it by your house and Brett said you were at work." Tyler frowned, wondering why Brett hadn't said anything, or why Sean hadn't left the mitt at the house. "I was curious to see the property—Emma's been talking about how busy she's been at work."

Tyler's heart sank like a stone in his chest. Had Sean come to the house? Tyler hadn't seen him and he still had his mitt, which meant—

"I saw you. With Emma."

Tyler's throat went dry. What was he supposed to say to that? "No, Sean, you have it all wrong. I'm only pretending to screw your sister, not actually doing it."

"Emma's better than the other women you've been with, you know that, right?" Sean asked, still not turning fully to look at him. Tyler swallowed hard. "She dated that asshat Alex Turner who used to play for C-Biscuit, I don't expect you to know him, but he was a raging narcissist. Messed with her head. Made her feel like shit and then love bombed her until she was convinced she couldn't live without him. Tossed her in the trash and then reeled her back in."

Sean looked up, his eyes hard. "I was there the night she finally stood up to him—the night she left." His jaw worked, and he drew a tight breath. "I don't know what this is for you, if it's a bloody challenge or distraction, but I think we both know she doesn't need more of this." Sean motioned between the two of them.

Tyler clenched his jaw, and Sean rubbed a hand over his buzzed head.

"I don't think you're a narcissist, and I know I'm not any damn better than you, so this isn't me passing judgement—" The door swung open, and Ryan, Fly, and Suraj bustled in chortling about something.

Sean dropped his eyes, nodded once, then stalked back to the other side of the room.

. . .

Message received, loud and clear. He would've been pissed if Sean hadn't been half-right. Emma was better than him, and he knew exactly what she wanted. Something he didn't know how to give anyone. But as of five seconds ago, he knew this wasn't a challenge or distraction for him. That realization felt like a cheap shot slamming him against the boards.

"Thank you for the apology," Emma murmured, reaching inside the fridge. They didn't say another word until the car pulled up to the entrance of the restaurant.

The warm glow of lanterns spilled out onto the sidewalk as Tyler and Emma stepped out of the car. He needed to pull himself together, but Emma's legs weren't helping him return to homeostasis.

The scent of warm spice and grilled meats enveloped them as they entered the colourful foyer.

"Have you eaten here before?" Emma asked.

Tyler shook his head. He hadn't eaten most places in Calgary, to be fair.

"Ah, there you are!" Troy greeted them with a wide grin, standing beside Gina. She wore a strapless dress with a blazer draped over her arm and smiled as if she'd practised the expression in front of a mirror.

Tyler clapped his hand on his dad's back, noting the dark circles under his eyes and his sunken cheekbones. This afternoon in the sunshine, bundled up in his coat, he hadn't looked so fragile.

"Emma, lovely to see you again." Troy's voice dripped with charm as he took her hand, planting a light kiss on the back of it.

"You, too." Emma smiled and waved to Gina.

"Come, let's sit." Troy led them to a low table surrounded by plush pillows in vibrant hues. As they settled onto the cushions, servers dressed in traditional attire circulated, placing small plates filled with marinated olives, hummus, and colourful salads. After washing their hands with warm cloths dipped in hot water and lemon, they dug in.

Tyler didn't have to work to move the conversation along as he tore off a piece of steaming, pillowy pita bread. His dad was always happy to storytell, and surprisingly, so was Gina. Emma asked her questions about the Calgary market, and Gina had barely come up for air during appetizers.

And Tyler was back in that dressing room holding his mitt, Sean's words echoing in his head. What the hell was he supposed to do now? He'd seen the schedule. Emma was almost finished with the shoots for the menu, and then Lindsey and Vaughn would take over for room-by-room promos as the contractors finished up.

Would she take on the next property? Even if she did, they wouldn't keep this ruse going, not after what happened today. Because he was going to keep breaking Emma's rules. How could he not? Emma shifted on her pillow and her hip grazed the side of his thigh.

"Tyler, have you tried these stuffed grape leaves?" Troy's voice pierced his thoughts. "Absolutely divine."

"Uh, no, not yet." His heart felt like a helicopter about to lift off as he reached for one. Troy and Gina turned to each other, arguing the benefits of red versus white wine. When Gina stood and announced her need to find a bathroom, Troy insisted on walking with her.

Emma waited a moment, then turned to Tyler. "Are you doing okay?"

Tyler nodded as he took a bite. Troy was right. This was delicious.

"You haven't said more than a few words."

Tyler held up the half-eaten stuffed leaves. "I've been eating."

Emma rolled her eyes, and if it was possible, more heat flooded his veins. He took the last bite and wiped his fingers on his napkin, then took off his sweater. Emma still looked up at him, and he allowed himself to turn toward her for the first time since she'd taken off her coat.

It was a terrible life choice. Emma's hair cascaded over her shoulders, smooth and soft. The golden light softened the edges of her face. His eyes slipped over the curve of her jaw, the arch of her brow. The neckline of her dress hit high on her chest, all straight lines and thin straps. Nearly the same silhouette of her sleeveless sweater earlier. *What was it about that cut that drove him insane?* He wanted to rip the fabric just to get a glimpse of her collarbone.

His pants grew tight, and he reached for his water. "I'm not feeling chatty, I guess."

Emma twisted on her pillow and slipped a hand under the table, resting it on his knee. "This must be so difficult. Do you know his latest results?"

Tyler ignored the liquid fire searing his right thigh and glanced up. Emma thought his mood was because of his father, and maybe it should've been. Half a stuffed grape leaf still sat on his father's plate, and the rest of the white surface looked mostly untouched. He'd worked to avoid staring at how Troy's skin hung off his cheeks and how his eyes wouldn't stop watering. *He had to be on a disturbing amount of pain medication.*

A pit opened up in his stomach, and Tyler reached around Emma's waist, pulling her into him, burying his nose against the top of her head. She didn't push back, just wrapped her arms around his middle, her chest rising and falling against his.

He couldn't keep her rules, not anymore. *He wanted her.* Seeing his dad fade away in front of him only made it more obvious. He wanted her annoyed looks, all her different laughs, her obsession with marinated chicken and old English phrases. He wanted her honey crullers and the way she breathed out slowly through her mouth when she was setting a piece of chocolate or twirling a garnish for a shot.

He wanted *her*, and Sean had been half right.

Troy and Gina returned to the table. He reached down and

squeezed Gina's thigh as they sat, his fingers trailing a bit too high for decency in public. Two weeks ago, it had been Melanie next to Troy. *When has that ever stopped the Bowen men?*

Tyler relaxed his grip, and Emma looked up at him, her eyes deep chocolate pools. "Thank you." He murmured, then pulled his arm to his side and reached for another scoop of Basmati rice.

Sean knew who Tyler was. *He* knew who he was. He didn't know how to give Emma what she deserved, even if every cell in his body screamed out how much he wanted to. That meant he had to cut this off.

Tonight.

CHAPTER Eighteen

EMMA AND TYLER waited for Troy and Gina at the VIP entrance on the northeast side of the Saddledome. Emma had changed out of her dress at the restaurant into jeans and a long-sleeve shirt for the game, which she'd brought in her backpack. She hadn't been able to decide on an outfit and was glad she'd decided to split the evening.

She'd be lying if she didn't admit she enjoyed how Tyler looked at her when he picked her up, and then again in the restaurant. Her pulse quickened, thinking about the way he'd held her before their main dishes arrived.

He was hurting. That much was obvious. After what happened in the storage room, she hated that she cared. No, of course, she cared. She hated that Tyler breaking the rules and making her feel things she didn't want to feel made it obvious how *much* she cared.

Troy and Gina walked up to the door, flashed their tickets, and the four of them strode into the bustling arena. Troy and Gina wrapped their arms around each other as they stepped into the elevator. Tyler and Emma stood across from them with arms hanging at their sides. *He didn't take her hand.* Of course he didn't after she'd treated him that way in the car.

"What a night, eh? Good food, excellent company, and hockey. Nothing better in my book." Troy planted a kiss on Gina's temple.

"Thank you so much for this." Emma smiled in gratitude. She'd been able to summon anger and hold a standoffish front right up until she'd seen Troy at the restaurant. Had he even eaten more than a few bites? He seemed to be aging years by the day, and the visual reminder of suffering and looming loss crushed her wall of indignation to dust.

Which meant she had to stare the thoughts lingering behind those bricks straight in the face. What if I gave in? What if I told Tyler how I felt? That thought wound tight springs in her chest.

Tyler didn't want what she wanted. He loved the attention from women, the laissez-faire life, and he'd told her directly that she was exactly the kind of girl he couldn't keep. Or at least the kind Troy Bowen didn't think him capable of keeping. *Couldn't or didn't want to?* That seemed like an important distinction.

Emma pondered this as they found their seats behind the plexiglass among the sea of silver Blizzard jerseys. What if Tyler hadn't wanted to hold onto girls like her in the past . . . but he wanted it now? Was it possible that he was over the pink bras and Jell-O shots? Not that she was against pink bras, she had one but didn't wear *only* that and dance on bartops. What if what Tyler wanted, what he was capable of, and what he did were correlated but not causal?

He had been the one to seek her out. He'd broken the rules. He'd kissed her. In the car he said he missed her and that he found her attractive. Had he been trying to tell her something all this time, and she'd been so caught up in holding back that she'd missed something real?

Emma's skin began to hum as the teams took to the ice, the blades on their skates carving intricate patterns into the frozen surface. She could barely pay attention. She took her cues from the crowd and cheered, then groaned when she was supposed to.

Troy and Tyler analyzed plays and argued about strategies. It took the duration of a power play for enough pressure to build in Emma's midsection that she finally reached out and twined her fingers in Tyler's.

He flinched, losing his train of thought momentarily, then picked back up as he relaxed his hand around hers. Her heart rate jumped up another notch. *This wasn't the same.* He was holding back, and in seconds she'd flipped from wishing she could walk away from Tyler Bowen permanently to worrying she'd already done it.

Images of him laughing with that blond's fingernails scraping his skin or him walking into One Place with Ginger on his arm flashed through her mind, and the mixture of ground lamb, hummus, and cucumber tomato salad roiled in her stomach.

Troy started to fade mid-way through the second period, and Gina insisted they head home. She took Troy's arm after he embraced both Tyler and Emma, then walked with him back the way they came. Troy laughing and Gina putting a hand on his back to steady him.

Emma wasn't any better than Gina. She wasn't better than Ginger, or even pink-bra-on-the-bar-girl. Who wouldn't want to be in Tyler's orbit? To feel like for one brief moment in time, he shone for only them? The only difference was Emma knew what it felt like to have to float through space alone. Or worse, to still be circling when men like him turned to face another direction.

They sat back in their seats.

"We don't have to stay," Emma murmured, laying her hands flat on her lap.

"Since when does Emma Thompson leave a Blizzard game when the score is tied?" he teased. Emma looked up at the jumbotron. She hadn't even noticed the score. Tyler stretched his arm over the back of her seat. "We can go if you want. I know this wasn't in your schedule for tonight."

Emma fought to keep her breathing even. She could talk to

him in the car on the way home if they left. But trying to be real with him now would be next to impossible. Here she sat, staring at two men pummeling each other next to the blue line, barely able to keep tears from pooling in her eyes.

"Let's stay." She choked out, settling into her seat, pretending to be entranced. She didn't know if Tyler bought it, but he didn't argue.

Emma bought a drink so she'd have something to do with her hands, then kept her eyes glued to the rink. A Canucks player made a daring deke to slip past two Blizzard defensemen. "Was that Boeser?" Tyler leaned forward to see the back of his jersey. "He's too pretty to make plays like that."

Emma snorted. "Oh, that's rich coming from you." Tyler grinned, and she couldn't help herself. "You'd think the Blizzard D-line would be more motivated to press him." Tyler laughed out loud.

The game continued, and the Blizzard made a breakaway play. A fast pass to Gaudreau saw him slipping the puck between a Canuck's skates and then firing a wrist shot, only to be deflected off the goalie's pad.

Emma groaned. "Gaudreau should've passed. He had Tkachuk wide open on the left."

Tyler clicked his tongue. "Those who can't do, yell from the sidelines."

Emma flipped him the bird, and Tyler slapped her hand away. She elbowed him in the ribs, then sat a little closer to his side of her seat than before.

By the third period, neither of them would shut up. Emma argued against his suggested strategy while the Blizzard were on the power play, and Tyler mocked her praise of almost every player she mentioned.

Lazy on defence. Too predictable. Selfish.

Emma pretended to swoon. "If only Tyler Bowen were on the ice, he'd be our hero!"

Tyler threw up his hands. "I don't know how it took you that long to figure it out."

It was still tied one to one in the middle of the third, and the energy in the arena was palpable. The instructions on the Jumbotron turned full propaganda, whipping the fans up into a frenzy.

Then, with two minutes left in regulation, the Blizzard's defence intercepted a hasty pass from the Canucks near the blue line, initiating their counter-attack. Giordano, the Blizzard veteran defenseman, took control of the puck. Spotting Lindholm on his right, he fired off a crisp pass, avoiding a charging Canuck. Lindholm deftly received, pausing just a fraction of a second to pull a Canuck defender toward him before relaying the puck to Gaudreau on the left wing.

Gaudreau danced past a defender with a series of swift dekes, drawing another opponent toward him. As the Canucks' defence began to close in around the threat, Gaudreau dropped the puck back to Monahan, who'd patiently hung back.

Monahan didn't hesitate. With the Canucks' defence off-balance and the goalie anticipating a direct shot from Gaudreau, the netminder was slightly out of position. Seizing this brief window, Monahan snapped the puck upwards.

The biscuit soared and the Canucks' goalie lunged desperately, his glove hand reaching out a fraction too late. The red goal light illuminated as the puck brushed the underside of the crossbar and nestled into the top right corner of the net. A perfect top-shelf goal.

Fire burst from flame throwers at both ends of the rink, sending a wave of heat over the rabid crowd. Emma cheered until her voice was raw, then flowed with the crowd after a satisfying Blizzard win.

"Ugh. If only all centres could play like Monahan," Emma crooned, pulling on her coat.

Tyler pursed his lips. "You know I'm searching up food stylists tonight so I can show you how flawless their work is."

"Well, we all know how much you love searching the internet."

The cool air calmed the flush on her cheeks as they made their way to the car waiting for them at the curb. Tyler opened the side door for Emma with over-the-top gallantry, and she slid into the leather seat, laughing as Tyler walked to the other side.

"Did you see the look on that player's face on the bench when number six missed that goal?" Emma clutched her stomach as he sat and closed the door, her muscles aching.

Tyler wiped at his eyes. "That shit is ending up on Hockey Evening in Canada guaranteed."

The car moved forward, and Emma reclined her seat and played with the buttons until she found the one that opened the skylight. "Okay, if you could only eat one type of candy for the rest of your life, what would it be?"

Tyler pretended to ponder the question seriously. "Are we talking chocolate or—?"

Emma shook her head. "Candy, candy."

"That's unnecessarily restrictive, but I'd have to go with Twizzlers."

Emma grimaced. "What? Please tell me you're not talking about the black licorice ones." Tyler shook his head, and she groaned. "No, ugh! Those are like wax with a little flavouring mixed in."

Tyler held up a hand. "That from the girl who was eating Wine Gums the other day?"

Her jaw dropped. "I ate those in secret."

Tyler asked her what else she ate in secret, but Emma refused to answer, instead asking him what he missed about Toronto. She laid her cheek on the seat and turned to her side, watching him as he talked. The way his hair fell over his ears, mussed and perfect. The way his lips curled, like he was always seconds away from finding something funny. *Those damn crinkles around his eyes.*

Tyler finished and turned toward her, then frowned as he looked past her shoulder.

"What is it?" She sat up and glanced out the window. It was dark. How long had they been in the car? She glanced at the clock. Twenty-five minutes had passed since they left the arena. Even with terrible traffic, they would've made it to her apartment by then.

Emma leaned forward and rapped her knuckles on the glass. The partition lowered. "Hey, I think you might've taken a wrong turn . . ." She trailed off as a green sign listing the distance to Canmore and Banff popped up on the side of the road.

The driver shook his head. "No wrong turn. This is a gift from Troy. I thought he told you."

Emma whirled to Tyler, but his eyes were as wide as hers. A pit of dread settled in her stomach. "What kind of gift?"

"Rooftop suite. At the Canmore Cascade."

CHAPTER
Nineteen

EMMA BIT her lip as Tyler's thumbs flew across the screen of his phone. "Sent."

"A rooftop suite?" she hissed. "What is Troy thinking?"

Tyler dropped his phone in his lap. "He's thinking, 'My son has an amazing girlfriend, and I'm about to die, so I'm going to send them on a romantic trip to Canmore.'"

That shut Emma up. Right. Troy thought they were together and clearly in love since Tyler's longest relationships were typically shorter than the gestation of a chicken egg. This was his fault. *And hers.* She fell back against the seat and ran both hands through her hair.

Tyler's phone buzzed.

Emma jolted. "What did he say?"

Tyler held out the screen for her to read Troy's texts.

> I'm sorry I didn't give you a heads-up, but I wanted it to be a surprise
>
> You two have something special
>
> Enjoy tonight

Emma pursed her lips, staring at the two emojis at the end of his message. "How does your almost seventy-year-old dad know about eggplant and peach emojis?"

Tyler coughed a laugh. "He's only sixty-four."

Emma groaned and dropped back to stare out the skylight. The Canmore Cascade was *the* hotel. Only twelve rooms and over a thousand dollars a night for lower-level accommodations. She knew because she'd looked at it for her parents' anniversary last year in November. They'd opted for the Prince of Wales in Waterton because Kelty had a corporate discount. She didn't even want to know how much Troy paid for the rooftop.

"I can tell the driver to turn around," Tyler murmured.

They *should* tell the driver to turn around. They definitely *should not* continue the last twenty minutes into Canmore and stay the night in a romantic rooftop suite when they weren't even together.

But that little voice clawed at the back of Emma's consciousness. *What if he wants this? What if he wants you?*

"Or . . . we could go." Emma swallowed hard. "Not as—just as friends, I mean. I've heard the hotel is incredible, and I don't have plans tomorrow. If you do, then—"

"No, I don't have plans." He twisted the cap to his water bottle. "I assume they have a gym there."

Emma scoffed. "Spending a night at the Cascade, and you're thinking about the gym?"

Tyler didn't answer, and Emma couldn't make out his expression in the low light. What *was* he thinking about?

Emma played with the zipper of her coat. At some point tonight, she would talk to him. Tell him how she felt. Preferably before her rabbit heart gave out.

———

Emma couldn't help but stare wide-eyed at the gorgeous building nestled against the backdrop of the majestic Rockies. The sight was straight out of a fairytale—the way the moonlight glinted off the stone walls, the elegant archways sure to be framed with lush greenery in summer, and the warm glow spilling from the vast windows.

Vaughn had raved about this place purely from pictures he'd seen online, but witnessing it in person was on a whole other level. Emma turned and pulled her bag from the car as Tyler closed his door and rounded the vehicle.

Her heart danced like butterflies in a mason jar as he approached, his sweater open, his dark hair curling over his ears. She didn't have any toiletries. No toothbrush—

"Welcome to the Cascade."

Emma turned to see a young man dressed in a tailored suit with a name tag that said, "Quinn" atop an Australian flag.

"I'll take your bags if you'd like." Quinn held out a hand as their car pulled away from the curb. *This was happening.* Tyler was standing next to her, and their only escape route was vanishing up the manicured drive.

Emma looped the strap over her shoulder. "No need. This is all we have."

Quinn nodded, unfazed and motioned for them to follow him into the lobby. He pushed open the heavy, ornate wooden door with aged brass handles, and the grandeur of the entryway took Emma's breath away.

Wooden beams stretched across the vaulted ceiling and a rustic chandelier cast soft golden light across the polished stone floor. To her left, a grand staircase with a hand-carved wooden balustrade spiralled upward.

In a corner, a grand stone fireplace rose from floor to ceiling. Plush velvet sofas in deep greens sat around a refurbished farmhouse coffee table atop inset herringbone wood flooring.

Quinn walked to the left toward a check-in desk constructed of repurposed barn wood juxtaposed with elegant gold leaf embossing on its front panel. Ornate brass lamps illuminated the back wall where there were two short rows of hooks, some holding tagged keys awaiting their guests.

"Sir, what name would I put in for the reservation?" Quinn asked.

"Bowen," Tyler answered, stepping up to the counter.

A petite woman with a Swedish flag on her nametag set a basket on the worn wood. Emma's curiosity got the better of her, and she stepped up to look inside. Glistening glass bottles of artisanal shampoos and conditioners were arranged on one side, their labels scripted in elegant gold lettering. Soft pastel soaps embossed with intricate designs lay next to petite vials of essential oils. A silk ribbon tied the plush hand towel that lay atop two aluminum toothbrushes with Wintermint toothpaste, completing the ensemble.

She breathed a sigh of relief and pulled the basket from the countertop.

"Thank you." Tyler took the key from Quinn and turned, nodding to the staircase. "All the way to the top."

Emma's breathing quickened as they ascended the staircase, and for once in her life, she hoped another human being would assume it was because she was out of shape. Tyler didn't say anything as they reached the top. He only turned to the right to proceed down the hall.

"This place is gorgeous," she murmured. The hall leading to their rooftop suite was lined with exquisite photographs of the Rockies, lit by singular goosehead lamps.

Tyler stopped in front of a carved wooden door and inserted the key into the lock. "This is it, I think."

The lock clicked, and they walked through the doorway. For a moment, Emma couldn't speak. She stood next to Tyler and stared slack-jawed as the door closed behind them.

The design was unabashedly modern—clean lines, minimalistic decor, and a monochromatic palette of greys and whites, broken only by the occasional accents of brushed steel and gold.

A plush dove-grey sectional sofa framed a low-profile coffee table, its polished surface glinting in the light of a sleek chrome floor lamp. But what truly took her breath away were the floor-to-ceiling back windows. Through them, the majestic Rocky Mountains, bathed in silvery moonlight, seemed to butt up against the rooftop patio.

"Holy shit," Tyler whispered.

"Exactly."

Tyler walked toward the kitchen counter. "Looks like Troy didn't hold back." Tyler motioned at a pristine white dessert plate filled with delicate chocolate truffles, ripe strawberries, and flaky pastries nestled among elegant silverware. A bottle of sparkling cider chilled in a bucket, dew glistening on its glass surface.

"Huh." Tyler ran a finger over the label.

"What?"

"Troy hardly ever remembers I don't drink."

Emma set the basket on the counter, her heart hammering in her chest. What did they do now?

"I need to see the bathroom," Tyler announced, and Emma laughed.

"I have to show Vaughn this place. He's obsessed. Do you mind if I give him a quick tour?" Tyler raised an eyebrow. "If you don't want—"

"No, go for it." He stalked to the bedroom. What the hell was that all about? Emma thought of Tyler walking into the kitchen when Vaughn had been dancing with her.

"Do you not like Vaughn?" She called after him.

"He's fine." Tyler called from the bedroom.

Emma grinned to herself and pulled out her phone, opening her video messaging app. As soon as she started recording, Vaughn's profile image appeared. He was watching live.

"Vaughn, make sure you're sitting down. This place is . . ." She shook her head and hit the button to turn her camera, walking through the living area and zooming in first on the view out the back then on the plate of desserts.

Vaughn sent a quick reaction with a shaking camera and unintelligible screaming.

Emma chortled and turned the camera back to her face. "I know, right? Here, let me take you into the bedroom. I haven't seen it yet."

"If it has a bidet, I'm moving in."

"That's all it takes for you to move in?" Tyler quipped from the bathroom.

Emma's heart jolted. "Ignore that please," she whispered to the camera, then held it out in front of her as she crossed the threshold. She barely made it three steps before she froze and looked up in awe.

Skylights stretched across the entire ceiling, exposing the night sky. She moved the camera in a wide arc. "I don't even know what to say about this." Emma tore her eyes from the twinkling stars and scanned the room. An antique writing desk stood against one wall, and then . . . there was the bed. Sleek, matte black pillars rose from each corner, framing the sleeping space with an air of minimalistic sophistication. The canopy was clean and geometric, and the *bedding–all* soft greys and whites. Crisp and inviting.

Emma turned the camera back to her. "So, there you have it. Wish you were here." She blew Vaughn a kiss and pressed the red square.

Tyler appeared in the shadows next to her, and the air in the darkened room grew thick.

"Perfect," Tyler murmured behind her. "What did Vaughn think?"

"He may be having a stroke."

"Understandable." Tyler's voice rumbled through her. Emma cleared her throat and walked past him to peek into the bathroom.

Three lights patterned around twin oval mirrors glowed softly, making the space feel reverent. Mosaic tile. Double sink. Wide glass shower with double heads and wall sprayers.

"It's a car wash," Emma whispered. "I've always wanted a car wash shower."

Tyler chuckled, and she jumped. He was standing behind her. His breath whispered against her neck.

She had to tell him. Either he would tell her he felt the same, and then this magical shower and bedroom would get a lot of use, or he wouldn't. And it would be the most awkward night of her life. But, based on the fire licking her bones, it was already going to be torture. *Nothing to lose.*

"Tyler—"

"There's a hot tub!" he called from the other room.

Emma re-entered the bedroom and found Tyler pointing out the sliding glass doors onto the patio, grinning.

"We don't have suits." Emma strode toward him. The hot tub was on. Steaming. Looking out over the Rockies under the most perfect night of stars.

"You could get in first. I won't watch. Then you can turn your head, or don't, and I'll jump in."

Emma blinked, looking at his profile silhouetted by the light in the other room. "You're saying we should skinny dip?"

Tyler shrugged. "Why not?"

Emma opened her mouth, then closed it. *Why not?* She could think of a million reasons why not. But one very compelling reason *why*.

"I'll grab dessert." Tyler retreated, leaving Emma alone in the bedroom. Her hands began to tingle. Was she actually going to strip naked and walk out onto a rooftop patio in a room half-covered with windows?

Yes. Yes, she was. Her body felt like she'd just downed an energy drink as she pulled off her shirt before she could change her mind. She laid her clothes over the writing desk, then pulled off her bra and underwear. Her nipples pinched against the cold as she slid the glass door open.

This was insane. The pebbled deck numbed the soles of her feet as she cupped her breasts and ran toward the hot tub. If Tyler was watching, she didn't want to know. She carefully ascended the steps and stepped into the hot water.

Emma sighed as she lowered herself into the corner seat, then pulled the hair tie off her wrist and pulled her hair into a bun on top of her head. When she was safely obscured by the water, her shoulders finally relaxed. This was the right choice. The chilled mountain air pressed against her cheeks like a mask, and she tipped her head back, staring at the stars.

Music wafted from somewhere down the street. She couldn't hear it well enough to determine the style, but it didn't matter. This was perfect. Almost.

Movement caught her eye and she turned to face the mountains, crossing her arms and resting them on the edge of the tub. *Turn your head or don't?* Every cell in her body screamed that "don't" was the correct option in this scenario, but she couldn't move.

The sound of his feet against the deck sent blood rushing through her ears. He was standing behind her. Six-three. *She'd felt his hard muscles under his shirt.* The surface of the water wobbled as Tyler stepped into the hot tub.

"Good?" she asked, her voice catching. She covered it with a cough.

"Very good."

Emma turned, careful to keep the water lapping at her collarbone. Tyler's chest was half visible above the water, and Emma couldn't keep her eyes from straying. She snapped them back to his face, but not before he noticed.

Tyler stretched an immaculately sculpted arm back to the stairs and grabbed the plate he'd set on the edge. He held it out to her, and she picked up a strawberry. The chocolate crunched after being outside for only a few minutes but then melted on her tongue.

Tyler chose a truffle, then set it back on the step. "I didn't bring the cider. Figured we could have that later if we wanted."

Emma nodded. Later. Tyler's foot brushed hers under the water, and she sucked in a breath.

"Sorry."

"No, it just surprised me. You can stretch out if you want, I can move over." She shifted to the seat opposite him and accidentally lifted a little too high in the water. "I—" Her cheeks flushed as she sunk into the corner bucket, allowing Tyler to stretch his legs diagonally. "That was—I'm sorry."

"I'm not." Tyler smirked, and Emma laughed so nervously she thought she might give herself the hiccups. She dropped her head back and lifted her knees onto the bench. "Skittles."

Emma frowned and looked back at Tyler. "What?"

"You hate Twizzlers, so you must love Skittles."

A slow grin spread across her face. "You think Skittles are my favourite candy?" She sighed. "Oh, Tyler, you have so much to learn."

"Educate me, then."

Emma drew a deep breath and lay her head back. "Skittles are too much work. You can only eat four to six of them before you have TMJ."

"Four to six? That's specific."

"I've done extensive testing. Starburst, same thing, but eating those you also risk pulling out any fillings you have on your molars."

"I don't have any fillings."

Emma dropped her knees and sat straight, sending water in a wave toward Tyler. "Zero fillings?"

He flashed a cheesy smile. "Zero."

"So you sold your soul to the parking and dental gods."

Tyler barked a laugh then met her eyes. A boyish grin flickered across his face, and Emma's heart buried itself against her spine.

"It's been a year." Emma swallowed hard as she curled her knees back toward her chest. "Since I broke things off with my ex."

"Alex."

Emma's brow furrowed. *Had she told him that?* "I didn't think —I didn't know when I'd be ready for something new." Tyler watched her, the pale light from the hot tub moving in slow waves across his skin. Emma's pulse raced until she felt weightless. "I don't want to do fake, Tyler."

Tyler drew a deep breath and ran his hands through his hair, his chest muscles stretching and shifting as he lifted his arms. Emma felt dizzy.

"I know. Our fake relationship was fun while it lasted, though." The corner of his mouth lifted.

"What if . . ." Emma pressed a hand against her chest, willing her lungs to expand. "What if it didn't have to be over? What if it was real?"

CHAPTER
Twenty

TYLER'S HEART pounded harder than Frank Zummo. *What if it was real?* Did those words really just come out of Emma's mouth? He stared at her, stars winking around her in a halo, baby hairs curling around her ears.

One move. He could push out of his seat and be next to her. Pressing up against her bare skin, running his hands over the curves he'd snuck glances at too many times to count. He hadn't slept well for weeks fantasizing about a moment exactly like this, and now she was inviting him to act on it.

You know she doesn't need more of this in her life.

His throat tightened, shutting down all the words begging to burst out of him. *I want it to be real. I want you. You have no idea how much I want you.*

Pressure built behind his eyes as he remembered her standing in his living room with the phone to her ear, talking to Sean. *You know that's not what I want.*

Emma's toes grazed the outside of his thigh, and he was breaking. His body lit on fire from the inside out. If he didn't touch her, he was going to lose his damn mind.

But if he touched her? He wouldn't stop. He would consume her, body and soul, and where would that leave them? Emma knew what she wanted. She'd made it abundantly clear she wasn't looking for nights of Jell-O shots and fast pleasure.

She knew who he was—who he'd always been—but that hopeful look in her eyes wasn't saying she wanted *that* Tyler. She wanted him restored. A history stripped down and refurbished. Old, rotten beams ripped out and replaced with materials built to last.

His chest tightened. "I don't think that's a good idea, Emma." He pushed himself up to the edge of the hot tub, not even trying to hide the evidence of what her touch did to him. *He didn't have a damn towel.*

Tyler twisted and dropped his feet to the freezing cold ground. Pressure built behind his eyes as he stalked back to the sliding door, the mountain air snapping against his dripping skin. His insides churned as he walked into the bedroom, not daring to look back.

He stumbled into the bathroom and turned on the shower. Cold. *"I've always wanted a car wash shower."* Tyler gritted his teeth and slapped his hand against the tile.

Tyler hung his head under the freezing spray and shivered, goosebumps lifting on his flushed skin. *He'd hurt her.* He'd walked away, and he'd hurt her.

He didn't know how long he stood there forcing himself to breathe before changing the temperature, but it felt like hours. How could he go out there and face her?

He finally turned off the water when his hands and feet were wrinkled. She probably wanted to rinse off. He'd left the dessert plate there for Emma to clean up, and she didn't have a towel either.

Shit. What a mess. He was a self-centred asshole, and now Emma was paying for it on a night that should've been an escape. He could've at least talked with her, though at the moment, all the blood wasn't exactly circulating in his brain.

The cold water clung to Tyler's skin as he stepped out of the shower, his body still recovering from the numbing deluge. He wrapped himself in a towel and reached for his boxer briefs, pulling them on with clumsy fingers.

He hung the towel on the hook behind the door, then hesitated before opening the door. Steam billowed into the bedroom, and he waited for it to clear. The room was dark, the only light coming from the stars visible through the skylights. *Maybe she was still on the patio?*

Tyler stepped out, feeling along the wall as he searched for his clothes. What was he going to say to her? How could he explain?

He'd tell her the truth like an adult instead of being a coward.

Tyler found his shirt on the end of the bed and pulled it over his head, then froze.

There she was.

Curled into a tiny ball so close to the edge of the bed, she'd fall off if she moved. He padded across the plush rug and knelt down in front of her.

Asleep. Mascara smudged. Fully dressed under the covers.

His ribs ratcheted, squeezing his lungs until they ached.

Tyler stood and saw the desserts sitting on the writing desk. The door was locked. He rounded the end of the bed, his head spinning. Lifting the comforter and top sheet, he slipped into bed, not even bothering to go back to the bathroom and brush his teeth. He thought of the basket of toiletries still sitting on the counter in the kitchen. The way Emma's eyes had lit up in the lobby.

He twisted his hands in the sheets and clenched them until his nails bit into his palms.

Emma held her breath as Tyler moved around the room, each sound making it less likely that her lungs would fill with air. If he'd stayed ten more seconds in front of her, she would've exploded. She was sure of it.

Sobs threatened to escape her lips, but she gritted her teeth and clutched her pillow like she'd just jumped out of a plane and it was her parachute. At the moment, it felt like the only thing keeping her from shattering on the ground.

Finally, the soft scuffs of his feet silenced, and then the mattress moved as he laid down on the other side of the bed. Emma couldn't relax. She could barely breathe. Tears leaked down her cheeks as she laid in the silence, waiting for Tyler's breath to slow and deepen.

Sleep must have claimed her at some point because when her eyes flew open, the moon was directly over the skylights. Her eyes felt like they were lined with sandpaper, and her head throbbed. She grappled for her phone on the nightstand and checked the clock. Five-thirty.

The night before downloaded into her brain, and her stomach heaved. She rushed as quietly as possible to the bathroom in case she threw up and splashed water on her face when the initial wave of nausea passed. *She had to get out of here.* The idea of seeing Tyler's face when he woke made her want to burrow in a hole and starve to death.

Emma tiptoed out of the bathroom and began gathering her things. Despite her best efforts, her eyes were pulled toward the bed like iron filings to a magnet. Tyler slept on his back, one arm draped over his chest and the other curled under his pillow. His lashes splayed across his cheeks, his chest rising and falling with slow, steady breaths.

Emma popped a truffle from the plate on the writing desk into her mouth. They were probably supposed to be refrigerated, but it couldn't make her stomach roil any more than it already was.

With one last look at the moonlight glinting off Tyler's golden skin, Emma picked up her bag and padded into the living area. Emma crossed the room and slid the hotel room door open, careful not to let it creak and sound the alarm.

The hallway stretched out before her, a dimly lit path to freedom. She paused momentarily, holding her breath as she listened for any stirring from Tyler behind her. When all remained quiet, she slipped into the corridor and closed the door behind her.

She leaned against the wall and sucked in a breath, then marched toward the stairs, pulling out her phone to search for a rideshare. This was Canmore, and even though it was mud season, there had to be someone out driving tourists.

Her fingers trembled as she tapped at the screen, summoning a car that would take her back into the city. The wheel spun, but finally, confirmation came, and Emma sighed with relief.

"Morning, love!" Quinn greeted her with surprise. "You're up early."

Emma smiled. "I have some things I have to take care of at home."

Quinn cocked his head to the side. "We'll be sad to see you go. At least have something for the road, then. Since you won't be joining us for breakfast." He left the desk and walked through a door to the left of the entrance, then returned with a chocolate croissant wrapped in a napkin.

"Thank you." Emma took it from him. *The buffet. Couples massages.* Ugh. She'd been so stupid. It all made her want to kick something.

"Take care now," Quinn flashed her a sympathetic smile.

Emma nodded, not trusting herself to speak, then walked through the heavy wooden door. Outside, the morning was cool and crisp, slapping her awake. A Jeep pulled up into the circular drive, and a ski bum with a mop of unruly curls and a friendly grin greeted her cheerfully.

"Hey there! Headed somewhere fun?" he asked, his enthusiasm grating against her nerves. Emma hated morning people under normal circumstances.

"Home" was all Emma could muster as she climbed into the back seat.

"Ah, gotcha. Long night?"

Did she miss a setting? Wasn't there some box you could click to let your driver know you weren't interested in conversation?

"Yep." Emma stared out the window, her short responses a brick wall she hoped would deter further questioning. He got the hint and turned on some Nickelback.

That was apropos.

Emma pulled out her phone and texted Lindsey.

> Heading home. I'm an idiot. And Tyler's a dick

She felt a little guilty as she pressed send. Tyler wasn't a terrible person, but he had led her on. All of his flirtations and signals after she'd been crystal clear about her boundaries and the type of relationship she sought.

Anger and hurt welled up in her. *No.* It was justified. Never mind that she felt the same disdain for her own actions.

As they sped along the Trans-Canada Highway, then eventually entered the city limits, Emma stared out the dark window as her fingers traced the screen of her phone. When the sun rose, the sky was bleak and grey, and in a place with over three hundred sunny days a year, that felt like a message.

When they pulled up to her apartment complex, Emma thanked the driver and hurried into the lobby. The place was dead, as it should be so early on a Saturday morning. Her body finally relaxed as she slipped into her apartment. *Home.*

Emma kicked off her shoes and strode to the bedroom. She peeled off her clothes, the fabric sticking to her damp skin that still smelled lightly of chlorine from the hot tub. A shower would eventually be necessary, but her eyes were already drooping. She left her bag on the floor and stumbled into bed, her blotchy face sinking into the pillow.

She slept like the dead until a loud banging jolted her awake.

Confused and disoriented, Emma tried to hide under her pillow as if she could smother the sounds of the world outside. *Was there construction planned for today?*

More banging. "Emma, open up!" Lindsey's voice filtered through the door.

Groaning, Emma forced herself out of bed, her body leaden and sluggish. She opened the door a crack.

Lindsey took one look at her and winced. "You look terrible." She pushed the door open and walked inside holding a folded paper bag.

"Thanks," Emma muttered. "I was sleeping."

Lindsey flopped down on the loveseat.

Emma yawned and rubbed her eyes. She had no idea what time it was. "Why are you here?"

Lindsey shot her an exasperated look, then tapped on her phone and held it out so Emma could see the screen.

Emma groaned, reading the text message she'd sent that morning. "You didn't need to come all the way—"

"Ems, if you don't start talking right this damn minute, I'm going to eat this honey cruller myself." Lindsey held up the bag, and that plain paper bag released the floodgates.

Tears filled Emma's eyes. "You're going to think I'm an idiot."

"Oh honey, I thought you were an idiot the second you told me you were pretending to date that hockey god." Lindsey patted the cushion next to her. "You're a sweet idiot, if that helps?"

Emma laughed and flopped beside her, snatching the bag from her hands. Between bites of donut, her words tumbled out. She recounted the kiss in the storage room, dinner, the hockey game, and finally, the disastrous trip to Canmore. Lindsey gave all the appropriate reactions. *He did not!? What the hell was he expecting you to think? You said that?*

When she finished, she lay with her head on Lindsey's shoulder until the cruller was gone and her eyes were dry.

Lindsey slapped a hand on her knee. "Alright. First things first: rinse off, get dressed, and let's get you some fresh air."

"I don't want to go anywhere, I just want to sleep."

"Well, too bad because Vaughn's waiting for us at the farmer's market."

Emma sat up, glowering at her friend.

Lindsey gave her a look that said, *It's out of my hands*, and Emma forced herself to retreat to the bathroom.

Emma felt slightly more human as they entered the bustling indoor farmer's market. The air was littered with the earthy scent of fresh produce and the excited chatter of vendors and shoppers. The sight of colourful fruits and vegetables, homemade jams and pickles, and artisanal cheeses and breads buoyed her spirits, even if she wasn't yet ready to admit that to either of her friends.

Vaughn greeted them with open arms, his infectious energy warming Emma from the inside out. Together, they navigated the maze of stalls, sampling gluten-free baked goods and admiring handmade crafts. As Lindsey filled Vaughn in on the details of what had happened in Canmore, his face darkened with indignation.

"Hockey players, am I right?" Vaughn shot Emma a look of sympathy. "You deserve so much better, Em."

"Thanks." Emma busied herself with reading the label on a tin of loose-leaf tea. That was the problem, wasn't it? She didn't *want* better. She wanted Tyler. She wanted him to look at her with that smug grin on his face. To laugh when she teased him and find her eyes when he went on the ice. She wanted to be on his arm when he walked into One Place, not Ginger or pink-bra girl.

But Tyler didn't want her. He didn't want to tie himself down, and she'd known that from the second Sean had texted her and told her not to get involved with him. *Was she broken? Was she forever going to search for something she couldn't have?*

"Emma, you coming?"

Her head snapped up, and she set the tea back on the shelf, then followed Vaughn to the next aisle. As they continued through the farmer's market, her mood continued to lift. She marvelled at the vibrant hues of fresh flowers and laughed at Vaughn's reaction to trying curry-flavoured honey.

"See?" Lindsey nudged her as they walked back out onto the street. "I told you it would help."

Vaughn scoffed. "Taking all the credit, as usual."

Lindsey pulled them both to a stop, her eyes bright. "Hey, why don't we go to the bar tonight? It's ladies' night at Soto's. Sorry, Vaughn."

Emma squeezed her friend's hand. "I think I'm more in an eat-ice-cream-and-watch-trash-TV kind of mood."

"You're always in an ice-cream-and-trash-TV kind of mood. This shit show deserves something special." Lindsey flashed a cheesy smile.

Something itched at the back of Emma's mind. She pulled her phone from her back pocket and opened the calendar. When the day's schedule filled the screen, she groaned.

"What?" Vaughn peered over her shoulder, then hissed air through his teeth when he saw it. "Team barbecue," he murmured to Lindsey.

"I'm not going." Emma clicked the screen to black.

"Fair enough. Which means you're free to come barhopping." Lindsey linked her arm through Emma's and continued on toward their car.

Emma laughed. "You guys, thank you for getting me out of my own head for a second, but I seriously need a night in. Long shower. Lounging in my underwear. You know the drill."

Lindsey sighed. "No, you need to get drilled. You're thinking about this all backwards."

Emma snorted. "Pretty sure that won't solve my problem. If I wanted that, Tyler and I would've gotten along perfectly."

They said their goodbyes to Vaughn, then drove through the still sleepy city. The streets were dotted with people strolling leisurely in the warm sun while others sat on patios with coffee and a book.

Calgary always put on a show like this in April, but Emma wasn't fooled. In another week, they'd be up to their knees in spring snow. Emma rested her head against the window, watching the world drift by in a blur of colours and shapes.

The car slowed, and she lifted her head. "Thank you for forcing me out of my comfortable bed."

Lindsey pulled her into a hug over the console. "If you change your mind . . ."

"I know. I'll phone you, I promise. Love you, Linds."

Emma grabbed the bouquet of flowers she'd purchased from the backseat, then stepped out of the car. She waved and turned toward the doors.

The morning sun glinted in her eyes as she walked up the path, and it wasn't until she passed into the shadow of the building that she saw a familiar figure past the glass of the lobby doors.

Tyler. His hands were shoved in his pockets, his hair more tousled than usual.

Emma froze on the walkway as Tyler turned and stared directly at her.

CHAPTER
Twenty-One

EMMA'S HEART fluttered against her ribs like a caged bird. She couldn't run, could she? He'd already seen her, and he was probably faster anyway. She squared her shoulders, drew a shaky breath, and then forced herself to march forward and enter the building.

Tyler's hazel eyes locked onto hers as she pushed open the heavy glass doors. He was still in the clothes he'd worn the night before. Had he come straight here? Did he even have a vehicle?

A muscle in his jaw jumped as she approached. "Emma." He whispered her name like a prayer, and something inside her cracked. *She couldn't do this.* She dropped her eyes and tried to walk past him to the elevator, but he caught her elbow.

"I woke up, and you were gone—" His voice caught, and Emma couldn't turn. Couldn't look up. She tried to swallow the lump in her throat, but it still threatened to choke her. "I can pay for your ride if—"

Emma tugged her arm out of his grip. "I don't need you to pay for my ride, Tyler." Her insides twisted. "I need to get up to my apartment." She reached out and pushed the elevator call button.

"Are you going to the team barbecue later?" Tyler asked.

Team barbecue? Was he serious? Emma whirled, her eyes flashing. "Doubtful."

Tyler flinched. His tongue flicked over his lips. "I thought that might be the case, so I wanted you to know I'm not going."

She shook her head and turned back to the elevator. "You couldn't have texted that?" It felt like someone was pressing their thumbs against the backs of her eyes.

"I wanted—" He sighed heavily behind her. "You should go. The Snowballs were yours before they were mine."

The light above the elevator blinked, and the bell dinged, echoing through the empty lobby. The doors couldn't open fast enough. Emma stepped in and clutched her flowers as she hit the button for the third floor.

By four o'clock, Emma's kitchen was spotless. She furiously scrubbed out the last refrigerator drawer, rinsed the plastic, then slid it back into place.

The barbecue started at five. Her parents had blown up their family text chain, talking about last-minute items they were picking up at the store and asking what else they should grab. *Salt 'n Vinegar or All Dressed? Molson or Stella? Clearly Canadian or the mineral water that smelled like a flavour but tasted like salt?*

That last one had been from her dad. They wanted her to be there, but despite her rage cleaning, she was still barely functional. Would she really have to do much? Nobody would think anything of it if she sat in the corner and nursed whatever drink her parents decided on.

She entered her bedroom and stripped off her clothes. Finally time for that shower. She pulled up her hair and stared at herself in the mirror. Her eyes were still red-rimmed, the skin surrounding them a bit puffy.

Why would she let Tyler Bowen determine whether she went to the team barbecue? This was her family, and the Snowballs were in the playoffs—in the semifinals. She should be celebrating with them.

Emma slapped her hands against the counter and straightened. She would shower, dab some vitamin C and concealer under her eyes, and drive to the damn barbecue.

The acrid smell of disinfectant filled Tyler's nostrils as he stepped off the elevator. He walked to the nurse's station and got directions to Troy's room, then continued on down the hall. He hesitated before the door to Room 314, the beige paint peeling slightly at the edges, the small frosted window allowing only a ghostly glow to seep out. He took a deep breath and gently pushed it open.

The room flickered with light from the television set mounted on the opposite wall, playing a muted nature documentary. The sterile white walls were only interrupted by pastel paintings and the gleaming chrome and digital feeds on the equipment. The faint rhythmic beeping of a heart monitor sang a soft, haunting melody.

In the centre, Troy's frail figure was swallowed by his bed. His father's once robust frame looked frail, and his usually tan, rugged skin now papery and sallow.

Tyler put a hand on the end of the bed to steady himself as the room spun around him.

Thirteen years ago. The walls then were a cheerful shade of blue, but the rooms were disturbingly similar. That time it had been his mother lying with her eyes closed, a halo of brunette curls framing her pale face.

The flurry of doctors and nurses had left, and the machines were quiet. He hadn't been allowed in when he'd arrived, and then it'd been too late. He remembered sitting in the chair next to her and picking up her hand, already growing cold.

Tyler squeezed his eyes shut and waited for his head to clear. *These machines were still beeping.*

"Ty?" His father stirred, and Tyler straightened.

"Hey, Dad." He forced his feet to move and rounded the bed, pulling the chair pressed against the wall to the side of the bed. Tyler reached out, taking his father's limp hand into his own.

Troy gave him a weak smile, the corners of his eyes crinkling with warmth. "How was Canmore?"

The wound he'd been working to patch all day split wide open. "The hotel was gorgeous. Emma and I were both floored."

"Then why didn't you stay?" Troy wheezed.

Tyler frowned. "We did, we—"

"I had a voicemail asking if I wanted to reschedule the couples massage."

"You're checking your voicemails?"

Troy grinned. "What else do I have to do in here?"

Tyler patted his dad's hand and leaned back in his chair. "Where's Gina?"

"Don't change the subject."

Tyler coughed a laugh and ran a hand over his face. "Well, it turns out I'm a lot like you."

Troy didn't answer, just watched him with watery eyes. A lump formed in Tyler's throat, but the words he'd wanted to speak for over twenty-four hours now wouldn't be held back any longer.

"Emma and I aren't together. We met the way I told you and then found out we had a connection through my hockey team. I won't go into details, but for various reasons, we pretended to be—"

"That's bullshit."

Tyler stiffened. "Yeah, I realize—"

"Bullshit that you two aren't together! You're telling me you came to work on property for *weeks* for a ruse?" Troy shook his head. "I see the way you look at her."

Something pinched under Tyler's ribs, and he shifted in his

chair. "It was stupid. She got attached, and I can't give her what she wants."

"What does she want?"

Tyler leaned forward and rested his elbows on the side of the bed, dropping his head into his hands. "Not a guy with a rotating door to his bedroom."

Troy exhaled slowly. "You know doors can always be switched out."

Tyler looked up. "That coming from you?"

The corner of Troy's mouth lifted. "I said 'can.'"

"So why didn't you change yours?"

Troy reached for the handle of his plastic cup. Tyler stood and helped him bring the straw to his lips. He took a long drink, then laid back on his pillows.

"I loved your mom, Tyler. If that's what you're asking."

"Funny way of showing it," Tyler muttered.

Troy flinched. "I guess I deserved that."

The machines beeped, and the lights flickered on the walls. Tyler dropped his eyes. He hadn't planned on walking in and accusing his dad of ruining their family on his deathbed, but there it was.

Tyler pointed at a clipboard on Troy's tray. "What are they saying about your stay?"

Troy shrugged. "Mostly pain management. Getting some nutrition in me."

Tyler's shoulders tensed. "Dad, I—"

"I was young and selfish." Troy dropped his eyes to his hands. "I took her for granted. There are some mistakes you can't come back from."

Mistakes. Was he really trying to pretend he'd accidentally ended up in someone else's bed? Then *accidentally* continued that pattern for thirty more years? But as he watched Troy adjust his hospital gown over his bony shoulders, Tyler couldn't bring himself to argue.

Troy turned. His smile didn't reach his eyes. "Don't make the same mistake, Ty."

Tyler scoffed. "I won't." He couldn't. Because he would never let himself get close enough to let somebody down.

Troy patted Tyler's hand. "I didn't mean betraying her. I meant taking her for granted."

CHAPTER
Twenty-Two

AT THE BARBECUE, Emma tried to act normal. She didn't succeed, but thankfully it didn't seem like anyone noticed. Curtis was showing Brett how to play chords on her dad's ukulele while Fly, Mike, Ryan, and Suraj were deep in an intense game of corn hole. It was warm enough to eat outside with jackets on, and her parents had pulled out the patio furniture from the garage just for this occasion.

Emma took a bite of her bison burger just as Kelty dropped into the seat beside her, balancing a plate piled high with potato salad and chips. From the looks of it, her parents had decided on All Dressed.

"I've missed you, you know." Kelty popped a chip into her mouth.

Emma sighed. "I know. We have our final shoot on Monday. As long as everything goes well, things should calm down from there, at least until we start on the next property."

"You're going to keep working there, then?"

Emma twisted her napkin, and she forced a smile. "Not sure yet. I've got some other irons in the fire."

Kelty nodded and took a swig of her water that smelled like a flavour but actually tasted like salt. She turned and scanned the backyard. "It's a bummer Tyler couldn't make it, eh? I feel so bad for him."

Emma frowned. *She felt bad for him?* What excuse could Tyler have given that would evoke pity? "Mmhmm." She took another bite of her burger, hoping a mouthful of food would disguise her annoyance.

Kelty sighed. "I'm sorry, you probably know more since you work for Troy. Have they given any updates on his condition?"

Emma chewed and swallowed. "I think he's doing relatively well. When I saw him yesterday—"

"Oh, Emma, had you not heard?" Kelty put a hand on her shoulder, and her stomach dropped. "Troy had a medical emergency during the night. He's in the hospital."

The world around her seemed to slow as Kelty's words sank in. *Medical emergency. In the hospital.* Emma's thoughts raced back to the tense conversation she'd had with Tyler that morning in front of the elevator. Was that why he'd come? To tell her Troy was in trouble?

"I have to go," she whispered, and Kelty nodded. Emma offered a tight smile as she rushed to drop her plate in the trash. She gave her parents each a quick hug, then raced out the door to her car.

Had Tyler found out while he was still in Canmore? Her chest tightened as she thought about him waking up to find her gone and then discovering that. She didn't regret leaving, but guilt niggled at her for how she'd treated Tyler in the foyer that morning. Yes, she was hurt, but Tyler's father was dying. There was no competition as to which one took precedence.

And, since he'd stayed away from the barbecue—away from the only family he had in this city besides Troy—Tyler was doing this alone.

The drive to Tyler's house felt both too long and too short, the streetlights blurring together as she navigated the familiar route. She hit too many red lights, and by the time she finally pulled onto his street, the sun was setting, and her nerves were frayed.

She pulled up to the curb a few houses down and put the car in park, then flung the door open and got out. The night air prickled Emma's skin as she slammed the door and hurried up the street.

There wasn't a guarantee Tyler would be here, but she had to try. *He might not want to see her.* That thought made her skip a step, but she clenched her hands into fists and kept walking. He might not want to see her, but she'd leave that up to him. She wasn't going to avoid him at a time like this because she was worried about making him uncomfortable.

Her heart pounded faster when she spotted a silhouette up ahead. A woman. Tall, with long blond hair, wearing a trench coat. A stone settled in Emma's stomach, and she slowed.

The woman's stiletto heels clicked softly against the concrete. She was beautiful. Stunning, even. Emma stopped altogether as the woman turned up Tyler and Brett's walkway, ascended the front steps, and knocked on the door.

Brett was at the barbecue. This woman could only be coming for—

The door opened. Emma only caught the side of Tyler's profile before she spun on her heel and dashed back to her car.

Emma arrived at the property Monday morning feeling like she'd been hitched to the back of a truck and dragged. She'd barely slept at all Saturday night and hadn't made up for it Sunday.

Neither Tyler nor Troy had texted her over the weekend, which in some ways, made things easier. Emma didn't relish the idea of talking to them, but as much as she tried to convince herself she didn't care about Troy's health, she did.

She cared less about Tyler's feelings now that she knew he most definitely wasn't doing this alone. Her stomach clenched. That woman walking up the steps and entering Tyler's townhome had lived rent-free in her head all weekend. *She'd been so stupid.*

Emma walked into the kitchen, not even pretending to be in a good mood. Lindsey and Vaughn trodded carefully as they set up for their final product shoot. They'd already done the specialty soaps and luxury towels. Today was marinated olives and spiced nuts. Then Emma was on to editing.

Lindsey would continue to shoot the property as the contractors finished up and the rooms were furnished and decorated, but Emma wouldn't have to be there for that. She should have a couple of weeks off to work from home before they decided on their next project.

Time away couldn't come soon enough. Everywhere she looked, she was reminded of Tyler. The way he'd grasped her waist and kissed her next to the sink. The way his head moved on the other side of the stained glass. How he filled the entire doorway when he heard them having fun and couldn't help wanting to be a part of it.

She meticulously arranged the glossy olives while Lindsey's auburn curls danced around her face as she fiddled with the camera settings. Vaughn shifted the light, then decided against the new position and moved it back.

"Ugh, my baby is acting up again," Lindsey grumbled, her brow furrowed in frustration as she fiddled with the settings on her camera.

"Adorable to pretend it's not user error," Vaughn teased, and Lindsey shot him a look.

Emma turned to find her mister and froze. Someone was standing in the doorway.

"So sorry to interrupt, but I'm having trouble with the WiFi." The woman nodded toward the other room, and Emma's heart flipped in her chest. It was the woman from the street. Her hair was pulled up into a chignon, and she wasn't wearing heels today, but it was definitely the same person. "Would you be able to help me? I might just be entering the password wrong."

Emma's lips drew into a line. "Sure." Blood rushed in her ears as she followed the woman into the other room. This was what Tyler was doing now? Spending the night with a woman and then giving her a job in the morning? *Or had he been seeing her all along?*

It wasn't like they were actually dating. She mentally berated herself. Of course he was seeing other women. How could she have been so deluded?

The woman pointed at her screen, and Emma stepped up. Her fingers trembled as she entered the password.

"You're Emma, right?" The woman asked.

Anger flared in her veins. What had Tyler told her? Emma stepped back and gave a curt nod. The WiFi symbol lit up in the right hand corner of the screen, and Emma turned to go back to the kitchen.

"Troy mentioned you. He said he was so grateful you took the job here, mostly so he could see his son more often. But he did say he was thrilled with your quality of work." She put her hands on the keys and typed something into the search bar.

Emma's brow furrowed. There was so much to unpack in those few sentences. She started with, "How do you know Troy?"

The woman laughed lightly. "I claim the title of ex-wife number six." She straightened and turned toward her. "I flew out from Toronto two days ago. Tyler was nice enough to put me up. Troy told me he didn't know how long he had left, and there were some business decisions he needed help with." She shrugged. "I'm a lawyer and was happy to help." She put out a hand. "Grace."

Emma took it, all the pieces of Tyler's life she thought she'd put together over the past few days suddenly jumping and shifting, then snapping into place to form a brand new picture. "I'm glad Troy is happy with my work, but I don't understand how me working here would allow him to see Tyler more. He was here anyway."

Grace dropped her arm and observed her curiously. "For the

past eight months, Tyler has worked solely from home. The best Troy could get out of him was a dinner every few weeks. He sometimes wondered what the point of Tyler relocating was in the first place."

Emma's world tilted on its axis. She shook her head and took a step back. *Tyler hadn't worked here?* Hadn't stepped foot on the property until she'd started working? She glanced at the table where he'd set his laptop. The empty space made her throat constrict.

"Thank you for the WiFi help." Grace smiled, then got back to work.

Emma spun and walked back to the kitchen.

"I think I'm going to have to get a new battery," Lindsey was saying as Emma rushed in and snatched her purse from the counter.

"I'll be back. Taking my lunch break." Emma dashed out of the kitchen, her heart pounding wildly in her chest.

"It's only nine-thirty?" Vaughn's voice floated after her as she sprinted to her car. Every second felt like an eternity as Emma pulled away from the curb and sped north.

"*Come on, come on,*" she muttered under her breath as she hit red light after red light. She had to talk to Tyler. He would be home wouldn't he? Unless he was at the hospital. She had no idea which hospital Troy was at, and even if she did, she wouldn't show up there unless someone invited her. *Please be home,* she silently pleaded.

She finally pulled up to Tyler's townhouse and took the spot directly in front of the walkway. Her hands trembled on the steering wheel as she parked, her body awash with adrenaline. Drawing a deep breath, she climbed out of the car and ran up the steps on legs that seemed to have transformed into jelly on the way over.

Emma knocked. When she didn't hear anything, she knocked again. Then, a third time even though she knew it was pointless. Tyler wasn't there.

She pulled out her phone and typed out a text, then deleted it and rewrote it. Then deleted it and shoved her phone back in her pocket. She didn't want to send him a message, *she wanted to see his face and talk to him in person.*

Emma cursed under breath and turned back to the steps. She couldn't wait here all day. They had to finish this shoot, and she wasn't about to leave Lindsey and Vaughn to finish it themselves.

Tonight. It was Monday. Tyler would have practice at the arena at seven. Emma jogged back to the car and got in. She could go finish the shoot and get to the arena early.

Olives and nuts. She'd have plenty of time to talk to Tyler before practice.

CHAPTER
Twenty-Three

DARK CLOUDS ROLLED in from the mountains as Tyler drove from the hospital to the Ice Arena. It was definitely going to snow tonight. Kind of perfect since he didn't have to go anywhere the next morning. No more driving to the property for work.

His stomach flipped inside out as he sped through a yellow light. He'd probably get a photo radar ticket for that, but he couldn't bring himself to care. *Not betraying her. Taking her for granted.*

Tyler clenched his hands over the steering wheel. He didn't take Emma for granted, that was the problem. Walking away from her had made it disturbingly clear how much he wanted her. Needed her. Like he'd been living his whole life not knowing he had a hole punched through his chest until her smiles, her sarcastic comments, her soft skin, *her sunny laughs* had filled it.

The sight of her curled up with tear stains on her cheeks corroded him like acid, and he had no way to neutralize it. Any possible solutions terrified the shit out of him.

He parked the truck and yanked his bag from the back, then pulled his hood over his head against the bitter wind. At least it seemed like Troy would still have a little time. Based on what the nurse said, he'd be able to go home the next afternoon as long as his pain was still manageable. They upped his dose of meds and gave him shakes to up his nutrition.

Tyler's throat tightened as he stepped into the airlock, the wind whistling through the doors. He needed to pull it together, and that's why he was here. The guys had given him their blessing to miss practice—had even stopped by the house yesterday and dropped off burgers and enough fries to feed him for weeks from Peters. He hated being anyone's project, but coming from the team, it felt genuine.

This was hockey. A physical outlet. Comfort. Comic relief. Brotherhood. He was barely finishing his first season with the Snowballs, and they already felt like family. Fights and all.

He pounded his chest twice before descending the stairs. He was going to fly tonight. Skate the shit out of that ice. Burn himself out so all he could do was shower and collapse when he got home.

Sean, André, Country, and Fly were already in the dressing room. He was early, but since they had first slot tonight, the high school kids weren't dinking around on the ice. They had the week off for spring break, which was fortuitous for them. More ice time before the semis.

Just as he set his bag on the bench next to Fly, a hand landed on his back. Tyler turned to see Country standing next to him shirtless.

"Man, I'm sorry I couldn't stop by yesterday. Calving season." He pulled Tyler into a tight hug.

"All good, Country. Appreciate it." Tyler clapped his broad, bare shoulders.

Sean nodded to him as Country sauntered back to his gear. "Brett coming?"

"Yep. I was at the hospital this afternoon, so we drove separately."

André put a foot up on the bench as he slapped baby powder

into his compression shorts. "Poor Brett, no strong man to get him to prac—"

The door swung open and Brett, Ryan, and Suraj walked in.

André sighed. "Ah, Bretty-boo, we were just talking about your sensitive ass."

Brett looked at the powder in André's hands. "Looks like your ass is more sensitive than mine. Your tender Quebecois skin not built for chafing?"

André barked a laugh. "You wouldn't understand. It's only a problem for men with . . . how do you say, large packages, yes?"

Brett dropped his bag then lunged and caught André in a headlock. Powder plumed into the air as he ran his knuckles over André's skull.

Tyler laughed and turned back to unload his gear.

"Rough weekend, eh?" Fly looked down to pull up his hockey pants.

"You could say that."

"Sorry to hear about your dad."

Tyler nodded. "Are both your parents still alive?"

Fly shook his head. "No. Lost my mom last year. Dad went a few years before that. They were both in their eighties."

It was easy to forget Fly was seven years older than him since he was still in such impressive physical shape. This would probably be his last season in the Elite league, and then he'd age up to Masters.

"And Emma?" Fly's voice was low. Tyler frowned as he continued to rummage through his bag even though everything he needed was already out on the bench. "You know, when I met Jess, I was a mess. Partying all the time, smoking just enough weed to keep me stagnant and happy about it."

Tyler snorted and stripped off his shirt. "Seems like it worked out for you."

Fly looked up and drew a deep breath. "It did, but not because I sorted things out before we got together. If we had to be perfect before we met the right person, all of us would be alone, eh?" Fly sat on the bench and reached for his skates. "Half the fun is figuring it out together."

Emma tried to focus on the marinated olives and spiced nuts, but by six o'clock her thoughts were tangled around each other. It had taken until three to get the camera dealt with, and now they were rushing to get their shots in the shifting light from the window.

At six-thirty, Emma looked at the display on the camera and hissed through her teeth. "We need to get a bit more texture on those nuts. They look dull."

"I know." Lindsey chewed on her lower lip. "I was thinking the same thing."

Emma turned and slammed her hands on the counter. If she didn't leave now, she wouldn't be able to catch Tyler before practice.

Lindsey pursed her lips and set her camera down. "Emma—"

"He wasn't there." Emma dropped her head, beginning to hyperventilate.

Vaughn put a hand on her back. "Who wasn't there?"

"I went to Tyler's apartment, and he wasn't there, and I was going to go to the Ice Arena and talk with him before practice, but their practice starts at seven, and the almonds look like *dehydrated rabbit turds* and—"

"Whoa, girl. Whoa." Vaughn grabbed her shoulders and turned her to face them. Tears pooled in her eyes, and she reached up to flick them away. "You need to talk to Tyler?"

Emma bobbed her head, her face twisting. "His dad's in the hospital, and I thought he was with someone, but he wasn't, and then I found out he was working here only because I was here, and I don't know why he left the hot tub in Canmore if he was doing all that to be near me, you know?"

Lindsey and Vaughn exchanged a glance.

Vaughn dropped his hands and rounded the counter, picked up her purse, and brought it to her. "No. I don't know because you're not making any sense, but I want you to take this and leave."

"But—"

Vaughn snapped his fingers. "I said leave. Lindsey and I will figure out how to make people salivate over the almonds, okay?"

Emma's lip trembled. "I—"

"Get out!" Lindsey threw up her hands, and Emma jumped.

She clutched her purse to her chest and strode toward the door. "I love you, you know that?"

"We know," Vaughn murmured, already bent down over the bowl of nuts.

Emma's heart raced as she sprinted through the dimly lit parking lot, the wind howling around her. She looked up and saw someone ducking into a car that looked oddly like André, but with the haze and sputtering snow, she couldn't be sure. *Why would he be leaving practice early?*

The two London Fogs warmed her hands, though she had to get creative not to drop the crullers as she burst through the arena doors. Her pulse pounded in her ears as she scanned the foyer for any signs of life.

"Emma?" Sean leaned against the wall next to the closed ticket window.

"Why aren't you on the ice? Isn't practice till eight-thirty?"

Sean frowned. "Practice was at five-thirty tonight."

Emma's stomach swooped out from under her. "What? Why?"

Sean blinked. "Because the team that normally practises before us is out this week. We took the earlier slot."

Emma pressed her fingers to her temples. "Don't people have work? Day jobs?"

"Yes, but—"

"Why would you change practice times without telling me?" Her breath came in short bursts and her hands started to tingle. "And why are you just *standing here?*"

"Umm, okay, Emma. My car's in the shop and I'm waiting for Kelty. She hates driving in the snow, and since when have you wanted to know what time we—?"

"Is Tyler still here?" Emma ran to the railing to look down the stairs.

"Tyler? Did you bring him food?"

Emma turned, her eyes flashing. "Yes, Sean. Is he still here?"

Sean must have seen the fire in her expression because he only shook his head. "I didn't see him, but you could check the—"

Emma felt like a ball of yarn beginning to unravel. *He had to be here.* She'd already been to his apartment twice and found it empty. Emma bolted around the railing and started down the stairs.

Sean called something after her, but she couldn't answer. It felt like an eternity before she reached the bottom of the stairs and ran down the hall to the dressing room. She didn't even think to knock before she set the cups and bag on the concrete floor, flung the door open, and dashed inside.

Steam billowed around her. *Was the water running?*

"Whoa!" Fly yelped and grabbed a towel to wrap around his waist with impressive speed. "I thought everyone was gone!"

"Sorry!" Emma squeaked, heat flooding her cheeks. "I didn't mean to—" She spun and rushed back out into the hall. Fly was the only player in there, wasn't he? She hadn't seen any other backsides glistening in the steam.

Emma groaned and leaned against the cool wall. *He was gone.* Tyler had already left for the night, and even though she'd rushed over, she'd missed him. Adrenaline made her shaky as she picked up the cups and bag, then trudged back to the stairs.

Maybe it was a sign. She should've just texted him in the first place and set up a time to meet and talk. But if he didn't text back? She didn't want to give him the chance of ignoring her—of shutting her out like he had in Canmore.

Tyler had kissed her. He'd started showing up in person the same time she'd started work there. She wasn't misinterpreting this, which meant there had to be some other reason why he'd bolted from the hot tub the other night, and she needed to know what it was.

Emma turned and started up the stairs when something caught her eye. A card. Kicked up against the edge of the stairs.

A driver's licence.

CHAPTER
Twenty-Four

EMMA SET the cups on the stairs and bent down to pick up the rectangular piece of plastic. She flipped it over. Tyler's face stared back at her.

She squeezed her eyes shut. *That man needed a better wallet.* Her eyes popped open and she stared at his black and white GQ photo.

She wanted to buy it for him. She wanted to know the things he needed—she wanted to bring him London Fogs and crullers.

With tears blurring her vision, Emma turned and sat on the stairs, hugging her knees to her chest. She should go home. The snow was probably already coming down, and Tyler was most likely headed to the hospital again.

She had just reached out for the railing and pulled herself up when a low crack pierced the quiet. Emma knew that sound. A puck slamming against the boards. *Someone was on the ice.*

Her heart fluttered. Sean had said they took the first slot because the other team was out for the week, but that didn't mean there couldn't be other players or teams booking ice time.

Emma followed the faint echo down the hall until she saw him. A player in baby blue, no helmet, slapping puck after puck toward the net.

She felt like she was treading water in a rising pool as she opened the door and started down the rink, walking next to the boards. Tyler's body twisted, swinging his stick and sending each puck whistling toward the net. Just like in a game, his movements were fluid and graceful as he lined up shot after shot.

Emma stopped before the plexiglass rose up from the boards and set the drinks and donuts on the bleachers behind her. When she turned back, Tyler was standing still on his skates, watching her.

Neither of them moved for a long moment, and then Emma held up his licence. Tyler dropped his stick and skated over to her.

"It feels like this is becoming a habit." Emma set his licence on the boards. Tyler glanced at the Tim Hortons cups on the seat but didn't comment. Her heart jumped into her throat. "Isn't practice over?"

Tyler nodded once. Sweat beaded his brow, and his dark hair was damp, curling at the ends.

Emma couldn't bear the silence. "I heard about Troy. I tried to stop by after the barbecue—"

"I was at the hospital." Tyler's voice sent a feeling of fingertips tapping down her spine.

She nodded, wetting her lips. "How is he?"

"As good as can be expected."

"And you?"

He exhaled. "Fine."

Emma pursed her lips. "Fine?" Tyler rested his hands on the boards. "Well, that's good to know." She clasped her hands in front of her and rocked on her heels, then spun and started back the way she came.

"Emma, wait—"

She whirled. "Don't tell me to wait unless you're planning to make it worth my time."

"Emma, *wait!*"

She stomped back to stand in front of him. "Why did you leave the hot tub, Tyler? And before you answer, don't you *dare* tell me it was because you didn't think doing *this* was a good idea." She motioned between the two of them. "That's such bullshit. I know you didn't used to work on property, which means there was no reason for us to have to pretend at work. We wouldn't have had to do anything to prove to Troy that we were dating if you continued to work at home. And then you *kissed me*—"

Tyler muttered a string of curses and bent over the boards. When he rose, his eyes were wild. "I don't know what the hell I'm doing, okay?" His voice boomed across the empty rink. Emma's mouth snapped closed as he slammed his gloves on the boards. "I left the hot tub because I don't know *what the hell I'm doing*."

"That much is obvious," Emma muttered, beginning to pace. "But you know what, Tyler? *Neither do I.* Nobody knows what they're doing, but at least I had the balls to be honest about it. To tell you how I felt, and then—"

"No, you didn't." Tyler shook his head.

"What?" Emma hissed.

"You told me you wondered if this could be real, that wasn't telling me how you felt!" He scoffed, "But I didn't need you to, did I? I'd seen it written all over your face. When you saw me at the bar, or when I walked into One Place with Ginger. Even there in the hot tub when we were alone, that look was still plastered on your face."

"What look?" Emma ran her hands through her hair in exasperation.

"The look that says 'I want you *if*.' I want you, Tyler, *if* you can stop acting like a slut at the bar. *If* you can be in a committed relationship. *If* you can change who you've been for the past thirteen years!"

"Of course I want you to change! We all have to change, Tyler! Don't you think *I* need to change? I'm terrified of getting into another relationship because I don't trust myself not to get sucked into someone else's shadow and lose my way again. Or to see the signs soon enough to get out if it's terrible." Her cheeks warmed, and her eyes filled with tears.

Tyler's expression softened. When he spoke, his voice was rough. "I don't know if I can be those things. I don't want to keep doing this, but I don't know any other way, and if I try to figure this out, I'll hurt you, Emma. I know I'll—"

"I'm *already hurting*, Tyler." Emma flicked a tear off her cheek, her breath coming in short bursts. She forced her lungs to expand, then exhaled. "Is this what you do?"

Tyler threw up his hands. "Yes, that's what I'm trying to tell you, it's exactly—"

"No, Tyler! Is *this* what you do? Give up? Refuse to try? When you're lacking a skill in hockey, do you avoid it?"

"Emma, that has nothing to do—"

"Or do you get on the *damn ice* and practise until you get it right?" She stared at him and pointed at the pile of pucks behind them, her eyes flashing. Tyler didn't move. He didn't speak. "I don't want you *if*. I want you because this is the first time in a year I haven't felt broken. And even though I know this scares us both shitless, I don't want anyone else to have this first with you."

The words were so honest, they felt like a punch to her own gut. Emma clenched her middle as her eyes burned. She wouldn't let him see her break down, not when he was going to stand there against the boards like a coward. She turned before another tear spilled over and stormed away from him.

There was a sharp slap of a blade on ice, and then a rumble and scrape against the boards. Emma turned, but before she could see what was happening, Tyler grasped her face between his hands. He kissed her hard, and colour exploded across her vision. Emma sighed against his lips as Tyler's hands ran through her hair, tensing and releasing.

"Did you use a hockey metaphor because you didn't think

I'd understand anything else?" He growled, then slipped his tongue past her lips.

She tipped her head back, reaching for something to grab onto, but only finding hard hockey pads. "Absolutely." Her back arched as one of Tyler's hands travelled down her spine. Why was she wearing this coat? *Why was he wearing his hockey equipment?*

"I didn't want to leave the hot tub," he forced out before hungrily attacking her mouth.

"It didn't—" Emma whimpered as Tyler tugged on her hair and trailed his lips to her neck.

"It didn't, what?"

His voice rumbled against her voice box making every hair stand on end, as if lightning were about to strike.

"It didn't *look* like you wanted to leave, but then I thought—" She gasped as Tyler pulled her skin into his mouth.

"What did you think?"

Emma swallowed hard. "That maybe the water was just hot."

Tyler chuckled. "Something was hot." He pulled on her zipper and pushed his hands into her coat, his lips never leaving her neck. "Did you flash me on purpose?"

Emma panted out a laugh. "No, I—" She couldn't think, couldn't force her mind to focus on anything other than the ripples of pleasure radiating across her skin or the heat pooling at her centre. She needed to take her coat off or she was going to have a stroke.

As she lifted her hand, the sound of metal gears and squeaking panels split the silence. Emma squealed and jumped as Tyler gripped onto her waist. He spun around to see Jem throwing up his hands atop the Zamboni. With his dark blue coveralls and thinning hair, he stood up and scanned the ice, then spotted Tyler behind the boards.

He threw up his hands and shouted something. Tyler lifted an arm and pointed at Emma. "I'm a bit busy at the moment!

Give me a sec!" He turned, but Jem hit the horn in successive bursts.

Tyler's nostrils flared.

Emma laughed and shoved him forward. "Just go get your crap off the ice. I'll wait, I promise."

Tyler shook out his hands, then jumped back over the boards and skated over to the pile of pucks. Emma leaned against the boards, trying to catch her breath. The cold air did little to cool her flushed cheeks.

Tyler skated effortlessly across the rink, leaning over to scoop up puck after puck and throw them in the bucket. She couldn't take her eyes off him as his body bent, his jersey stretching tight over his pads. When the ice was clear, he picked up the bucket, then skated over and dragged the net with him to the other side of the rink.

He hoisted the net over and stored the pucks, then skated back across the ice as the low rumble of the Zamboni echoed through the arena. Jem shouted at Tyler as he pulled the machine onto the ice, but Tyler ignored him.

He stopped next to the boards, sending a spray of shavings into the air. Emma's heart skipped as his hazel eyes fixed on her.

"I need to grab my stuff and change." His gaze dropped to her lips, lingering for a fraction of a second too long.

Emma nodded, her throat suddenly dry. "Sure."

"Meet me at the top of the stairs?" Emma bobbed her head. Tyler pushed off from the boards, then stopped and turned back. "Promise you won't leave?"

Emma tucked her hair behind her ears and flashed a teasing smile. "Depends on how long I have to wait."

Tyler set his jaw and sprinted across the ice. Emma laughed and grabbed his licence off of the boards, then slipped it into her pocket.

―――

Tyler's heart thudded as he raced toward the dressing room, his skates biting into the rubber floor. He skidded to a halt, nearly losing his balance and dropping his stick and helmet in his haste to reach the door.

Inside, he fumbled with the straps and buckles of his gear. Why were there so many things to undo? He cursed under his breath as he wrestled with the layers of padding, not bothering to pack his bag nicely as he stripped.

Finally, he managed to shed the last of his gear, leaving him clad in only a sweat-soaked T-shirt and compression shorts. He tore them off his skin and bolted to the showers, not even waiting for the water to warm up. He scrubbed his hair and skin, then rinsed off as fast as humanly possible and towelled off.

His hair was still dripping when he emerged from the dressing room, panting and dishevelled, but no longer smelling like sweat and iron.

He slung his bag over his shoulder and gripped his stick as he jogged to the stairs. When he reached the top, he was out of breath.

Emma took a sip of her drink and handed the other cup to Tyler. "That was impressive."

Tyler dropped his bag, then set the London Fog on the thin strip of the ticket counter behind her. He grabbed the drink in her hand and the paper bag she was holding and set it next to his cup.

"Tyler, what—" Emma's breath hitched as he grabbed her hips and pushed her back against the wall, her hair covering the paper taped there announcing the upcoming summer free skate schedule.

He couldn't wait another second to pick up where they left off. Tyler pressed his body against hers, the wet tips of his hair brushed her forehead as she looked up at him. Her coat was still undone, and he moved his hands up the sides of her body.

Emma's eyes flicked to the offices with lights on down the hall. Tyler brushed his nose against her cheek and watched her eyelids flutter closed as she inhaled. "Who told you I didn't work on property?" he whispered.

Emma's throat worked, and seeing the effect he had on her was intoxicating. "Troy's ex. She came by today, and—" She sucked in a breath, as Tyler pulled her earlobe into his mouth. "I went to your house on Saturday night, and I saw her. I thought—"

Tyler pulled back and looked at her. "You came to our house Saturday?"

Emma nodded. "When I heard about Troy. I figured you'd found out that morning, and then the way we left things—I wanted to make sure you were okay."

"And you thought I was sleeping with her?" he asked. Emma smiled weakly. Tyler smoothed her hair out of her eyes. "I haven't been with anyone since we met."

Emma raised an eyebrow. "Since we met? At Tim Hortons?"

Tyler nodded. "Couldn't do it."

Something flickered in Emma's expression. "Why not?"

She knew the answer, or she wouldn't be asking, but he could see in her expression that she needed to hear him say it.

"Because all I can think about is you." He kissed the tip of her nose. "It's been annoying as hell."

Emma laughed and slipped her hands under the edge of his shirt, brushing his lower back.

"Bowen! Why the hell are you still here?"

Tyler spun to find Nora, the assistant manager of the Ice Arena, stalking toward the front doors. Her eyes widened and she stopped. "Oh, Emma. I didn't—" Nora cleared her throat. "We're closing for the storm, so I suggest you get home before the roads freeze over."

Emma's cheeks were stained pink as Tyler pulled back. His pulse quickened. He didn't want to go home, at least not alone, but he had no idea what Emma was thinking.

Tyler picked up his gear, then snatched the paper bag from the counter and opened it.

"You're eating that now?" Emma laughed.

"I would've eaten it sooner, but I've been a bit distracted." He pulled out his honey cruller and bit into it. "Mmm," he groaned. Emma held both of their cups and walked next to him toward the front doors.

"Goodnight, Nora," Tyler said between bites.

Nora grinned at the two of them. "Don't stay out too late. You've got semis this weekend, and I want that cup to stay right where it is."

Tyler saluted her, and they walked out into the swirling snow. Emma shifted his cup into her other hand and pulled her hood over her head. Tyler popped the last of his donut into his mouth and they lowered their heads against the wind.

"My truck's over there," he called out, then felt like an idiot. There were only four vehicles in the parking lot, and his was more than obvious.

Emma nodded, then nudged his arm. He stopped, and she handed him his Fog and took the paper sack. His heart sank. She was going to tell him goodnight, and then he'd have to do something drastic. He couldn't watch her get in her car and walk away right now.

She folded over the edge of the bag, then reached into her pocket. Tyler laughed when he saw what was in her hand. Had he seriously forgotten that on the boards? Again, he'd been a little distracted.

Emma held it out, then, seeing that his hands were full, reached down and slipped it into his pocket. His skin burned where her fingers brushed. She wet her lips and looked up with snowflakes on her lashes. "My place?"

CHAPTER
Twenty-Five

TYLER FOLLOWED Emma's car through Calgary, his knuckles white on the steering wheel. The slick roads forced them to drive slowly, and it felt like a personal affront. *My place?* Her words and the coy smile on her face played through his mind, making it impossible to sit comfortably in his seat. *He should probably turn the heat warmers off.*

"Come on, come on," he muttered under his breath as yet another red light forced them to stop. His leg jittered impatiently, toes tapping against the car floor as if that could force the light to change.

Finally, after what felt like an eternity of traffic-induced torture, Tyler pulled up to the curb outside Emma's apartment building. The engine rumbled beneath him as he put the truck in park and watched her car continue on, turning into the parking garage. *He should meet her inside the lobby, right?*

Tyler reached into his centre console and pulled out his floss, toothbrush, and a sleeve of condoms. He didn't want to be presumptive, but . . . he was sure as hell going to be presumptive. Everything in his life up to this point had taught him to be prepared, at least he could be grateful for that. *Would Emma find it unattractive?* Knowing that he was always ready for a sleepover?

He sighed and reached for the door handle, then paused and narrowed his eyes. Condensation had built up on the glass on the drive over, and he spotted a tiny heart streaked amidst the haze.

Emma had done that. The night he'd driven here after the bar when she'd told him the console between them was necessary. He laughed out loud, remembering her nearly scaling the door to stay as far from him as possible.

And here this was. Sitting there all this time, just waiting to reveal itself.

His hands shook as he stepped out of the truck and made his way into the apartment lobby. Inside the airlock, he stomped off his shoes and drew a deep breath to steady himself as he waited, trying not to look like a creep with his toothbrush sticking out of his jeans pocket.

Each second stretched like an elastic band until, finally, time snapped back into focus as Emma walked through the door from the parking garage. Her cheeks were flushed, her eyes bright. Tyler had to remind himself to breathe.

"Hey." Emma dropped her eyes and fiddled with the strap of her purse before hitting the elevator call button. Three times. Tyler smirked.

They stood there next to each other, the air so thick it felt like he was breathing in maple syrup. The elevator doors slid open with a soft whoosh, and Tyler followed Emma into the metal box. She hit the button for her floor, and as soon as the doors slid closed, Tyler moved.

His body trembled as he pushed her up against the wall and kissed her, so pumped full of adrenaline he could barely stand straight.

The elevator dinged, and Emma looked up. "Second floor. Someone else—"

The doors opened, and Tyler called out, "Wait for the next one!" to the group of girls gaping at them from the hall. He hit the button to close the doors, then scooped his hands under Emma's butt and thighs to lift her up to his level. She wrapped her legs around his waist, and he dropped his head back as her hair fell against his cheeks.

He could live here. Right where they were standing. With her weight on his hips, her chest lifting and falling against his, her tongue on his lips.

When the doors opened again, Tyler didn't let go. He carried her giggling out of the elevator, barely able to see where he was going. Though he'd only been to her door once, he didn't need directions. He'd thought about retracing his steps enough times to have the route memorized.

Tyler reluctantly dropped Emma to the ground when they reached her door. She fumbled with her keys, her lips flushed and swollen. Her hands shook, but she finally got the key in the lock. She pushed the door open, and as soon as they stepped inside, he pinned her against the door, pushing it closed.

Emma laughed. "Tyler, I really have to pee."

"Great. I'll come with you."

She slapped his chest, then dropped her gaze and smirked as he stepped back. "Is that a toothbrush in your pocket, or are you just happy to see me?"

Tyler rubbed his neck. "I always brush my teeth after practice, but you were cracking the whip at the arena, and I didn't have time."

Emma shot him a look that said, *Nice excuse*, then kicked off her boots and hung her coat on the hooks. "I've got some food in the fridge—"

"I'm not hungry." That was a lie. He was starving but wouldn't be able to eat a thing when his body was riled up like this.

Emma put a hand on her hip. "I haven't had dinner, and you

just had practice. I doubt one donut—" He reached for her, and she wriggled out of his grasp, scampering toward her bedroom.

Tyler held up his hands. "I'll make you something. Hurry up."

Emma shot him a look, then disappeared behind the door.

Inside the safety of the bathroom, Emma's heart threatened to burst through her ribcage. She leaned on the counter and stared at herself in the mirror, noting all the pink patches of skin where Tyler had kissed and nibbled.

They'd touched and kissed before, but not like this. This was an expansion of what happened in the storage room, all desperation and need. This was real, and it was so much hotter than anything she'd ever fantasized about. *That was saying something.*

She closed her eyes and forced herself to draw a deep breath, then held it before exhaling. This was just a mild panic attack, no big deal. She dropped her pants and sat on the toilet, continuing to breathe deeply.

Tyler was standing in her kitchen. Tyler brought a toothbrush.

Emma flushed the toilet and stood up to wash her hands. She should shave. Maybe shower?

"Hurry the hell up! Your dinner's ready!"

She snorted. Never mind. Despite her rabbit heart spasming in her chest, she ran her hand through her hair, swept her fingers under her eyes to smooth the smudges of her mascara, and then walked back out into the living area.

"What is this?" She stopped and stared at the plate on the counter.

"Egg salad."

Emma blinked. "You made that in the last two minutes?" *Hot. Funny. And now he could cook?* Again, blatant oversight by the personality gods.

"You were in there for five, and the eggs were already

boiled." Tyler turned and pulled a glass from the cupboard, filled it with water, then guzzled it down.

"Thirsty?" She grinned.

"You have no idea."

Tingles shot through her from head to toe as Tyler's eyes darkened. She slipped onto the stool, never dropping her gaze from his as if she were trying not to disturb a wild animal. "You're not eating?"

"There's more in the fridge. I'll eat later." He clamped his hands onto the lip of the counter. His toothbrush now sat next to his hand.

Emma picked up the sandwich. "So you're going to stand there and watch me eat?" Tyler nodded, and Emma shook her head. "Nope, that's not going to work for me."

Tyler huffed and stalked out of the kitchen, moving to the back patio window to stare out into the storm. Emma took a bite and nearly groaned. There was celery and onion in this. *So. Good.* "Thank you," she murmured, her mouth still full.

She got about halfway through the sandwich before she felt something brush her shoulder. Every nerve ending turned into a live wire as Tyler swiped her hair off her neck and hovered there over her skin. Emma dropped her sandwich back to the plate.

"You can keep eating," Tyler murmured. She reached for a napkin and wiped her hands. "I just couldn't wait any longer to touch you."

Emma pushed off the edge of the stool and turned to face him. She snaked her arms around his neck. "That was delectable."

"Perfect choice of adjective."

"You make me wax poetic."

Tyler's eyes danced. "If I find a knight getup in your closet—"

"Then you'll obviously wear it for me."

A low sound hummed in Tyler's throat as he lowered his

head, but Emma stopped him. "I *will* be brushing my teeth, Bowen."

Tyler's brow furrowed. Emma grinned and pulled his head down next to hers, then flicked her tongue against the lobe of his ear. "This time, you can come with me." She trailed her hands down his chest, feeling every contour of his muscular body, then wrapped her hand around his and led him to the bedroom. "Promise you won't leave?"

"Depends on how long you take." His voice was husky.

Emma laughed, pushed him toward the bed, then walked into the bathroom. She left the door open and pulled her toothbrush from its charger.

"I like your bed," Tyler called from the bedroom.

"I'm sure you do." Emma brushed, trying to calm the ticker tape flashing through her mind reminding her how inexperienced she was, and how Tyler would have plenty of women in his head to compare her to.

She leaned over to spit, wiped her mouth, and steeled herself. *Get on the damn ice.* It was time she took her own advice. Emma flicked the light off and walked out to find Tyler staring at a picture on her nightstand.

He glanced up, his face lit by the dim light of the lamp. "How old were you here?"

"Sixteen, I think. It's one of my favourite family photos." She remembered that day. They drove to Prince's Island Park and spent far too long in the cold to get that shot. "I'm impressed you could tell which one was me." She and her sister looked a lot alike, especially as teenagers.

Tyler set the frame back down, and his jaw worked. Emma padded across the floor and leaned into his side. He rested his chin on her head.

When he spoke, his voice was barely a whisper. "I think . . . I want that."

Emma's heart ached for him. Here he was in a new city with his one remaining parent in the hospital, and Tyler didn't have anyone else. He didn't have five siblings to rely on. When Troy was gone, he would be the only one left who knew every piece of his story.

"You won't be alone, you know that, right?" Emma put a hand on his chest. "You're a Snowball now."

"And when Sean finds out about this?"

"He'll get over it. Because that's what family does for each other."

Tyler looped a finger through her belt loop and turned her to face him, then slipped his hands under her shirt and lifted it up over her stomach. The fabric grazed her skin as he pulled it higher, looping it over her head.

He took a step back and sat on the bed, pulling her with him. She twined her fingers in his tousled hair as he pressed his cheek against her, his breath whispering against her bare skin.

Tyler kissed each rib, then his hands crept up her back and found the clasp of her bra. She gasped as he flicked it open with only his finger and thumb. *That was a double hook.*

Tyler paused, feeling her tense. He looked up as her bra hovered loose over her flesh.

"What?" she panted.

Tyler's lips twitched. "You're not especially good at hiding your thoughts."

Emma set her jaw. "You find this funny?" Her bra straps slipped on her shoulders.

"You did tell me you were hilarious." He kissed her navel, his hazel eyes still fixed on hers. "But no, I'm not laughing at you. I love that I can read you like a book."

Emma's eyes shuttered as he nipped at the skin under her ribs. "And what exactly are you reading?"

"That you're nervous," he murmured. Emma's breathing quickened, and Tyler put a hand over her heart, making her bra slip another inch. "And that you're wondering if I'm thinking of the other women I've been with."

Of course, she was nervous. "I just don't want to be a disappointment. I haven't—there aren't many men in my past."

Tyler laughed, and his eyes crinkled. "I want to validate your thoughts right now, but do you know how crazy that is? Do you know how often I wished I could throw you onto the counter at the property or jump that bloody console in my truck? And don't even get me started about that night in Canmore…"

Emma's heart skipped a beat as Tyler pulled the straps off her shoulders and slid them down her arms. When his hands found her skin again, she sucked in a breath.

"Why didn't you? You obviously didn't care about the rules."

"I cared about you. And you cared about the rules." His lips dragged lazy circles over her. "From the start you were never like the others. So I'm going to take my time until you're convinced that you're the only woman in my head."

Emma opened her eyes and waited for him to look up. She nodded once, not realizing until he'd spoken the words how much she needed to hear them. She pushed his shoulders away from her, then climbed on top of him, nestling her thighs around his hips.

Emma tugged at his shirt until he got the hint and pulled it off, tossing it on the floor next to hers. She ran her fingernails over his chest, revelling in the way his skin prickled and his breathing sped up.

"There's only one problem with your plan," she whispered, pressing herself against him.

"Mmhm?"

She kissed the top of his jaw. "I don't want you to take your time."

Tyler rolled, flipping her onto her back and lying on top of her. "What the lady wants, the lady shall receive."

Emma laughed out loud, then writhed as Tyler proved just as adept at undoing button flys as bra clasps. She sank into his warmth and touch, cataloguing every new place she discovered on his body. The divet in his lower back, the taut muscles cording his abdomen juxtaposed with the baby soft skin along his sides.

The wind and snow howled outside her window, but Emma only existed in one moment. One symphony of pleasure. *One first.*

CHAPTER
Twenty-Six

TYLER HADN'T EVER BEEN SO ecstatic for a snow day. He didn't remember what time they'd gone to bed the night before, but it had been late. He ate his egg salad around two, and then they'd gotten distracted while attempting to shower.

He'd popped down to the cafe on the corner for breakfast and grabbed his computer from the truck. Since he'd taken it to the hospital yesterday, he had everything he needed to hole up and work from home. Emma's home, to be exact.

After a prolonged lunch break, where he tasted more of Emma's skin than his lunch, his phone buzzed. Tyler rolled over Emma to grab it from the nightstand, and she feigned suffocation.

"Hey, what's good?"

"Well, sounds like you're alive, bud. That's good news."

Tyler pulled Emma onto his chest. "Definitely alive. Sorry, I should've texted to let you know I wasn't coming home last night."

"We were all a tad worried. Did you check the team chat?"

Tyler exhaled. "No, I haven't looked at my phone much—"

Emma sneezed next to him, and Tyler's eyes widened. *I'm sorry!* she mouthed.

Brett chuckled. "Where'd you end up then, bud?"

Tyler glanced at Emma. The corner of her mouth lifted, and she gave a coquettish shrug. *Might as well rip off the Band-Aid now.* He'd already fake-dated Emma longer than anyone else in the past five years, and he wasn't planning on this being short-term. "I'm at Emma's."

Silence.

Emma held up her phone to show him her family chat.

> Just wanted to let you know Tyler and I are together

> Wanted to give Sean enough time to get used to that before playoffs on Thursday

Holy hell. Tyler laughed out loud. "Brett, I think I better go, but it really means a lot that you checked in."

Brett cleared his throat. "Should I—I mean, does Sean—"

"He knows. You're fine to blow up the team chat."

"Hell, yes." Brett dropped the phone. "And congrats, bud. Emma's a sniper."

"Thanks, man. See you at practice tomorrow."

Brett barked a laugh. "You're not coming home before *practice?* Shit, make sure you can still skate when—"

Tyler hung up the phone and dropped it next to him on the comforter.

Emma raised an eyebrow. "You going to check the team chat?"

Tyler shook his head. "Not while you can see."

She feigned offence. "Don't you think I have a right to read what they're saying about me?"

"You're adorable when you're indignant, but that text chain is sacred."

Emma sighed and dropped her chin on his chest. "Good adjectives."

Tyler went home Wednesday night after practice because he wasn't convinced he'd get any sleep if he stayed at Emma's before their playoff game. He regretted it the second he dropped into bed and didn't have her there next to him. He picked up his phone.

> You asleep?

> It's ten-thirty. What time do you think I go to bed?

> When you're not with me? Right after dinner. So the morning comes sooner

> Ha. You flatter yourself, Bowen

> I miss you

> I know

Tyler laughed, his fingers hovering over the keyboard. Before he could type a response, Emma texted again.

> Don't let all this time in bed deaden your killer instinct, got it? Stiff sticks have to go down tomorrow night

> Deaden? Unthinkable

> I miss you, too

> Goodnight, E

> Goodnight, T

Tyler plugged in his phone and turned on a meditation track. That was the only way he'd be falling asleep tonight with everything running through his head.

Troy was back home, and while Lindsey and Vaughn weren't able to finish the shoots with the snow, they were only a few days behind. The website was still planned to launch, and Gina had taken over the plans for the open house.

Everything was sorted so that he and Emma wouldn't be needed for the weekend. She didn't know it yet, but he had plans after the game. Win or lose, he was looking forward to Thursday night.

The Promenade Ice Center buzzed with palpable energy. The semifinal game had drawn a large crowd, and the stands were filled with fans. Stiff Sticks and Dangle was the home team, but since the playoffs were held in Calgary this year, the Snowballs didn't have to travel to Southern Alberta. The crowd seemed evenly split between baby blue and orange.

Both teams warmed up on the ice, and Emma immediately locked onto Tyler as she sat down next to Kelty and her parents. They hugged all around, and Sharla was the first to bring up the elephant in the arena.

"Is that him? Number four? Kelty was trying to show me, but it's hard to keep track with them all switching places every two seconds."

Emma grinned. "Yep, that's him." She wished she could run down to the edge of the rink and give him a kiss before the game started. She'd sent a few saucy texts and hoped that would be enough to let him know she'd been thinking about him non-stop since he left for practice Wednesday.

Kelty nudged her. "You going to tell us the deets?"

Emma laughed, her cheeks flushing. "It's a long story."

"Can't possibly be as long as your mom trying to tell me who she met at the store this morning." Rob chuckled as Sharla elbowed him in the ribs.

"Okay, short version is this." Emma launched into an explanation of their fake dating history, then how that led to her job with Troy, and then ended with how they both failed at the fake part.

Sharla looked flabbergasted. "Rob, I don't even know. Fake dates, dating apps where you swipe over people's faces—is anyone going to meet the old-fashioned way?"

Emma scoffed. "Didn't you two meet because Dad pretended to be a ski instructor?"

Rob chuckled, and Sharla's cheeks flushed. She took a sip of her pop. "He looked very official."

Emma leaned in so only Kelty could hear her voice. "How's Sean with . . . everything?"

Kelty sighed and leaned back on the bench. "He's Sean."

"But he's not going to punch anyone?"

Kelty laughed out loud. "Nope, he's on strict orders. And to be honest, I think he's happy for you."

"Just buried deep down."

"Oh, so far down."

Emma snorted just as the arena lights dimmed. The players lined up in front of the boards, and a spotlight focused on the corner of the ice where a carpet was rolled out. A tenor with a booming voice sang Oh, Canada and then the teams rallied their starting five as the cheers dissipated.

A referee stood at centre ice, and Sean won the faceoff. The puck slid to Country, who sped forward, watching for an opening. Tyler cut across the blue line, and Country passed it forward. Tyler received the puck in stride and wound up for a slapshot but was challenged by a Stiff Stick defender.

André swooped in to pick up a deflected pass. He zigzagged through two Stiff Sticks, drawing their attention. Just as he was about to be boxed in, he dropped a back pass to Country, who unleashed a shot toward the net.

The Stick's goalie deflected the puck, sending it bouncing toward the boards. Their group cheered every time the Snowballs had the puck, and Emma knew she wouldn't have much of a voice after this game.

Ryan subbed for Country, and the Snowballs maintained possession for a good minute, rotating the puck. Tyler took another shot, only to be blocked. The Stiff Sticks tried to clear their zone, but Sean intercepted, sending the puck back deep.

With only seconds left in the period, Tyler and Curtis executed a beautiful give-and-go play, leaving Tyler with a breakaway. The arena held its collective breath as Tyler deked left and shot right, sending the puck short side.

The crowd erupted as the buzzer sounded, signalling the end of the period and Tyler's goal. Emma jumped up and down with Kelty, her heart ready to burst. She turned to pick up her jacket from the bench and froze. As the crowd cheered around her, she stared at the top corner of the stands.

Troy pulled a hand out of his blankets and waved. Gina was next to him, making sure his oxygen stayed in place.

"I'll be right back." Emma slid out of their row and walked up to stand above Troy. "Is it smart for you to be here?" she asked, unable to keep the smile from her face.

"I think it's the smartest thing I've done in a long time." He patted the bench next to him, and she sat. He stared down at the bench, watching his son squirt water through the gaps in his helmet. "He's something else."

Emma nodded. "Why didn't you ever come before?"

Troy exhaled, and Gina put a hand over his shoulders. "I don't have a good answer for that."

"Well, I'm glad you're here now." Emma wished Tyler had his phone on him so she could text him and force him to look up. "This will mean so much to him."

"We might not be able to stay for the whole game. Troy has an early bedtime these days." Gina smiled warmly.

Emma watched the two of them and wondered what would

propel a fifty-year-old woman to care for a man she'd only met a few months ago. She didn't have to think about it for long. When someone like Tyler gave his attention, it was difficult not to crave it again.

"Emma, Gina has plans for the next two properties, and I'd love it if you and Tyler met with her in the next few weeks to give your input. Would that be possible?" Troy asked.

Emma nodded, her chest tightening. The next few weeks. Troy might not be around by then. "Of course. You're planning to continue with them, then?"

Troy looked at her, a twinkle in his eye. "Meet with Gina, and you'll get all the details." Emma smiled, amused by how tickled he was at being cryptic. "Now go be with your family, I didn't mean to pull you away."

The second period was about to start. Emma put a hand on his arm. "I was happy to visit with you."

She started to stand, and Troy grabbed onto her jacket. "Make sure you don't let him make excuses. And if he ever starts to pull away, pin him against the wall and force him to talk to you."

Emma nodded. "I don't know if I can force Tyler to do anything, but I'll try."

"He needs it. We all do. Someone who won't let us get away with just doing what we know."

Emma swallowed hard. "He's a good man, Troy. He loves you."

Troy blinked and dropped his hand. He nodded once, and Emma stepped over the bench and walked back to her seat.

———

On the bench at the start of the third, Tyler wiped sweat from his brow and guzzled electrolytes. They were still up one nothing, but the Sticks' attacks were relentless. They were cornered now, clawing for a goal.

"Have to shut down that pass through the centre." Brett pounded his fist against the boards.

Tyler nodded in agreement. Boyd was covering their asses in the goal, but if they didn't tighten up their D, their lead wouldn't last long. Tyler looked up into the stands and found Emma staring straight at him. Her face lit up. She lifted her hands in the air and waved like a crazy person.

He chuckled and waved. Yeah, I see you. Emma shook her head and waved both her hands in unison. Was she pointing at something? Tyler followed the direction of her hands and almost choked on his drink.

There, at the back of the stands, sat Troy bundled in blankets with Gina by his side.

"Is that your dad?" Brett asked. Tyler nodded and lifted his mitt so Emma knew he'd gotten the message. She clapped her hands together and sat back on the bench, beaming at him.

Fly slapped him on the back. "Focus, Bowen."

Tyler cleared his throat, then pulled his helmet back on. A few minutes later, he pushed back out onto the ice.

"Go, go, go!" Curtis shouted, sending the puck hurtling around the net.

With swift, powerful strokes, Tyler intercepted the puck and charged down the rink. He weaved through the opposing players with ease, his eyes never leaving the goalie guarding the net.

A check came out of nowhere, and he slammed into the boards. He growled and righted himself, searching for the puck.

"Three minutes left!" the announcer boomed over the loudspeaker. "Can the Sticks tie it up or will the Snowballs be facing Pucks Deep in the finals?"

Tyler saw it happening in slow motion. Everything seemed to blur except for the puck, which was clearly in the possession of a Stiff Sticks' forward.

Boyd sank low, eyes locked onto the puck, his gloves up, anticipating a shot. But the forward executed a no-look pass to his teammate far side. Tyler cursed under his breath and tried to close the gap, his skates scraping the ice as he pushed up the ice.

The Stiff Stick player wound up and, with a flick of his wrist, sent the puck sailing. The biscuit rotated end over end. Boyd lunged desperately across the crease with his glove flicking out, but he was a fraction of a second too late. The puck found its mark, nestling into the top corner of the net.

The sharp sound of the goal horn echoed. Sean slammed his stick on the ice.

The Snowballs circled up, knocked helmets, then got in position. As the puck dropped, Sean quickly wrestled it free, tapping it to Tyler, who accelerated down the left wing.

Spotting Brett in the centre, Tyler sent a crisp pass his way. As Brett received it, gearing up for a potential game-tying shot, a Stiff Sticks player came in from his blindside. The opposing player jutted out his elbow, clearly targeting Brett's head in an illegal check.

The impact was immediate. Brett's helmet took the brunt of the blow, but the force sent him sprawling onto the ice, the puck skittering away. Tyler started toward Brett as the arena erupted in outrage. Fans jumped to their feet, yelling for a penalty, but nothing came.

Seizing the unexpected advantage, the Stiff Sticks transitioned to offence. Brett waved Tyler off, scrambling to his feet, and Tyler bolted toward their end of the ice. He was going to hammer that player—was it number thirty-six? That headhunter deserved to be crushed against the boards.

Curtis challenged the oncoming players, and André swooped in to help, but it was three on two. Sean and Tyler rushed in. The shot went off. Boyd tried to keep pace with the sudden shifts and got a piece of the puck with his glove, but it wasn't enough. The puck ricocheted into the net.

"Bullshit!" Sean skated up to the refs, but Tyler's attention was drawn behind them. Brett was still sitting on the ice.

CHAPTER
Twenty-Seven

TYLER SLUMPED on the bench in the dressing room with his towel around his waist. The mood was sombre as the rest of the guys dressed and filtered out into the hall. Brett was on his way to the ER, but based on what he'd described as Tyler helped him from the ice, he had an inkling as to what they'd find.

That check had come from the side, and his knee had likely twisted as he fell. He'd put his money on an ACL tear.

Sean sat down next to him. "You played one hell of a game."

Tyler's jaw worked. They'd all played well, but it hadn't been enough.

Sean dropped a hand on his shoulder. "More importantly, you took care of Brett." He clapped him on the back, then turned to finish getting dressed.

"I care about her, Sean. This is different."

Sean looked back over his shoulder. "Will Emma finally come back to Sunday Suppers?"

"I mean, that probably depends on the food."

The corner of Sean's mouth twitched as he turned and kept walking.

The arena had mostly emptied out by the time Tyler trudged up the stairs. Emma ran to him and launched into his arms as he dropped his bag and stick.

"I'm so sorry," she mumbled into his chest. "You saw Troy in the stands, right?"

Tyler nodded and ran his hand over her hair. "How could I have missed the air traffic control arms?"

Emma laughed, clutching his shirt, then pulled back. "One Place? We could drown our sorrows in terrible karaoke since you don't drink?"

Tyler laughed and picked up his gear as Emma pulled him toward the doors. He was upset about the loss and worried about Brett, but it was something else entirely that made his pulse quicken as they stepped outside and started walking toward the parking lot.

He waited for Emma to notice the car idling against the curb. She glanced over, but it took her four more steps to slow. Her eyes narrowed, but she kept walking until Tyler pulled her to a stop.

"How about a do-over?"

Emma watched him, a slow smile starting at the corner of her lips. "What do you mean?"

Tyler ran a hand through his hair. "Well, our last trip to Canmore kind of sucked, especially for you. Now my season's over, and we don't have to meet with Gina until—"

"You know about that?"

Tyler laughed. "I do occasionally check my text messages."

"So . . . you want me to get in this car."

"I was hoping you'd want to."

She took a step closer to the curb. "I don't have any of my toiletries or a change of clothes."

"You didn't last time either."

She laughed. "What about a swimsuit?"

Tyler balked. "Absolutely not. I've been dreaming about a

do-over of that moment every night since we got back. You will not ruin this for me."

Emma raised an eyebrow, then slowly sidestepped to the door. "Is there a console?"

"I already requested it be stowed away."

"What about my car and your truck? They can't be here over—"

"Brett's taking my truck home—"

"And I'm taking your car." Kelty sauntered up next to them and held out her hand. Emma clapped a hand over her mouth, then dug in her purse and handed over her keyring. Kelty hugged her, then jogged off toward the pub.

Emma's smile widened. "You didn't know your season was going to be over when you planned this."

Tyler pointed with his stick. "Can you please just get in the damn car?"

As much as Tyler wanted to, he wasn't going to strip Emma's clothes off in the back of a car where the driver could lower the partition at any moment. Instead, they'd both gotten handsy until they couldn't take it anymore and now Emma was lying on his chest, drawing slow circles over his shirt. *Ten more minutes.*

"If you could have one superpower, what would it be?" Emma asked.

Tyler sighed and squeezed her upper thigh. "Right now? I'd say teleportation."

Emma laughed. "Funny. I was going to say x-ray vision."

This time when they arrived in Canmore, the ground was covered in snow. Emma squealed as they stopped next to the curb. She grabbed onto his arm as they waved the driver off without a second glance.

The same staff member, Quinn, walked out and looked

between the two of them. He quirked an eyebrow. "Should I tell our staff to prepare an early breakfast?"

Emma sighed. "You never know with this one."

Tyler feigned offence, and Emma winked at Quinn as they walked into the lobby. Anticipation bubbled beneath his skin, fizzing faster than champagne on New Year's Eve. He took their key and thanked Quinn, then took the stairs two at a time with Emma jogging to keep up.

"I assumed you'd be tired after the game." She laughed, slapping his butt as they reached the top.

"You assumed wrong."

They strode down the hall to the rooftop suite, and as soon as the door closed behind them, Tyler started stripping.

Emma's eyes widened as she saw the dessert plate. "Tyler. Bowen." She popped a truffle in her mouth.

"If you're not naked in thirty seconds, I'm taking those away from you."

Emma brought a truffle over to him, holding it in her teeth and making him take it from her. She kissed him, then stepped back and tugged at her shirt. "You're not going to wait in the bathroom this time?"

Tyler shook his head, blood pulsing through him as she pulled off her clothes, dropping everything in a puddle on the floor. Tyler watched as she slipped an elastic off her wrist and tied her hair up, then picked up the dessert plate and padded toward the patio doors, all curves and silky skin.

Tyler grabbed two towels and followed her to the tub. Emma set the plate on the side and dropped into the steaming water. She tried to settle into the same seat she'd occupied the first time, but Tyler hit the button for the jets and pulled her onto his lap.

He stared at her, the stars still poking through the cloudy night sky above her head. "I'm sorry about last time." Tyler's throat worked, and Emma brushed a hand over his cheek. "I don't ever want to make you feel that way again, but—"

She leaned down and brushed her lips over his. "We're going

to hurt each other, Tyler. That part's inevitable. But then we'll strategize. Change our training routine—"

Tyler laughed and pulled her into him. "No more hockey talk," he whispered. "There's too much I want to do to you."

"What, that doesn't put you in the mood?"

He chuckled. "I don't think there's a topic that could put me out of the mood right now."

"Is that a challenge? Because—"

Tyler's hands found her under the water, and Emma sucked in a breath. "You were saying?"

Tyler's hands moved over her skin, both of their bodies glistening in the starlight like freshly groomed ice.

In that moment, Emma wasn't scared anymore. Sitting there with Tyler was so good it ached in all the best ways. She wasn't naive enough to believe they wouldn't have their ups and downs, but there was no one she'd rather have on her team than him.

Emma curled over him and pulled his bottom lip between her teeth. "I was saying . . . I want to see every last move in your playbook. But we'd better get started because I'm *not* missing that breakfast buffet in the morning."

"So demanding." He tightened his hold on her, and she relaxed into his arms, letting him take control, body and soul.

Under the starlit mountain sky, both of them got on the damn ice and practised.

Epilogue

A MONTH LATER, Emma found herself sitting between Tyler and Sean at their usual Sunday Supper. The sun stretched high in the sky, warm weather finally upon them. Though Emma still didn't trust the forecasts until after Canada Day.

The long wooden dining table was crowded with players and significant others while Rob manned the barbecue. This time he was at least letting Fly help.

"Remember that time Brett tried to pull off a figure-skating spin on the ice and ended up face-planting into a snowbank?" Sean held his arms up in a mock pirouette and batted his eyelashes. The table erupted in laughter.

"You're lucky I'm in a boot, bud." Brett flipped up his middle finger and adjusted his leg resting on an extra chair.

"I'm going to go refill the lemonade." Emma stood and leaned over to grab the pitcher. Tyler smacked her butt.

"Easy, Bowen," Sean growled.

Emma glowered at her brother, then stalked off to the kitchen. She dumped more fresh-squeezed lemon juice and sugar into the pitcher and held it under the filtered spigot next to the sink.

She stirred it all together with a wooden spoon, then added two giant cupfuls of ice. She walked back out to the patio, set it on the table, and dropped back into her seat.

Tyler threw an arm over her shoulders.

Curtis held up a glass, and Emma clinked hers against it. "You two deserve all the love for that open house."

Tyler shook his head. "It was mostly Gina. She took the reins after Troy passed."

Emma squeezed his knee and exhaled when his fingers played along her neck. It had been three weeks, and she knew Tyler was still processing things. "Now on to phase two."

Jess asked about the restaurant and whether there were significant differences in the menu at the second bed and breakfast. Yes, they'd hired a French chef this time around. After discussing the timeline of renovations, they moved on to discussing Fly and Jess's landscaping project.

Emma sank back in her seat and took a long sip of lemonade.

Tyler leaned closer. "Thank you for this," he murmured, his voice low enough only she could hear.

Her blood heated. "For what?"

He squeezed her neck and nodded toward the scene in front of them. Suraj scooped salad onto his plate while Brett cajoled Sean into grabbing him another piece of garlic bread.

"I'm going to need to find a physical therapist after surgery. I'm not missing next season," Brett grumbled.

"Ooh! I have a friend who's an incredible PT. Let me text you her info," Kelty pulled out her phone.

Ryan was in the middle of a dramatic retelling of how Fly tried to deke at practice and ended up running into the goalpost. Tyler had already told her that one.

Fly scoffed from his place next to the barbecue. "It was a strategic move to confuse André. You had to be there."

André chortled. "I was fooled, Gramps. Excellent move."

Emma turned and kissed Tyler's cheek. "Move in with me," she whispered.

Tyler's eyes widened, and he searched her face. "You're serious?"

She nodded. "I'm sick of having to figure out whose stuff is staying where and then driving two cars over to the properties."

"Ah, so it's purely practical."

Emma scoffed. "Obviously. Have you seen gas prices?"

Tyler kissed her, his lips soft against hers. "Well, if it's to save money."

"And the environment."

Tyler flinched as a crouton bounced off his forehead.

Emma whirled. "Sean Thompson, I swear—" Sean had already jumped out of his seat, running away from the table so she couldn't hit him with anything bigger than a salad topping.

She folded her arms over her chest and glowered at him as he walked over to help their dad take the chicken off the grill.

Tyler looped his arm again over her shoulder, this time letting his hand droop a little lower over her chest. Emma burst out laughing as Sean's face reddened.

"Does Wednesday work?" Tyler asked.

Emma turned to him, her face lighting up. She grabbed his face and kissed him hard, not caring who on the team was watching. "Wednesday is perfect."

*　*　*

Available Now!
Find special edition e-books and paperbacks exclusively at www.CindyGunderson.com

About the Author

Cindy Gunderson is a voice actress and award-winning author. Since she has commitment issues, she writes both sci-fi and fantasy, as well as contemporary romance and women's fiction under the pen name, Cynthia Gunderson.

When she is not typing away in a quiet corner of her local library, you can find her traveling with her family, narrating audiobooks, or happily digging in her garden. She loves acting and performing, beating her kids in card games, and playing ultimate frisbee with her handsome husband, Scott.

Cindy grew up in Alberta, Canada, but has lived most of her adult life between California and Colorado. She currently resides in the Denver metro area. Cindy holds a B.S. in Psychology from Brigham Young University.

Cindy's first novel Tier 1 was awarded First Place in Science Fiction at the 2021 CIPPA EVVY Awards and her women's fiction novel Yes, And was honored with the Indie Author Award's first place prize for the state of Colorado, 2023.

Also by Cynthia Gunderson

Yes, And

I Can't Remember

Holly Bough Cottage

The New Year's Party

Let's Try This Again

Sugar Creek Series

One Last Christmas

Love in Audio

Canadian Played Series

Against the Boards

Called for Icing

Stickhandle with Care

On the Power Play

Guarding Home Ice

Find signed books and discounted bundles at

www.CindyGunderson.com

Instagram: @CindyGWrites

Facebook: @CindyGWrites

TikTok: @CynthiaGWrites

T 409410

Made in United States
Cleveland, OH
11 January 2025